THE KNIGHT
OF INNOCENCE

JULIUS A.M. BROWN

DIVERTIR
PUBLISHING
Salem, NH

The Knight of Innocence

Julius A.M. Brown

Copyright © 2021 Julius A.M. Brown

Cover image by
Emma K. Hill
https://www.instagram.com/emmahillphoto/
https://www.facebook.com/EmmaHillPhotography/

Published by
Divertir Publishing LLC
PO Box 232
North Salem, NH 03073
http://www.divertirpublishing.com/

ISBN-13: 978-1-938888-29-8
ISBN-10: 1-938888-29-4

Library of Congress Control Number: 2021945327

Printed in the United States of America

Dedication

To my mother, Gertrude S. Diggs, who first taught me to read. To my grandmother, Helen M. Diggs, who encouraged my imagination. To my grandfather, Franklin R. Diggs, who inspired me. To my wife, Adrienne D. D. Brown, who pushed me to share my work with the world. To my son, Julius A.M. Brown Jr., who personifies my every hope and dream.

This book is for you.

TABLE OF CONTENTS

CHAPTER 1

MY BACK HIT the glass door, and I had to dive to my left when a couch came soaring at me. I managed to barely get out of the way of the second piece of furniture to be flung at me tonight. The glass doors behind me exploded outward, and somehow I knew I was going to be blamed for it. It wasn't my fault this school decided to have an office with glass walls. Who the heck builds a high school with glass walls? No one! One ticked off student with a rock and that's the budget for the year. I rolled twice and then settled into a crouching position.

Two hours ago I was sitting in my favorite bar and grill with a burger on the way. That's when the news came over the television above the bar. Now, all the other patrons were pissed when the pay-per-view fight was interrupted by local news of the recent vandalism of a local high school, but I on the other hand was downright irate. I paid for the burger that I'd never get to eat and drove over to the high school in question. What do I find? A fully dressed yet still half-naked girl cowering in a corner with her strapping young boyfriend shoved into a trash can. Then of course there was the minotaur with lust in his eyes staring at the girl. Why couldn't it just be vandals that were vandalizing a high school?

The minotaur that had just thrown the couch at me bellowed in anger so loud that the remaining glass shook. "I heard you the first time," I said as I stood and leveled my sword before me. It was four feet long from the tip of the blade to the pommel with a cruciform cross guard. If you looked at the blade closely, you could see an inscription. "See this sword? Yell all you want. Either give me the girl and leave or I will have to kill you. Any other options went out the door with the couch."

The minotaur stomped his left foot and scraped it back across the ground. His chest muscles pulsed under the ripped-up football jersey he was wearing. He snorted and yelled in a surprisingly wheezy voice, "She's mine!" That's when he lowered his horns and charged me.

1

"No, no, no," I yelled. I started to jump out of the way, but the bastard leapt forward into a diving tackle. He hit me square in the chest. It was a miracle that his horns were too wide to impale me. The air was blasted from my body as we exploded through the glass wall out into the night. We passed the landing of the main office and were in free fall over the almost two dozen stairs that led to the parking lot.

My brain told me I was going to die if I didn't do something. My gut told me that my brain was right. I wrapped my arms around the minotaur's neck and arched my back with everything I could muster. I flipped him over me and turned as much as I could.

The ground came flying at us. When we crashed the minotaur was under me, and I smacked against his head and chest. I bounced off him and kept flying backward. My head smacked against asphalt as my momentum sent me tumbling across the parking lot. The passenger door of a red Dodge Charger crunched in as I crashed into it. I didn't want to get up after that. There are some things that seem pointless, but there was a girl at the top of the stairs scared out of her mind, and her boyfriend was probably hurt. I climbed to my feet as the minotaur came stomping toward me. My sword had landed between us.

I grunted and charged toward the monster. The minotaur roared and charged me. He ran over my sword and closed on me so fast that I wondered if he had even felt that fall. His head dipped down so he could gore me, but I jumped. Using his head as a springboard to clear the rest of his body, I dropped into a forward roll across the ground. The asphalt ripped through my jeans as I skidded on my knees across the parking lot. Blood trailed from both of my legs, but I had my sword again. The monster turned on me in an instant. He threw a punch, and I had to scramble to my feet to get out of the way. His fist added a new pothole to the parking lot.

At 6'2" and about 230 pounds I'm a big guy, but let's face it, I'm human. I was the underdog here. The minotaur was ten feet tall and weighed six or seven hundred pounds of solid muscle. I wasn't trading blows with him, but I wasn't backing down either.

"Come at me, you walking barbecue plate," I yelled. He did, and I couldn't have been happier when he reared back for a punch that would knock me clear out of the school district. I dove forward beneath his swing.

I rolled back up to my feet and spun around with my sword slashing across. The blade of my sword cut through the muscle of his leg with ease. He went down with a howl of pain. When he hit the ground the parking lot shook, and I almost lost my balance. I leapt at his back with the intent of stabbing him through the heart, but just as I did the minotaur rolled over. He caught me in two powerful hands and started to squeeze me as if he was trying to get the last bit of toothpaste out of me.

"You die now human, just like every other stupid monster hunter."

"I'm not a monster hunter," I wheezed. My ribs were straining. I had one last chance, so I drew my sword back and plunged it straight down at the minotaur's throat. There was a sound of steel scraping against stone as I buried my blade to its hilt in the monster's throat. Blood gurgled from his mouth, and his eyes bulged just as the life drained from them. His grip loosened, and I fell onto his chest. I just lay there for a moment coughing and gasping for air.

When I rolled off the minotaur onto the ground, something terrifying surged through my body. There was no pain, but I felt a piece of my life fade away. In the back of my mind, I could feel something akin to the loss of a distant cousin or a friend of a friend. It just felt wrong, like tearing a page from a thick novel. I closed my eyes as I felt my soul shake and quiver. The number thirteen was burned into my mind. I got up and wrenched my sword free of the monster's throat.

I was going to go up and rescue the girl, but she and her boyfriend were walking down the stairs. They looked a little banged up, but they weren't hurt. I waved them over. "You guys okay?"

The girl nodded, but the guy looked past me. His eyes filled with anger, and he shoved me. "You messed up my car, shithead."

I looked down at where he touched me. This guy was my height and a bit more muscular than I was. I was used to that. I wasn't used to being shoved by people that I had just saved. "I'm sorry, what?" I asked.

He got right in my face and yelled, "You dented my car."

"Yeah, with my head after I dented the ground the same way." I touched the back of my head and showed him my bloody hand.

"I just got that car. You had better be able to pay for it."

"So you have nothing to say about the minotaur? The huge monster that attacked you? The one I just saved you from?"

"What do you want, a medal? The fucking cops would have done that but without messing up my car. In fact, let's call them. You had better have insurance."

As he fished out his phone, I turned and walked over to his brand-new car. I took my sword and poked through one of his tires. He screamed. I walked around to the other three and repeated the process. Then I smashed through the driver's window and popped the hood. I stuck the blade of my sword through the GPS screen while I was leaning in. The young man ran over to voice his opinion once again. This time he punched me. He had a good strong punch. I hit him with an uppercut that lifted him into the air, and when he hit the ground, I put a size-fourteen work boot into his gut. Then I opened his hood and slashed every tube and wire I could see.

I took his cell phone and ground it into the parking lot. I turned to the young lady with my most polite and sincere smile. "Want to call your parents for a ride?"

She nodded.

While she called her parents, I went over to the minotaur's body. It was already breaking down into the basic elements of the mortal world. Bone to earth, blood to water, and flesh to grass. Mixed in with it all was a clear odorless gel. Some people call it slime, but those of us in the know call it ectoplasm, the byproduct of existing in a world that is not your own. It was shifting back to the world from which it came, our sister world, the Second Earth. In minutes, all evidence that monsters exist in the world would be gone. I said a prayer over the body and returned to the girl.

"What was that thing?" she asked me.

"Do you really want to know?" She nodded slowly. I looked her in the eye and said, "It was a creature called a minotaur. It had a mother and father like you. It was a monster, and it had a soul."

She looked at me with a skeptical expression. "A monster? Monsters aren't real."

"Monsters are as real as you and I. Are you religious?" I asked. She nodded. "Well tonight you met a monster. One day, hopefully a long way off, you will meet an angel. They're real too."

She smiled at that. A little light in the darkness is good. "Well what about you? What are you?"

4

I sighed and said humbly, "I'm a knight." I took her phone and ground it into the asphalt the same way I had done her boyfriends. Climbing into my old, beat-up Dodge Prospector, I turned the ignition. My truck creaked and clanked before it turned over. The cab rattled for a moment, and then I pulled out of the parking lot into the street. I drove through the streets of Baltimore, Maryland in the moonlight, thinking about that girl and her boyfriend. I thought about what must be going through both of their heads. It's hard when you first find out.

Ignorance Is Bliss. I have said it, you have said it, and just about every person in the civilized world has said it. That's why it is literally the worst curse ever placed upon humanity. Ignorance keeps us from seeing the world as it really is. Ignorance keeps us from learning the lessons our ancestors taught us. Ignorance keeps people from trusting what they know deep down in the core of their being. Ignorance has us make fun of, shun, imprison, and utterly disavow anyone that tells us the truth.

The truth is that we are not alone. The truth is that most people only see half of the world around them, if that much. The truth is that magic exists. The truth is that the bible is missing a lot of information. The truth is that everyone is right about their religion and wrong at the same time. The truth is darkness. The truth is scary. The truth is anger. The truth is painful. The truth may get you killed.

If you still want to know the truth, then I will give you what I know. First off, do not forget what you already think you know. Now take everything you have ever dismissed as childish, myth, fantasy, or blasphemy. It's all true! Not right but true. It is all connected. The Bible, the Quran, Scientology, the occult, Dungeons and Dragons, yesterday's crossword puzzle, Disney, Walmart, Atlantis, dinosaurs, the Loch Ness monster, and yes the fortunes inside of fortune cookies. Every bit of information that we have as a whole is connected to the truth. It has all been distorted, changed, and watered down so that people can be happy. So that we can be ignorant.

It sounds like a conspiracy theory, but it isn't. We did it to ourselves. Have you ever heard a rumor at your job about you? I bet it had an ounce of truth to it and ten gallons of fiction, right? Ever see that anywhere else? Like when you played telephone in kindergarten? You would think growing up would stop the confusion, but it just made it more vicious, right? The longer you are exposed to the curse the worse it is. But don't worry. It's easy to overcome. Just take your head out of your butt. You aren't always right! You aren't the smartest person in the room!

We are all children, and will be until we grow up and stop acting like we are the only intelligent beings on this planet. Monsters exist. Fairies exist. Vampires and werewolves exist. They are living right here with us, but most of us will never know it. Why? Because *Ignorance Is Bliss*.

Everyone has heard the creek of a door and thought it was the wind. Everyone has seen a scary shadow on the wall and thought it was a coat rack. Everyone has smelled something rancid and thought it was just something their kid spilled. But it's not the wind; it's a goblin sneaking into your house. It isn't a coat rack but a satyr stealing your beer. It's not a spill that you smell but a troll about to eat your family. Monsters are real. They always have been.

How do I know all of this? I am a Knight of the Crucifixion, the first true order of knights. You have heard of Jesus and the twelve Apostles. Well some things were purposefully left out of their tales. One hidden bit of knowledge was that Jesus gave each of his twelve followers a sword that represented an aspect of humanity. The swords didn't grant them special abilities or powers, but the swords did grant them a chance to fight back against beings that would harm any of God's children. The Apostles became the Knights of the First Order of Christ. When a knight retired or died, their sword was passed on to a person that represented the aspect that it was meant to defend. The knights that came after the original twelve were forever known as the Knights of the Crucifixion. I don't know who decides if someone is worthy of a sword, but they aren't human. They are probably angels, and I am guessing they take their orders from their boss.

Four years ago, I begged God for a chance to stop something horrible from happening. He gave me that chance by giving me a sword. Now I am a Knight of the Crucifixion and a member of The Church. The Church is a secret organization that has existed for thousands of years. It is not controlled by any particular religious faith or government, but it has its connections to just about everything. Its mission is to maintain the balance of power between humanity and the other beings of the world, to protect the entire world from supernatural evil, and not to pay me.

Seriously, I just found out I was supposed to be paid for this, and I haven't seen a check in four years.

My name is Michael White. I won't tell you my whole name because that can get you killed. I am the owner and sole employee of White Knight Construction. I am a part-time private investigator. I am the grandson of a Paladin. I am a Knight of the Crucifixion. When you have a problem that seems too big for you, when you think the police can't help you, when the shadows are surrounding you, or when you hear something go bump in the night, just ask for help. I will be there.

If you don't believe me that's fine. But on the off chance that I am right, if you have ever seen something dart away in the corner of your vision, if you have ever felt a presence that you couldn't find, or if you have ever heard something go bump in the night then keep reading. You might learn something.

CHAPTER 2

I GOT HOME and took a shower. My water heater works whenever it feels like it, so the warm water became ice-cold the moment I stepped under the shower head. The anxiousness of battle washed away along with the sweat and blood. The warm water came back just as my teeth started to chatter. When I got out of the shower, I looked at myself in the mirror.

Like I said, I am 6'2" and 230 pounds of evil-ass-kicking-awesomeness. My body has a runner's build of lean flat muscles that I got from getting my butt kicked by my grandpa while he taught me the business. I'm an American of the black variety with light skin. For simplicity, I keep my hair cut bald on the sides with a fade on the top. The only jewelry I have are a small stud earring in my left ear and a gold chain that holds a crucifix around my neck.

There are runic tattoos on my back, neck, arms, legs, chest, and stomach. The ones on my back run across my shoulders, down my spine, and around several random spots that I think are chi points. In my short life I have managed to get a few fading scars on my chest, face, legs, and stomach. On my left shoulder, there are five puncture wounds in the shape of a clawed hand. It shows no signs of fading. I don't have six-pack abs, but I keep trying to get them. Oh well. Maybe 200 sit-ups a day isn't enough.

I grabbed some shorts and went to bed. It felt like I had just closed my eyes when my alarm went off. Morning was here already, and I felt like crap. Today was supposed to be a big day for me. I did my usual 200 push-ups, 200 sit-ups, and 200 squats. No matter how much I do, I never really look like I am in shape.

Once I was done working out, I went into my kitchen pantry. I opened it and looked around at enough boxes of allergy medicine to last anyone else a lifetime. I would go through them in a couple of days.

On the floor was a clear storage bin; inside were the protein bars that my best friend, Aaron, made me keep. They were made from a bunch of plants that don't sound like grapes or watermelons and a bunch of chemicals that supposedly are healthier for you than the nutrients in grapes or watermelons. They smelled like fresh cow pie and tasted like a cow ate a cow pie then crapped it out again. I ate one, and having survived that attempt at suicide, I reminded myself that the life of a knight was supposed to be filled with peril.

Finally, I got dressed in a pair of jeans, a gray tee shirt, and a cheap pair of sneakers. It was the nicest stuff I had to wear since I don't spend much on everyday clothing. I clipped my gun and survival knife on my belt and pulled my shirt down to cover them. Then I grabbed my jean jacket, keys, and my sword before heading to the door.

My phone rang just as I was leaving. I looked at the screen and didn't know if I should be happy, sad, or terrified. The screen showed me a picture of an old man flipping me off as I tried to take his picture. I answered, "White Knight Construction, Michael White speaking."

A hard voice edged in mirth came back to me. "So, you finally came up with a name?"

"I figured I would go with what I know. My name is White, I'm a knight, and I do construction," I said. "What can I do for you, padre?"

"It sounds good, kid. The news this morning had some idiot talking about how some guy with a sword hacked up his car. You wouldn't know anything about that, would you?" he asked. There was a hint of laughter in the voice of Gregory Greyshadow. He was a catholic priest and one of the hardest men I had ever met. I had known him for a little over a year now and had come to love most of our conversations.

"Nope. All I did was save some dumb kid and his girlfriend from a minotaur and then got yelled at by the dumb kid. I don't remember hacking up a car," I said.

"Good. Did you see anything else last night?" he asked me. His tone had changed. The mirth that lined his voice had vanished.

"No. What's going on?" I asked.

"You at home?" Priest Greyshadow asked. I told him yes, and he told me to check the news. I didn't have cable, internet, or a converter box for my TV. "Get a paper. It's best if you see it for yourself. Call me back ASAP."

We both hung up. I put my sword in my baseball bag and headed out. My apartment is on the ground level of an old building near the center of town. There are four units to my building, so I have two neighbors above me and one beside me. The neighbors rarely interact with me, and I don't blame them. Most nights I come home covered in my own blood and with claw marks all over my truck. No sane person should want to deal with a neighbor like that.

The exception is Mrs. Faraday, who was always happy to see me. Mrs. Faraday lives next to me and is 87 years old. Her husband is even older than she is, but he lives in a home on the other side of town. She is a kind old lady with a few medical problems but nothing that has kept her from living alone. She never says much and just sits outside with her lawn ornaments. She has thirty or forty garden gnomes. She always waves just as she did today when she saw me running over to my truck.

"Michael, where are you running off to so early? Another job interview?" she asked.

"No ma'am. I am just off to run a few errands. Do you want me to mow your lawn this weekend?" I asked her.

She looked around at the shared lawn. The grass wasn't tall, but I know she liked it trimmed so she could better appreciate her gnomes. The landlord would come out to cut the grass every two weeks, but it had rained right after his last visit, and he wasn't due back for a while.

"Oh, if you wouldn't mind. If my Peter was well he would take care of it," she told me. "But your allergies, please take plenty of medicine before you do."

I chuckled. "I will, I promise. Also, if you want to go see Mr. Faraday this weekend, I would be glad to take you," I told her.

"That would be lovely. He loves when you tell him about your adventures," she said as she clapped happily. I waved and drove off to the nearest gas station.

I bought a paper and sat in my truck to look through it. There was a lot going on in the city the next few days. Nothing major. The Orioles were away this weekend. There was an art exhibit opening today, but a stone statue of a gladiator had gone missing from the exhibit hall, and as usual there was a lot of local government crap. I called up Priest Greyshadow and asked him what I was looking for.

"See that article about the dead guy found at Bear Creek?" he asked.

"Yeah," I said.

"Guy was strangled. Cops say he was also covered in claw marks."

"Since when do animals strangle people?" I asked.

"Right, but it gets worse," he said.

"How?" I asked.

"Get your ass over here first. It gets worse, but it gets a little more worse before that," he told me. Priest Greyshadow didn't give me a chance to argue and just hung up. I revved up my truck and hit the road.

CHAPTER 3

I ROLLED DOWN to 409 Cathedral Street and into the parking lot of a large Catholic Church. Well, the word large doesn't exactly cover it. This church takes up two city blocks. Its full name is the Basilica of the National Shrine of the Assumption of the Blessed Virgin Mary, but it was better known as the Baltimore Basilica.

The Cathedral is a monumental neoclassical style building whose main entrance is designed as a classical Greek portico with a double hex style pattern of columns. Behind the columns, you can see a pair of cylindrical towers rising to the sky. The church has existed since the early 1800s, and until recent years more priests were ordained there than at any other church in the U.S. That change may or may not have something to do with me showing up in town.

I walked up the front steps and into the entry hall. There were two people there. One was a deacon that immediately looked at me as if I was an intruder. The other was an older woman named Hillary who smiled at me from behind the visitor's desk. I smiled, waved, and spoke very politely.

"Hi," I said. "Is Priest Greyshadow in?"

Hillary started to nod and say something to me, but the deacon cut in. "He is, but why are you here?"

The deacon was an older man and as pious as any other Sunday Christian...or Catholic in this case. Don't misunderstand—not all the people in the world that follow Catholicism or Christianity are assholes, but a good number, just like with every other religion, exist. He was in his early forties, tall like me, broad shouldered, and black. I remembered his name was Darrel, and like most people, he did not like me. I have a winning personality, but sometimes people just don't warm up to you.

"Well, Darrel," I said.

"It's *Deacon*—show some respect," he said.

Older guys are really protective of their titles. I let him have it. "Well, *Deacon*, he asked me to come over and have a chat. You know, red phone business and such," I said with a smile. Darrel started to say something, but I leaned to the side and said to Hillary, "You can let Priest Greyshadow know I'm here."

Hillary smiled and picked up the desk phone. The Deacon calmly shoved me back around to face him. I saw something in his eyes but diverted my gaze slightly. He was angry, but he hid it well. "Young man, do you think you can just walk in off the street and demand to see Priest Greyshadow?"

"It's *Sir, Deacon*, not young man," I said. "Mutual respect. Try it."

"You do not belong here," he said in a soft voice.

"It's a church. Anyone that was created by God is welcome here," I said. "In fact, I think I have proof of my divine creation right here." I reached over my shoulder into my bag and pulled out my middle finger for him to admire.

His eyes went wide, and I saw rage flash over his features. "You don't deserve what he gave you," he said through clenched teeth.

"Well, I can't argue with you there. But you have no right to judge me. That's his job. Read your bible," I said.

Hillary spoke up, "Head on back, Michael. Father Greyshadow is waiting for you in his office."

"Thank you, Miss Hillary," I said.

Darrel and I exchanged glances. I walked past him into the church proper and marched back to the offices. The last office at the end of the long hall said in black letters 'Priest Gregory Greyshadow.' The door was cracked open. I knocked.

"Just get your ass in here, kid," said a voice that was already exasperated with me. I wasn't supposed to knock. Priest Greyshadow hated it when I knocked, so I did it every time I came to his office.

I walked in and found two men looking at me. The first was Priest Gregory Greyshadow. He was an older man, somewhere between sixty and a hundred. His head was bald, but he sported a devilish goatee of wizardly white hair. Priest Greyshadow was wearing his clergy blacks with his white collar. He was an average-sized man with a lean build. Scars could be seen on his head, face, forearms, and hands. His fists had been broken so many times in his youth that they were gnarled, large, and warped. I am sure they had broken even more jaws. He was sitting behind his desk with a cigarette that he wasn't supposed to have burning in the ashtray.

Priest Greyshadow pointed at me and said, "This is him, Michael White. Michael, this is Detective Garrett Clay." There were two chairs in front of Priest Greyshadow's desk. In the chair on the right, the one I prefer to sit in, was a man wearing a cheap suit. When he turned to look at me, Priest Greyshadow pointed to my bag and shook his head.

"Hello Michael," Detective Clay said as he stood up. He held out his hand to shake mine. We traded grips. He didn't try to crush my hand, but he had an ironclad grip. He was a little taller than me and more muscular than I was. His blond hair was in a buzz cut so sharp that it could slice you open. He was a handsome guy with a confidant, calming smile. He was the kind of guy women would like, men wouldn't trust, and that I had grown up in fear of.

"Hey," I said. I caught his eyes flicker up and down for an instant. He was sizing me up. He let go of my hand and went to sit back down. "I'm sorry. Could I have that seat?" He looked at me for a moment as if I was a little strange, but he moved over to the left chair. I thanked him and sat down in my spot. I put my bag on the ground beside my right foot as far from this man as I could manage.

"Now like I was saying, Detective, I don't do that kind of stuff anymore. Pretty much I just preach, tend to the flock, get drunk, rinse, and repeat," Priest Greyshadow said.

"I understood that the first time, Father. I just want to know if you have any ideas about what happened," the detective said. He tapped the manila folder that was closed on the desk.

Priest Greyshadow opened the folder and began going through the contents. They were crime scene photos. He picked up each one and took a long moment to examine it before setting it to the side, right where I could plainly see them while sitting back in my chair. The pictures were of either a very good horror movie or a gruesome crime scene. There were four or five bodies piled on each other in one picture. Some were ripped apart by the limbs and joints. One was simply split in two, and not the way you would think—there was a front and back picture.

15

"This was all in one warehouse?" Priest Gregory asked. The detective nodded. "Well, like I said, I don't do P.I. work anymore. As of the Baskin case, I haven't taken a case outside the interest of The Church. But Michael here, I taught him most of what I know. He could help you."

The detective turned to me and asked, "You're a P.I.?"

I shrugged. "The priest helped me get my license, but I have never taken a case," I said. Priest Greyshadow thought that it would be good for me to get my private investigation license. It had been time-consuming, but it was good training. Plus, it gave me an excuse to be armed at all times.

"How long have you had the license?" he asked.

"A few months," I said.

Detective Clay gathered the photos and closed the folder. "No offense, but I need someone that isn't wet behind the ears," Clay said.

"The kids good. He has a bad habit of solving problems," Priest Greyshadow said.

"It wasn't his name in the department's Rolodex, it was yours. I need experienced eyes," Clay said. He stood up to leave.

"The bodies were all of young people, right? Some teenagers and some just a bit older?" I asked.

Clay stopped halfway to the door. "Yeah. How did you know?"

"Some of the clothing on the females was pretty bright and flamboyant. Some had bunches of bracelets, and there was a pacifier on a necklace around one of their necks. They were at a rave," I said. Detective Clay sat back down. "There were three different scenes in those photos. The time stamp shows them as days apart. I am guessing you found claw marks on some of the bodies. Puncture marks as well, like something bit them, but the bite doesn't match any known animals?"

"Yeah, we were racking our brains over it. Father Greyshadow's name came up as knowing about stuff like this," he said. "Occult stuff, religious yahoos with god complexes."

"Nope. Just monsters," I said.

"Someone would have to be one to do this," Clay said.

"No. Monsters as in real monsters did this. Things with claws and fangs," I said.

Clay looked at me like I was an idiot. He stood up and walked to the door. "I knew your name before this case came up, Greyshadow. My father had mentioned you when I was growing up. Said you were a loose cannon and a nut job. This was a waste of time," he said. He left and slammed the door closed.

"Just had to throw it out there, didn't you?" asked Greyshadow.

"I don't see the point in lying about it. Either he believes the truth or he doesn't. His personal perceptions aren't my problem. My problem is that people are dead, and the monster behind it is going to kill again."

"Kid, you need to get your shit together. We lie about this all the time. Since you came back from seeing your grandfather, you haven't been yourself. I know Frank didn't tell you to start running your mouth," Priest Greyshadow said.

"Nope, but keeping magical beings a secret has worked out so well for us. We live in a world of fairies, vampires, werewolves, and wizards. Doesn't it bother you that less than a tenth of the world's human population knows that?" I asked.

"Kid, it isn't our job to tell the world. It's our job to defend it," Priest Greyshadow said.

I couldn't argue with him. Defending the world from the supernatural was our job. I was just sick and tired of keeping it a secret.

"It was the guy from a few months back. It's his M.O. Throw a rave, gather young people, summon demons," I said.

"What are you going to do?" Greyshadow asked.

"Go take a look at this murder at Bear Creek. They could be connected or not. But either way, if there is a monster killing people, I am going to find it and deal with it," I said.

"Keep your phone on and keep your head straight. I know you want to get this asshole, but you dying doesn't help. I'll let Aaron know you might need him. You want to call in the wizard?" Greyshadow asked.

"Yeah. This was her case. She came to us for help, and with a wizard summoning demons to his beck and call, I'm going to need back up," I said. I grabbed my bag and headed for the door.

"Michael, what's so different about today that's got you in such a get up and go mood?" he asked me.

"Kerri-Lynn is coming to see me," I said.

CHAPTER 4

I UNLOCKED MY truck, got in, and pulled out into traffic. I had a few hours before Kerri-Lynn was going to arrive. She had insisted on coming to see me even though I had basically told her that I didn't want anything more to do with her. Kerri-Lynn knew me better than anyone, and she knew the truth — the truth being that I wanted everything to do with that girl. That I always had and always would. Being a knight had gotten in the way. I told her that I could never do her justice, and that I was sorry for wasting her time. She had called me a week ago and told me she was coming to see me whether I liked it or not.

"You should focus on the road," a calm voice said from my passenger seat. I nearly jumped out of my skin. I swerved into the next lane and had to get control of my truck before I ran up on the median.

I had locked up my truck and gotten back in alone. Now there was someone sitting in my passenger seat telling me how to drive. When I looked over, I found a man that seemed relaxed and easy going. He wasn't a young man or an old man. He was physically fit without having bulging muscles. He wore the same white shirt and jeans that he always wore. His brown hair was playfully messy, and he sported a close cut beard. I called him Bill, and when I first met Priest Greyshadow he called him Fred, so now we both called him Bill Fred. I didn't know much about him, but to me if Priest Greyshadow was my handler for The Church then Bill Fred was my handler for the Knights of the Crucifixion. He was a hard guy to deal with, but if I was meant to understand angels, I am sure someone would have mentioned it by now.

"You scared the crap out of me," I said.

"That's how you want to start this conversation?" he asked me.

"No! I would like to start it in a restaurant, over breakfast, and with a tall cool glass of O.J. Instead you have to do the whole 'I'm magic so let me screw with the human' thing," I said.

He laughed at me and said, "I guess it could be a little annoying."

"A little? I could have hit someone," I said.

The mirth faded from his features. "Do you honestly believe I would have allowed that?" he asked in a flat voice.

I swallowed hard. The last thing I wanted to do was insult an angel that was charged with making sure I protected people. "Nope. Never crossed my mind," I said.

He looked at me and flashed me a smile of perfectly white teeth as he said, "I didn't think so."

Bill Fred creeped me out most of the time. Correction: all the time. He is an actual angel that could probably kick my butt with his mind, maybe even kill me. Whenever he smiles, you just want to buy him a beer. Oh yeah, angels drink beer. Bill Fred prefers Bud.

"I won't keep you, Michael. You already seem to be on the case," he said.

"The lake? It's connected with the rave murders?" I asked.

"That's not why I am here. It's Garret Clay," he said.

"The detective?" I asked.

"Be careful with him. He isn't what you think he is," he said.

"I knew it. I knew he couldn't be trusted," I said. From the moment we shook hands I had a bad feeling about him.

"Michael, do not go looking for a new problem when you have enough problems staring at you," he said.

"Problems like what?" I asked. When he didn't answer, I looked over and saw that Bill Fred was gone. I shrugged. It wasn't past breakfast time at McDonald's yet, and I was ready to call it a day.

Chapter 5

GETTING TO BEAR Creek and back wouldn't be a big deal. Since it wasn't past breakfast time, I got myself four bacon egg and cheese biscuits. They were on sale two for $3, so for seven bucks I had an orange juice to go with it.

Bear Creek Park was one of the recreation areas in east Baltimore built around Bear Creek, just a short one-hour drive in morning bumper-to-bumper traffic. I got to the park, and there was no one around to be seen. That was strange. The paper said the body had been found two days ago near the shoreline. I spotted an area that was blocked off with crime scene tape.

I drove down to another part of the park and parked right in front of a sculpture of a hawk. I found people galore here. Now this seemed right. A nice day with a clear sky and people living life not three hundred yards from a supernatural murder. I grabbed my bag and walked back toward the scene.

There was a trail that led me back to the taped off area. I got there and looked around before ducking under the tape. The tape went around some trees, a bear statue, and a long wide stone block with a placard on it to encompass an area of about the size of an average one-car garage. There were hearts and initials carved into the trees surrounding the area, and every so often, I noticed a discarded square of plastic. This was a place people came to be alone.

Now that I had a handle on the layout, I needed to check a few things. I entered the area and checked out the normal stuff first. There was blood on the ground in several spots and something else. I bent down and touched a brown substance. It was hard and gritty, like cement. I looked at the big block of stone and read the placard. It said 'Black Bear, Ursus Americanus.' The statue was sitting on its butt on the other side of the clearing. That was a pretty heavy prank to pull off. I didn't see any evidence of a mass exodus from the area, so whatever happened had been confined to the victim and the murderer.

Next, I took a deep breath, closed my eyes, and settled my mind. When I opened my eyes, I opened something else along with them. I opened my mind's eye. I am not a wizard, and I do not understand how magic works, but I can sense magic and the supernatural. It takes practice and a lot of getting used to, but anyone can do it. You start by remembering that your mind will try to trick you. *Ignorance Is Bliss*, and because of that, your mind will always try to hide the obvious from you with a simple explanation. You have to fight it.

I could feel the wind coming off the water. It was a cool air, but I could clearly see steam rolling off the closest part of the lake. There was no dew on the grass. I smelled blood and something else. It smelled like concrete or stone. Probably the brown substance from earlier. The trees surrounding the area were rustling with lush green leaves, but the murder scene was littered with fallen brown ones. There was magic used here, and it was powerful. I started to get dizzy, so I closed off my senses. I rubbed the bridge of my nose as a headache began to start.

There was a sharp snap to my side and a grinding sound from behind me. I felt something large and heavy enough to shake the ground coming at me from behind. I dropped low and looked over my shoulder. Then I jumped out to my left as an 800-pound bear statue came barreling at me. I did a sidelong roll so that I came up to my feet facing the bear statue. It was made of shaped black stone with crime-scene tape wrapped around its neck, and somehow it was moving just like a real bear would. It had too much momentum to stop, but when it wheeled around on me, it dug in and skidded into a charging position.

I got to my feet and employed Michael Combat Rule Number One: shoot first. I drew my handgun and took a stance just as the bear statue came to a grinding halt. My gun of choice is a .50 caliber Desert Eagle. It's a miniature hand cannon that I used to put holes in anything that needs to stop trying to kill me. This bear statue may have been made of stone, but it was currently trying to kill me. It charged and I fired three rounds. One hit it in the left shoulder, one hit it in the left arm, and one blew off a chunk of its back. But it kept coming.

I backed up and unloaded four more rounds as I backpedaled. All of my shots hit, and I saw stone go flying away as pebbles and powder. Still the bear charged. My back hit the stone block that the bear was supposed to be on. The bear swung at me as I jumped and rolled onto the block. The bear's claw sliced into the placard and cut through the stone beneath as if it was paper. It raked across with its right arm to rip huge trenches into the stone block. I kept rolling until I was as far back as I could get then readied myself in a kneeling position. I didn't have another magazine on me because a .50 caliber shell should have stopped almost anything, but I was dealing with magic. I needed iron or silver rounds, which were expensive. The rounds I had were lead, and though they did a lot of damage, they did nothing to magical beings other than piss them off.

The bear reared up on its hind legs. It was seven and a half feet tall with arms thicker than my chest and made of stone. As much as I didn't want to, I reached over my shoulder into my bag and closed my hand around the handle of my sword. Power, pure and raw, rushed over me. It's not something that can be described correctly by any mortal. I felt memories surge through me. The joy of the first time I rode a bike without training wheels, the joy of the first time I rolled a natural 20 in Dungeons and Dragons, and the joy of the first time Kerri-Lynn ever smiled at me. I felt the pride of my mother when I graduated high school, the pride of my grandpa the first time I changed a tire, and the pride of my family when they found out I was going to become a knight. I felt the power of something greater than I ever could be, far greater, focused into me. I felt the power of faith.

When I drew my sword, its blade bathed the clearing in white light. My sword was a four-foot medieval-styled long sword. The handle was wrapped in black leather. The cross guard was a simple crossbar of silver with rounded ends. In the center of the cross guard was a blue gem, and on the rounded ends were similar gems. The blade was just over three feet long, broad, and sharper than any sword should ever have been. I could easily manage the sword in one hand, but baseball is my game, so I took a right-handed batters stance with it.

The bear statue swiped at me with its left paw, and I jumped over it. It came back around with its left and right together. I leapt over them and charged at the bear. I planted a sneaker on its snout and leapt out into the open clearing. I landed and dropped into a roll to put some distance between us. I took a good look at the stone that the bear's claw had cut through and reminded myself that one hit from this monster and it was all over. I rushed forward as the bear was turning and slashed from my waist up over my right shoulder as I passed the stone bear. The sound of metal hitting stone rang clear, but my sword cut deep into the flank of the turning Ursa. I turned as it roared in pain. It was a sound akin to an actual bear but filled with the sound of stone rubbing against stone. I looked at the wound my sword had left and saw liquid stone ooze from it like blood. It wasn't hot like lava—it was just stone converted to liquid.

I ducked as the bear struck out at me. I parried another blow and left a long cut on its right arm. More liquid stone gushed from the new wound. I darted to my left, and when the bear swiped at me, I spun around back to my right and plunged my sword into its knee. It howled and backhanded me with such force that my sword ripped through the stone leg. I hit the ground and the bear fell over. Its ruined leg was bent inward, half ripped off, and useless. I struggled to get up into a sitting position. I saw blood. My shirt had been ripped open in several lines going from my left side abdominal muscles to my right shoulder. The cuts were deep enough to bleed and need stitches but not deep enough to have sliced bone or organs. The hit certainly was hard enough to break a few of my ribs.

I struggled to get to my feet, and so did the wounded bear statue. I was up first, so I went on the attack. I charged, and when the bear swung at me, I skidded to a stop to let the stone claw pass me. Then I cleaved down into its left shoulder. The arm fell lifelessly, but the bear snapped its maw up at me. I tried to jump back, but the earth beneath me was slick with stone blood. I started to fall but managed to get my sword up. The bears head surged forth, and I thrust my blade as I fell. My sword entered the monster's mouth and erupted out of the back of its head.

I braced for what was going to happen next. The reason I shoot first is not because I want God to sort out my problems but because there is a price to be paid when using one of the Twelve Swords of the Apostles. Some beings have souls and some do not. When you kill a being, any being, with a soul by using one of the Twelve you lose a day from your life as punishment, and the amount of days was burned into your own soul. Last night I had lost my thirteenth day when I killed the minotaur. I readied myself to lose my fourteenth. The bear's eyes flared with other-worldly light. Its blue hue clashed with the white light of my sword. The lights raged like little torches and then darted away into the distance. The light of my sword faded away as well. Nothing else followed. The creature had no soul, and that meant that I wasn't going to lose a day.

I pulled my sword free and breathed a sigh of relief. I had killed a monster and not lost a day of my life. Awesome. This was going to be a good day.

"Drop the sword and put your hands in the air!" yelled an angry voice from behind me.

CHAPTER 6

ISTARTED TO turn slightly and the person behind me yelled, "I said drop the sword and put your hands in the air."

I called back, "No chance you are just a park ranger and not a guy with a gun, is there?" I heard the sound of an automatic weapon chambering a round. I lowered my sword to the ground and lifted my hands over my head.

"Now the bag," the voice said. I pulled off my gear bag and tossed it down to the ground. "Don't move. Cover me—if he moves shoot him."

So there were two guys. The talkative one came down and flipped my hands down behind my back one at a time as he handcuffed me. He spun me around, and I came face to face with Detective Clay. I hadn't recognized his voice, probably because of the mix of adrenaline and the headache from opening my mind's eye. The timber of his "cop" voice had thrown me, too. I looked past him and noticed that he was alone.

"Where's the other guy?" I asked.

"What other guy? I just said that cover me shit because I figured you were stupid enough to believe it," he said. Well, I had fallen for it, so arguing was pointless. He took my gun and my knife before patting me down. "On your knees."

My brain started working harder than usual. The bad guy had me in cuffs and had a loaded gun somewhere on him. Fight or flight would be the normal reaction, but I wasn't doing anything that would leave my sword exposed to the enemy. I have no idea what kind of crazy super evil someone could do with a bad attitude and a holy relic forged by God.

"No," I said. I had to buy some time. I could rush him, but with the cuffs on and him armed, that would be a short-lived defiance.

Detective Clay looked at me with a smug smile on his face. "Oh, really?" he asked as he kicked one leg out from under me and pushed me down to my knees. I grunted as I hit the dirt. "I followed you. I figured you would lead me to more bodies. I didn't really expect you to be dumb enough to go back to one of your crime scenes, but here you are."

"My crime scenes? You asshole, this is your crime scene," I said. He hadn't taken my cell phone, but that wouldn't help since I couldn't see the screen.

"Now that's a new one. Blaming the crime on the cop that busts you," he said. He walked around me and picked up my gear bag. He tossed my knife inside along with my gun after ejecting the magazine and checking the slide. He picked up my sword and held it for a moment. He came back around to stand in front of me. "Now, I'm not about to take you in and have the department worrying about my sanity. So, you are going to tell me how you made the sword glow and how you made the statue move."

"Really? You want to play this like I'm the bad guy?" I asked. He had my sword in his right hand and my bag in his left.

"Seriously, kid, is it a button, some sort of special oil, what? And the bear, is it animatronic? Where is the real one, and who was controlling that one before you broke it?" he asked.

I looked up at him with the intent of spitting in his face. I didn't like this guy in the first place, and it turned out he was the bad guy. He had gotten the drop on me, and this was going to be it, killed by a bully. I can't say I didn't already know that was how it was going to be, but I never expected that bully to be a cop. I looked him dead in the eye and filled my mouth up with a morning's worth of allergy-related snot and spit.

God may be vengeful, and then again he may not be. God may be merciful, and then again maybe not. I can't say because I have never met the guy. Despite that, I do know for a fact he has a sense of humor. I prayed all of my life for a superpower. I didn't really care what it was as long as God gave me something that let me fight back against the numerous bullies I faced every day of my life. Something that gave me an edge over my oppressors, or at least let me escape the constant beatings that I was handed by bullies for as far back as I can remember. Instead, when I got my sword, I received an ability that not even the other knights had. I gained the power of Insight. A superpower I absolutely hate!

When I readied my super loogie, I looked Detective Clay dead in the eyes. Confusion swept through me, the same confusion that had been in me since I was a child. That confusion made me angry, and the anger made me violent. Violent towards others, when I didn't want to be. It came from my father. He and my grandfather both served on the police force. My father was a tough cop and a tougher father. He ruled the house with the back of his hand. He was a monster. It didn't matter how much of a good kid I tried to be or how well I did in school. My father would come home from seeing unexplainable murder after unexplainable murder, and he would drink. Then he would beat my older brother, my mother, and me.

My father hurt me, so I hurt others. My brother and I started working out. We fought back and lost. He beat us even more then, and I kept taking it out on other kids. My grandfather, whom never hurt me, would come over and try to help us. But my grandfather was old, and he couldn't always protect us. It was a living hell, until one day when my father came home, picked up his gun, and took his own life right in the living room. He left us broken and with a little sister on the way. I tried to be good for my family, to stay out of trouble, and grow up to be a good man like my grandfather. But here I am looking at the same strange shit that had driven my father to beat his wife and kids. Here I am facing his monsters and his demons, and all I want is a drink. Here I am turning into the monster that I spent my life fearing and running from.

They weren't my thoughts. They were Detective Clay's thoughts, his fears, and his pains. I felt every beating he received and the torment inside him as he beat up other children that were smaller than he was. I felt the anguish of getting stronger to protect yourself only to fail and use that strength to harm others. I felt his fear of the unexplained and of the darkness he feared was inside himself. I felt the fear he had of Gregory Greyshadow and of me. Even more pressing was his need to explain what he had just seen before he completely lost his mind.

I swallowed the super loogie. Somehow, I had managed to mix bile with it. I lowered my head and remembered what Bill Fred said. I had looked at this man as a problem when I shouldn't have. I'm a knight, not a saint. I have my faults, and bullies, or rather the fear of them, is one of them. "Detective Clay," I said, "let me tell you the truth. About a lot of things."

Chapter 7

I TOLD DETECTIVE Clay about the world he lived in, the one that he had been ignoring up until now. I tried to stick to only the pertinent stuff. First, I explained *Ignorance Is Bliss* to him. Next, I told him that I was a knight but not about my order or The Church. Then I told him about magic, monsters, and demons. The tutorial ended by explaining that I did not understand the stone bear or have anything to do with the mass murders other than failing to stop them several months beforehand.

Detective Clay listened to all that I had to say. He laughed at some of it, and he kept threatening to arrest me. Eventually he sat down on the stone block and thought about all that I had said. I was still on my knees. The adrenaline from the fight was gone, so the cuts along my abdomen and chest were aching. I wasn't too worried about the pain. I was more worried about what Detective Clay would do. He looked at my sword, and he kept looking at the statue I had destroyed.

"Do you have any questions, detective?" I asked.

"Why the hell should I believe anything you say?" he asked me.

I thought about it. "Why should you? You shouldn't. I could just be some nut job that doesn't want to go to jail. I could be a serial killer. I could be the host of a hidden camera show that wants to prove cops are gullible," I said. "You should just go home and hug your family as hard as you can. But after that you should look up why every culture in the world has a word for dragon, goblin, ogre, and troll."

He looked at me with wide eyes filled with anger. He got up and came over to me with the same expression he had when he walked out of Priest Greyshadow's office. He grabbed me under my arm and hauled me up to my feet. Then he took off the handcuffs. I turned to look at him, and he said to me, "You have to prove it."

"Huh?" I asked.

"You have to prove it to me. The monsters, the magic, the…all of it," he said. "Prove it to me."

My head was pounding and my chest was on fire. "How? I can't do magic. I'm a knight—the sword is magical, not me," I said.

He rubbed his hand over his head in frustration. "Then how about a monster? Show me a monster," he said.

Now that I could do. It would be risky, but I could do it. "I can, but not until 8 pm tonight," I said.

"Now," he demanded.

"What? Do you think I just have a vampire on speed dial? Tonight I can show you. I can show you a lot, but you have to leave them alone afterward. They are citizens of the city, and you are sworn to protect them. They don't all go around hurting people."

Detective Clay ground his teeth for a long minute. "Okay. But until then I keep your weapons," he said.

"Not the sword," I said.

"All of them. Until you prove to me that what you said is true, I keep your stuff," he said.

Without my sword I was a target, and something had already taken a shot at me. I couldn't let him keep my sword. "You can't just confiscate my sword on suspicion," I argued.

"Call the cops. See who they side with," he said.

He had me over a barrel. I needed my sword, but it looked like I was going to have to play his game. I nodded to him and said, "Fine, but I want your word that you will return my gear tonight, and you will let no one else know about it. It's an artifact from God, and I don't feel like telling my boss I lost it."

He held out his hand to me. I took it. "You have my word on the monsters being left alone, as long as they aren't hurting anyone, and on your weapons, but you have to show me a concealed carry permit for the gun," he said.

"Deal," I said. We shook hands, exchanged phone numbers, and I told him where to meet me. He left, and I hurried back to where The Rust Bucket was parked in front of the statue of the hawk. At least that's where it should have been parked. My truck was still in the same spot, but the hawk was gone. I checked the inscription of the pedestal, and sure enough a hawk statue should have been there. Someone had stolen the statue but left my truck alone. I would take any win I could get.

My chest hurt too badly to wear my seat belt, but I still hightailed it home. I made good time considering traffic and nearly passing out on the way back to my apartment. I stumbled from my truck to the door and somehow managed to get inside. Pulling my shirt off, I walked into the kitchen. I opened the first cabinet, grabbed a bottle of alcohol, and dumped it over my wounded chest and abdomen. Then I grabbed an industrial-sized first aid kit from under the sink and went to the living room. I fell on the couch and started treating my wound. Antiseptics, more alcohol, and then bandages. That's all I remembered before I passed out.

Chapter 8

THERE WAS A knock at my door. I ignored it. My head was pounding, and I felt like I was exhausted. Not to mention that my chest was on fire. There came more knocking, and I ignored it again. I leaned over and lay on my couch. My soft, comfortable, warm couch. Then someone started knocking harder. I grunted as I got up. I walked over to my door, and like every tired human ever, I opened it with the intent of killing whoever was on the other side.

I opened my door slightly and started to yell, but the words froze in my mouth. There on my doorstep was every fantasy I ever had in my short life. The sun flashed off Kerri-Lynn Briscoe's golden skin. She was barely five feet tall in her sneakers. She wasn't a thin woman, but she wasn't fat. Her body had found that comfortable area that all men love but never admit to. Her hair was done in fresh tight braids then pulled into a ponytail. She had on the standard nerd traveling gear of jeans and a tee shirt. The shirt was one of mine, a Green Lantern shirt that she had taken years ago. It had shrunken since then, or maybe her breasts were just better looking in a men's 2XL. She wore tight jeans that showed off her hips, butt, and the rest of her perfectly sculpted legs. Her dark eyes were framed perfectly by fire engine red glasses.

I may have been struck silent, but she wasn't. She looked me in the eyes and said, "Hey Mikey! Did you miss me?"

I replied in a calm and cool fashion. "I...um err...eh yeah...um ah..." I said with a suave resolve.

"Okay, sweet talker, your mama taught you better than to keep a guest at the door," she said.

The human ability for speech reasserted itself in my brain. Consonants and vowels lined up, and I was suddenly able to perform simple speech again. "Come in," I said. But I said it like it was my idea, not as if it was in response to the mention of my mother. I'm not a child.

I opened the door and her eyes went wide. She looked at my chest and back to my face in a quick motion. "What the hell happened to you? Go sit down," she ordered. I moved and did as I was told. She carried in five large plastic bins, two duffle bags, and a backpack. She tossed it all beside the door, locked up, and then came over to me.

"Did you even try to clean this?" she asked as she started going through the already open first aid kit. She sat on my cinder block and board coffee table as she worked. She moved back and forth between my hallway closet, my kitchen, and my table. She complained that my cabinets had more painkillers than a hospital, and they did. Aaron saw to that. My kitchen wasn't for food—it was for medical supplies.

After cleaning the wound, disinfecting it, smacking me on the head for squirming, and telling me I was being a big baby, Kerri told me to stand up. She wrapped bandages around my chest and waist. She did the same with the cut along my arm that I hadn't noticed. After that, she had me sit down, and she pounced onto the couch next to me with her knees folded beneath her.

"So how did you do that," she asked.

"A bear attacked me this morning," I said.

"I thought you fought monsters. Bears are bad but not monsters." She held up a hand and then went back to the bags she had thrown to the side. She dug around in one for a few seconds, and then she came back over to me. "Except this bear, he isn't bad," Kerri said as she set an old teddy bear in my lap.

I looked down at the black and brown bear. It had brown fur with tuffs of black here and there. The marble eyes had been a matched set of green with black pupils, but one had fallen out to be replaced with a black button. He wore overalls, and there were patches of cartoon superhero emblems on them: GI Joe, He-Man, Silverhawks, Thundercats, Transformers, and Voltron. The strap across its chest that held a matching shield and sword across its back was new. Other than that, he looked exactly as he did when he was sitting on the bookshelf of my old home.

"Horace?" I asked. "You brought my old teddy bear?"

"Yeah. Since you were being such a big baby about me coming and how dangerous your life was I figured you could use a body guard. I fixed him up. I have another marble for his eye on order. I even gave him a sword and shield so he can keep you safe from the big bad monsters." She ruffled the tuff of hair on the bear then kissed me on the forehead.

I set the bear to the side of the couch and cleared my throat. "It was made of stone. The bear that attacked me. Someone animated it," I said in a matter of fact tone.

"So a wizard? Witch? Warlock?" she asked.

"All of the above. I won't know until I call up Eden," I said.

"Eden?" she asked as she scooted closer and propped her face against her hand.

"Yeah. She is one of the resident wizards in the area. Pretty powerful and smart. She'll know," I said.

"So Eden is pretty," Kerri said.

"Yeah," I said. Then I realized what had just come out of my mouth. I panicked and tried to correct myself. "No, I mean she is pretty powerful, not pretty and powerful!" I said.

"So she isn't pretty?" Kerri-Lynn asked as she slid closer.

I thought about it for a moment. "Well, yeah she is pretty, but not like you. She's older than me and kind of hates me," I said.

"So you do think she is pretty?" she asked me.

I was stuck between a rock and a hole that was getting deeper by the second. I was used to dealing with monsters, not women. Monsters were scary, but Kerri scared me more than any monster. Women are hard to deal with when most of your experiences with them have been them wanting to castrate you.

"Kerri—" I started to say, but she cut me off.

"Michael, I just drove all the way from Virginia to see you, and you are telling me that you need to talk to a pretty woman? Boy, if you don't get your head on straight right now I am going to make you wish that bear had killed you today. You haven't so much as hugged me since I got here," she said.

I turned to her with the intention of hugging her, but when I lifted my head, I found her face inches away from my own. She kissed me like she had been waiting for me all of her life. Her lips wrapped around mine as she took my face in her hands. Kerri floated over to me and fell into my arms as if she belonged there and nowhere else. My arms closed around her to hug her with all my strength, and the world around us melted away.

There was no pain, there were no monsters—there was nothing but her. Nothing but us. Kerri-Lynn took away everything that was wrong like she always had. As a child, she had warned me about the boys that wanted to beat me up, and she had bloodied more than a few girl's noses for teasing me. As a teenager, she had come to every one of my baseball games, played in every Dungeons and Dragons game, and been there every time someone sent me to the hospital. She had waited for me to get over my fears and to come back to her.

Kerri was my saving grace. She was my light in the darkness. I had been hated by every man, woman, and child in Virginia except my family. Everyone except her. She loved me and I loved her. We even shared a birthday: February 29th, 1992. When she looked at me, I felt like everything was possible. When she laughed, I knew that there was a God. When she cried…I would kill anyone that made her cry.

I lifted her into my arms and carried her into my bedroom. Our clothes fell from our bodies to the floor. I laid her down and slid my body between her legs. She looked at me, and her eyes met mine. There was no flash of Insight, and I prayed to God for it. I wanted to see what could have created this girl short of God forging her out of clay. But all I saw in her eyes was happiness, happiness to be with me. I leaned in to kiss her just before I entered her.

"KNIGHT!" a booming voice said. "KNIGHT OF THE FALSE GOD!" it continued. "I HAVE BUSINESS WITH YOU!"

Kerri looked at me, and there was confusion in her eyes. I looked at her not knowing what to do, but then something caught my eye. There was a tear in the corner of her left eye. I got up, got my pants on, and went to my closet. I put on an undershirt and grabbed my Louisville Slugger baseball bat, knocking the weights off it. I grabbed the pistol that I used as a backup and clipped its holster to my left hip. I walked into the living room and picked up my Orioles baseball cap.

Kerri followed me into the living room. She was getting dressed as fast as possible. "Michael, what's going on? Who was that?" she asked.

I put my cap on and pulled the brim down to cover my eyes. I slung my bat over my shoulder and put my hand on the doorknob before saying, "Someone that has no idea how violent nerd rage can be."

CHAPTER 9

THERE WAS A man standing beside a black sedan with an open back door at the edge of my sidewalk, roughly fifteen yards from me. He was older than I was by two decades at least. I judged his height at around five and a half feet tall, and he was thin as a rail. There were bags under his eyes, and his face was drawn. His hair was pulled into a ponytail of dark brown and gray. Of course, his clothing had come straight from Men's Evil Warehouse. A black shirt was tucked into black dress pants. To complete the ensemble, he wore a charcoal gray long coat with a matching fedora. I always get the stereotypical jerks that dress like cartoon characters. If there was any question remaining whether he was a wizard or not, the five-foot oak staff he held was enough to convince me.

The two goons with him looked like your standard henchmen from any movie you can think of. They were dressed in Men's Evil Warehouse's fall line of black short sleeve button downs, dress pants, and athletic casual shoes. I had heard that look was all the rage this year. In fact, I was sure I would see it on most of the henchmen this season if I lived through it. I had armor and a bulletproof vest inside, but in my rage I had neglected them. At least I had remembered my baseball cap.

"I'm going to say this once: I am going to stick my foot up all three of your butts if you don't leave right now. This is my home. My neighbors have a strict rule about me bringing my work home," I said.

"Well that wasn't witty at all. I had heard you were witty, but you just sound like some thug," the man in black said.

"Typically I go find the bad guys. They don't come to me," I said.

"Typically I hear about you being backed by a female wizard and a vampire. I know why one of them isn't here. Where is the witch?" the evil wizard asked.

"Not here and not important. You came to see the knight; well here I am. Say what you have to say while you still have teeth in your mouth."

"I had come prepared to be entertained, but this thuggish report isn't worth my time," he said.

"Well you caught me at a bad time for banter. We could reschedule, but since its high noon already I say we get on with the showdown," I said.

"Never let it be said that Michael White wastes time. But I am not here to fight; I came to talk," the wizard said.

"I'm sorry, you seem to know me, but I have never seen you before, sir. Did you Facebook stalk me?" I asked.

"Oh, my apologies, we haven't formally met. My name is Alistair Dyhart, and I'm a wizard. I am here on behalf of our mutual acquaintance, Mr. Ophalistis," he said.

"I'm sorry, who?" I asked.

"Ophalistis, the demon you hit in the face with the hammer at the rave several months ago," Dyhart said.

I remembered a few months back when a short, foul-mouthed lady wizard had led me into a fight with a demon in the middle of a rave. She had blown it up with a grenade. Something wasn't adding up. That demon was dead. I had seen its body burn. Then again, I was dealing with the supernatural, so what the hell did I know.

"So you are the jerk that invites people to parties and then summons demons in the middle of the dance floor," I said.

"Yes, if you must say it so mundanely. I prefer to think that I presented my associates with the entertainment they requested," he said matter-of-factly.

"How about we just cut to the chase. You came to talk, so talk," I said. I wanted Dyhart to talk—I needed him to talk. Rule number one when dealing with villains: monologues are your friends. Let the bad guy tell you his plans. It makes it easier to thwart them later...and you get to say 'thwart'!

"I want your sword," he said.

I was expecting a lot more information than that. "No," I said.

"Mr. Knight, before you say that, you may want to consider this. The statue that attacked you this morning was deliberately enchanted to attack you. The young boy that died there died trying to protect his young lover. I have her and two other girls. Give me your sword and I will let them go. Refuse and their blood is on your hands," he said.

Amendment to rule one when dealing with villains: sometimes monologues also reveal how twisted they are. The bastard had three hostages and was bargaining with their lives for my sword. This meant I couldn't just shoot him, because now I had to find these girls. My day was getting complicated.

"Why?" I asked. Now I needed to think. I didn't have my sword, and once he found that out I was expendable and those girls were dead.

"Simple. You are a human," said Dyhart.

"Same as you," I said with a smile.

"Let me expand on my previous statement. You are a normal human. You have no special powers, no magical aptitude, and are very much mortal. Without that sword you are no threat to me," Dyhart said with a sinister and knowing smile. He was right on some points. I was a normal man. I was mortal. I could die just like anyone else.

"You come to my home. You tell me you have people held hostage. You admit to killing for entertainment. You demand I hand over my sword to you. I thought you were smart, but you obviously don't understand the can of whoop ass you just opened," I said. I took my bat off my shoulder so that he could see what I was holding.

"A bat. You came out here with a bat?" he asked.

"I like bats. They break bones pretty easily."

Dyhart held his hand out toward me, and I got ready to move. He lowered his head but made no move to attack or threaten me. His eyes opened wide when he looked back up at me. "The sword isn't here. Where did you hide it? Where is it?"

"Why would I tell you, jerk?" I said.

We stared off, and I started doing math—distance, age, and the odds of goons one and two being willing to take a bullet for their boss. I wanted to go for my gun, but I had a problem killing people. Call it conflict of duty, call it humanity, or call it cowardice. I have never taken a human's life. God gave me my sword to protect an aspect of humanity. How was I protecting it if I was taking human lives? As evil as Alistair Dyhart sounded, his blood still ran red, and he was a child of God. Someone had to stop him, and I would, but not by killing him. He was the monster, not me.

"You don't know, do you? That officer…the bag he took from you had your sword," he said with a spurt of laughter. I didn't reply. "This is perfect. The police want to stop me and have no idea how to do so. Then they solidify my plans by crippling the one man in the city that could pose a threat to me!" He broke out into evil maniacal laughter, a huge 'bwahahaha' that needed some serious practice.

Behind me, I heard Kerri snicker. "Really? Every villain you ever rolled up for us in Dungeons and Dragons could give this guy pointers on evil laughter. Shoot him. Twice for monologing," she said.

I couldn't help but smile. Kerri was awesome. She had no idea how deep in trouble we were, but she had my back. Alistair Dyhart mistook my smile for something it wasn't. His smile faded and a scowl returned to his face.

He scoffed at me, "You still think you can stop me? I have hostages. I have power. I have allies, both human and demonic. I even have the powers of Jezzepus. What do you have?"

"A baseball bat and a size fourteen boot that I bet is a perfect match for your butt," I said. "Oh, and that whole chosen warrior of God thing. Remember that?"

"Your false god. He picked a muscle-bound fool for a champion. That shows his inferiority," Dyhart said. I was shocked. No one had ever called me muscle bound. I didn't know whether to be flattered or insulted. "Well it doesn't matter. Without your sword, you are no threat to me. In fact, you aren't even worthy of my time." Then he flicked his hand as though he were waving me away. Normally I wouldn't care, but in this case, a sphere of green fire came at me.

I slammed the door shut behind me and used the momentum to spin out of the path of the fireball. It passed me, and I felt its heat wash over me. The fireball hit my door and blasted a hole in it the size of a baseball. Kerri was in there. She could have been right behind the door and have a hole in her gut right now. I turned and charged the wizard and his goons. Before I could close the distance, they drove off in their black sedan. It didn't have a license plate. I ran back to check on Kerri. When I opened the door she was standing there, dressed, and with no holes in her that weren't supposed to be there.

"You alright?" I asked. She nodded and I took a step toward her. Something caught my leg and pulled it right out from under me. I hit the ground, and suddenly I was being dragged across the yard. I tried to turn over, but whatever had me lifted me into the air and held me upside down. I couldn't see anyone. There were no goons, no monsters, not even a giant gorilla. I looked up at my leg and saw a rope around it. No, not a rope. A tree root.

"Holy crap," said Kerri.

I craned my neck to see her and saw something that was out of the ordinary. Lawn gnomes, dozens of them, had surrounded the ground beneath me. Some were raising their hands and wiggling their fingers. Others were rubbing their hands together, and the more they rubbed the more fire I could see sheathing their ceramic mitts. I thought of the bear statue and got the feeling that this was the same type of magic.

I tried to wiggle free but couldn't, so I did a sit up and grabbed hold of my trapped leg. The root wouldn't budge. I dropped my bat so I could take hold of the root in both hands. It tightened the moment I touched it. My fingers wedged into the vice grip of the enchanted plant. There were flashes below me, and I panicked when I felt the heat around me rise.

"Mike!" Kerri screamed. I pulled with all my strength and screamed as the first of the flames reached me. My body jerked in pain, and that gave me the push I needed to break the root apart. My shirt, pants, and body became sheathed in flames as I fell. When I hit the ground, I scrambled and rolled as much as I could. The fire died away, and I escaped with only minor burns.

I started patting myself down to make sure all the fire was out when a jet of flames came at me. The flames barely missed me as I fell back into a roll. Dozens of multicolored, bearded, pointy hatted, ceramic gnome lawn ornaments had come to life and were wielding magic. My hand closed around my bat, and I struck the closest gnome with a back handed swing. It shattered like a cheap lawn ornament…which I guess it was.

Gnomes were magical beings. Not exactly fae and not human. They were like dwarves. I wasn't sure if they looked like their lawn ornament counterparts, but I knew they possessed power over earth and fire. So these constructs, created in the mythical image of the noble and powerful gnome, were probably magical powerhouses.

As I stood up, another root took hold of my right leg and pulled it out from under me. I fell on my back as another gnome shot a jet of fire at my face. Before the flames hit me, I rolled up and away from them. Then

43

I smashed the little fire gnome with my bat before trying to break free from the root. Fire hit my back, and I rolled onto the ground to put it out. I tried to swing at the new attacker but found my arm gripped with another root. My free hand snatched up the bat, and I tried smashing anything within reach. The gnomes started moving back, and more jets of fire came at me. Tangled up like this left me unable to dodge, so flailing about was the only defense I had. More roots snaked up from the ground at me, and I was pulled at awkward angles. My legs were pulled in opposite directions, and I gritted my teeth in pain.

A root closed around my throat. I grunted and had to drop my bat so I could try to pry my throat free. Desperation set in as I struggled against the magical strength of the root. The heat of small fires were building around me as I was pulled in four different directions. The root around my neck finally broke, and I gasped for air just as a jet of flame passed over my face. My nose was burned, and my lungs took a hit of fire and smoke.

My left hand swung down to my hip, and I grabbed my pistol. Then I started filling gnomish fire starters with lead. They were close enough that I couldn't miss. Four shots took out four of the bastards, but then my gun clicked empty. Undaunted I flung my gun and took out another gnome. There were still too many left, and I had only broken some of the ones shooting fire. I sat up to try to free the rest of my body. That's when the ground shook and five thick, powerful-looking roots erupted from the ground around me and started to entrap my body.

Those roots were as thick as tree trunks at their base. They thinned slightly every few inches until they were spear points sharp enough to pierce through my flesh. Five of them spaced around me in a star like pattern towering above me and threatening to close around me. The ground beneath me began to crumble. The air around me became hot, violently hot, and in the back of my mind, I felt something old and dark. The animated garden gnomes had started this, but something else was in play. These roots. This heat. This was a claw from Hell, and it was here to drag me away.

I couldn't move. I couldn't fight back. I was hurt and I was unarmed. I was done for.

There was a bark and a gnome head exploded. There was another bark and another gnome bit the dust. Gunshots rang out in rapid succession. Each shot was followed by a ceramic explosion. I heard a magazine eject, and a half-second later another baker's dozen of animated pyrotechnic gardeners were smashed to pieces. I looked over to see Kerri in a weaver stance picking off targets faster than I could blink. The second her gun ran empty she ejected her magazine and slapped another into it. She killed each gnome with a single shot, and I didn't know if I should be excited or terrified.

She looked at me after she had finished off all the gnomes and said, "No power in the verse can stop me."

I was excited. Definitely excited.

The magic around me died away, and the hot air began to cool. I still felt that ancient power in the back of my head. It didn't feel angry, just patient—like it had all the time in the world to wait for me. My limbs pulled against the roots binding me, and without magic backing them they broke away. When I got up, the ground beneath me felt like it could crumble away at any moment. Stepping aside, I kicked one of the claw roots. It was still as strong as a tree. There was still magic coming from it, and the more I felt it the more I missed my sword.

I looked off in the direction the wizard had fled. He had threatened my city, my home, my neighbors, and my girl. I walked over to Kerri as she eased her black gun into her holster. "What is that?" I asked.

"It's a Baby Desert Eagle. I heard my favorite superhero carries one that's a little bigger," she said with a smile. "Iron rounds mixed with silver jackets. I keep a magazine of incendiary rounds in my purse just in case."

I dragged her inside and locked up before I started asking questions. "First, thanks for saving my bacon," I said.

"Not a problem," she said.

"Second, where did you learn to shoot like that?" I asked.

"From my daddy when I was ten. You're the one that didn't learn to shoot until you were eighteen. I've owned a gun since I was eleven."

"Okay, I didn't know that. But third, where did you get that kind of ammo?" I asked.

Kerri walked over to one of the plastic cases that she had carried in. This one had wheels, so she just had to pull it. She opened it and my eyes went wide. Inside the storage bin were boxes upon boxes of ammo.

Silver jacketed rounds, iron shells, white phosphorous rounds, and explosive bullets. Thousands of rounds, all in .50 caliber size. Redneck Christmas was here!

"Where the heck did you get all of this?" I asked as I dropped to my knees and started looking over my new treasure horde.

"Care package from your Grandfather," Kerri said as she walked over and opened up her backpack. "But this is from me."

I managed to pry myself away from the ammo, and my eyes met something of pure beauty. In Kerri's hands was a Desert Eagle of the same design as mine. The difference was that this one was blinged out in chrome. She handed it to me and the weight felt familiar. I took aim and the balance was perfect. She laid out a holster, laser sight, and extra magazines.

I set down my new favorite thing in the world and pulled my old favorite person in the world in for a kiss. Our lips met, and she started to fall into me. Kerri caught herself and pushed away. "Hold it. Shouldn't you figure out what to do about everything that just happened first?"

She was right. Baltimore was still in danger. Every knight was given a territory to look over. My Grandpa, Franklin White, wielder of the Sword of Justice that was given to Peter by Jesus, was in charge of the Eastern United States. From the Mississippi River to the Atlantic Ocean, he was the man that stood between good and evil for both the mortal and the magical worlds. He had assigned me to look after Maryland.

This problem wasn't just in my territory, it was in my city. I made Baltimore my home because it was a hub for supernatural activity and the home of my favorite baseball team. It needed people that could intervene whenever some nut job decided to play super villain with magic or when a supernatural being decided coexistence with mortals was unacceptable. It had a few good Samaritans, but when it came down to it, I was the only one that could say it was his job to step up and push the bad guy down.

I got up and went over to my bookcase. There were about six dozen books crammed on the top shelf. My hand reflexively reached for and pulled out a large thick tome with a brown cover. On the front of the book were the symbols for most of the standard religions in the known world. Mixed with them were the symbols for most of the known organizations of Second Earth. All those images surrounded a broken cross set in gold. I opened it just as Kerri sat down next to me.

"What's this?" she asked.

"The monster manual," I said.

"What? This doesn't look like a Dungeons and Dragons book to me," she said.

"Not that Monster Manual. The Church keeps records of every type of creature they encounter," I said. "Fey, cryptid, demonic, celestial, ecto-plasmic, demigod, old world, and even extra dimensional. They update it every few years if there is significant new information. It's literally a book about anything not human. An actual monster manual."

"Holy shit, are you serious? You have a book on actual monsters?" she asked.

"Yes. Alistair Dyhart gave me a name," I said. "Here it is, Ophalistis." There on the page was a picture of the demon that I had thrown down with six months ago. I thought he was dead. Apparently he had survived.

"It says here that Ophalistis of the Thrall is a true demon with power seated in sin and frivolity," Kerri said. "He has power over fire and regularly associates with two other demons: Anfalar the Beast Bringer and Jezzepus the Stone Caller."

"He did have two other demons helping him," I said. I looked up Jezzepus, and his picture matched the demon whose throat I had slit on one of my first missions in Baltimore. "Jezzepus is able to breathe false souls into earth wrought golems. Any stone can become his vassal, and if the stone is fashioned after a creature, it gains the natural abilities of the muse."

"So the gnomes were animated by this guy?" Kerri asked.

"No. I killed him. I am sure of it," I said. I had lost a day of my life for it, which still bothered me. Why did that demon have a soul?

"It says he is a true demon too," said Kerri. "What does that mean?"

I turned to the page explaining demons. Past that page was another page that explained true demons. We read it together. Demons were any being that was born of chaos and malice. They were barred from the earth unless specifically invited by one of our world's inhabitants. They drew their powers from the suffering of those in Hell. A true demon was created with a soul. The only being capable of doing this besides God or Jesus was the Fallen Angel Lucifer. True demons drew their powers directly from Lucifer as Angels draw their power directly from God. The only way for a mortal to kill a true demon is with one of the twelve Swords of the Apostles or to strike a killing blow while they are on the plane in which they were created. Any other time they would be destroyed would result in banishment back to their original plane of creation.

My spine began to tingle. I had killed one of these true demons, and it had drawn its power straight from the Devil. More pressingly, I needed my sword to kill the other two. Now that sword was in the hands of a police officer with no idea of its importance. I had to get it back. I had to get myself moving.

The adrenaline from the fight was wearing off. I could feel the burns on my body, and the injuries from this morning hadn't healed yet either. Luckily, I could trust in the runic tattoos that the Church had placed on my body to heal me while I worked. I would have to rely on my own stamina as well. There wasn't time to wait for my body to fully heal.

I got up and loaded my new gun and several of its magazines. In the kitchen, I opened one of the drawers. There was a spare key underneath the top of the compartment. I tossed it to Kerri. "I have to get some business done. You will be safe here, but if you want to go out just lock up behind you. Keep your cell on and your gun handy," I said.

"I should come with you," she said.

"No. Not right now. I need to meet up with a wizard. But I am going to need every bit of help later if you are up for it," I said.

She nodded. I went to my room and grabbed a new shirt. This one was dark blue. Kerri walked me outside, and for the first time I noticed the Red Dodge Journey that she had shown up in. I got into The Rust Bucket and hit the road. It was time to see a lady about a demon.

CHAPTER 10

I KNOCKED ON the door of an old Victorian-styled home on the good side of town in Roland Park. My truck was out on the street and looked completely out of place among the convertibles, expensive SUVs, and new pickup trucks. I looked a mess of course, with the blood and the bruises—plus the gun that I wasn't even trying to hide in its brand-new holster. But my baseball cap looked nice.

When the door opened, I was greeted by a woman with a pleasant smile. She smiled at me and said through gritted teeth, "Mr. White. Why are you at my home unannounced, during the day, and dressed like a vagabond?"

Eden Freeman stood five feet tall in her heeled house shoes. Eden was a heavy-set woman that looked to be in her mid to late thirties if you were close enough not to mistake her small stature and cherubic face for that of a child. She was wearing a sundress and apron that covered her too-large chest. She was holding a steaming hot pie in her mitted hand.

"Well, Mrs. Freeman, you aren't answering your phone. I figured I would swing on over and make sure everything was alright," I said with a smile.

"Well thank you, Mr. White," she said with enough sugar in her voice to give me diabetes. "As you can see I am perfectly fine. Now you run along and play with someone else today."

"Those party demons that killed all of those kids are back in town, and they're kidnapping people," I said.

Eden didn't say anything. She slammed her door in my face, and I heard a minor commotion inside her home. There was a loud thud behind the door and footsteps going back and forth. After about ten minutes of listening, the door swung open. Eden stepped outside in clothing that I was more accustomed to seeing her in. No longer was she the picture-perfect homemaker but a streetwise wizard. She was dressed in brown cargo pants, a red tee shirt, and combat boots. There was still a pie in her hands, but now it was in a plastic container. Her eyes were covered by a pair of dark sunglasses, and she was pulling a jacket on. The little wizard pointed to a large hockey bag that was almost as long as she was tall. I picked it up to carry it for her because chivalry isn't dead. She pulled a hockey stick from behind her door and walked over to my truck.

I put her bag into the bed of my truck while she climbed in with her hockey stick. Once I got in, we hit the road. Eden had come to Priest Greyshadow six months earlier because she needed help dealing with these demons. We had fought side by side, and I respected her. Heck, I had a healthy amount of fear of her. She could throw magic around as easily as I can throw a baseball, and with a lot more force. She was older than me, smarter than me, and more powerful than me.

"Can you please buckle up?" I asked her.

She looked at me and swore under her breath. She did buckle up though. "Tell me something Church Boy? How does trouble keep finding you?" she asked.

"How do you know trouble found me?"

"It's you! Holy sword, witless, and a bad attitude. Those three things don't add up to staying under trouble's radar," she said.

I had to smile. She was right. Trouble did find me more often than I found it. I filled her in on the day's events while I drove through town. Eden listened to me patiently as I laid every detail out to her.

"You let a cop take your holy sword?" she asked me.

"I'm going to get it back," I said.

"Good, because without it, you aren't going to be much help," she sighed. She pulled out a Zippo lighter and started flicking it. "No offense, but you aren't exactly on the same level as the vampire or me."

"He has a name you know," I said.

"Yes," she said. "But he is a vampire. He may be special to you, but he is just a monster to me. I won't blow him up unless he tries something, though."

"Thanks," I said sarcastically. "I don't need you killing my best friend."

"He's already dead," she stated as a matter of fact. I hadn't thought about it in a while, but it was true. For all intents and purposes, Aaron was dead. It seemed so strange, though. He had a lover, he was a Harry

Potter fan, he was a doctor, and he had a gnome barbarian that liked pop-up books in our regular RP game. Still, at the end of the day he was a vampire. He drank blood and would do so for all eternity if he wasn't killed at some point.

Aaron had patched me up, saved my life, and was always willing to back me up when things got rough. He may have been a monster, but he wasn't evil. Aaron was my friend, and that was the end of it.

"Have you heard of a guy named Alistair Dyhart?" I asked Eden.

The little mage looked at me and sneered. "Is that the guy that came after you?" she asked. I nodded, and she flicked her lighter closed. "No, but I can ask around."

"I don't know how much time we have," I said. "Do you think it would be good to go back to the place we fought the last demon?"

"Yeah," she said. "Let's go take a look. Maybe we missed something last time."

As we drove to the sight of the last rave, we traded information on demons. I told her about the difference between a normal demon and a true demon. She told me that normal demons were created from the hubris, sin, and fears of other beings. Potentially, if you were arrogant enough, bad enough, or scared enough, you could create a demon. It was terrifying how easy it was to do something as bad as creating a demon.

"Eden, you're a wizard, right?" I asked.

"Yes, Church Boy. Just like I was the last time you saw me," she said.

"I never asked you what made you a wizard. What is the difference between a wizard and everyone else?" I asked.

Eden was quiet for a while. She played with her lighter and looked thoughtfully out of the window. "You really aren't like the rest of the Church kids," she said. It always made me laugh when she called me "kid." Eden looked like a schoolgirl in her street clothes.

"All magic users are mages. The old world term is magi. To keep it simple it means that a person has awakened a greater level magic beyond the basics of life within them by some means. 'Magic' is one of the basic components of reality. It is in all things. Sometimes it is called mana, and other times it is called energy or many other names. You have it, I have it, and the shit that dog just took has it. Magic is existence. A mage can utilize the magic within them," she said.

"Beyond being a mage, a person can become many things. The most common are the sorcerer and the wizard. A sorcerer is a person that has gained power from a source beyond the mortal realms, like a demon. Sorcery perverts the surrounding universe. A wizard is a person that has gained power through effort of will. They may sometimes gain power from other sources, but the powers base is always within them. Wizardry is the manipulation of the world around you," she told me.

"So what is Alistair Dyhart?" I asked her.

"He summons demons. He is either a foolish wizard or a sorcerer. I'm betting on the latter," she said.

"So a wizard can summon demons, too?"

"Anyone can summon a demon, Michael. Anyone. You are missing the point. Sorcerer and wizard are labels, titles. You aren't born as a sorcerer or wizard. You become one. There are many things a magi can become in life, but these two are the most widespread."

We pulled into the parking lot and found the building in shambles. It had been condemned before the rave, and no one was going to try to fix it up after what had happened. There was blood on the floor and walls on the inside. We spent about an hour going over the open area inside. I watched Eden's back as she tried to magically sniff out anything that we had missed. I had my baseball bat, and she had her hockey stick. Eden also kept waving around a little wand. Every time she did, she seemed to get a little more frustrated.

"What's wrong?" I asked her.

She bent down and touched the ground with her wand. "We never found a summoning circle," she said. "You remember the fight we had when I tried to intercept the summoning. My circle took hours to make, and I had to borrow a pressure washer to make sure it was cleaned up. There is no sign of one here."

I looked around at the ground. There was no debris to speak of, and the floor was solid stone. Someone could have cleaned up the summoning circle, but not while the demon was running amok on the dance floor. A thought occurred to me, and I shined my flashlight over at Eden.

"What if the demon wasn't summoned from inside the building?"

The little wizards turned to face me and smiled. She led me outside, and we found an access ladder to the roof. Up we climbed. Sure enough, there on the roof were the remains of a summoning circle. It was done in chalk, so I wondered how it had survived. When I asked how that was possible, Eden smiled at me.

"Maybe you aren't so dumb, Church Boy. The magic gives it longevity. The circle has to be destroyed, as in someone has to actively try to break it," she said.

Eden moved alongside the circle and knelt down next to it. She looked around for a long while. I didn't want to get in the way, so I walked outside the perimeter while making sure I kept my distance from the circle.

"Whoever did this was an amateur," she said. "There are little mistakes that you just do not make when you learn properly."

"Such as?" I asked.

"What do you know about magic circles, Church Boy?"

"I am a clean slate," I smiled proudly.

Eden chuckled. "Alright. Magic Circles for Idiots," she said.

"You mean beginners," I corrected.

"I mean you, idiot," she corrected. "There are three things all magic circles have in common. The first is that they can all be used to summon otherworldly forces. The second is that they must all be constructed with the intent of their use in mind. The third is that they can be broken by acts of will. Magical circles can be structured to protect what is inside from the outside world or vice versa. When a magic circle is activated, it draws power from the latent magic all around it. You don't have to keep feeding magic into it; it is self-sustaining. Little known fact among young wizards, until a magic circle is activated it has no magical properties. It's just a circle."

"So how do you break a magic circle?" I asked.

"I'm glad you asked. You break a magic circle by actually breaking it. You have to disrupt the flow of magic. You can physically destroy the circle, you can send magic across the barrier from the protected area to the unprotected area, or you can cross the circle with the intention of breaking it," she told me.

I watched as she pulled out her phone and took pictures of the circle. I kept walking around and checking the area for any clues. Looking over the edge of the roof, I saw my truck in the empty parking lot. I remembered a photo I had seen online of Eden and myself and guessed that this had been the spot used by the photographer. I started pacing backwards to see if I could spot anything else. A sudden rush of electricity surged through my body. Nothing painful, but it was substantial.

Eden snapped her head up at me and asked, "Michael, what did you do?" We both looked down at my right foot. I lifted it and found a strange looking symbol cut into the roof. It started glowing. I jumped back but nothing happened. Eden rushed over to me and put her wand to the symbol. She began chanting. Her wands tip began to light up in several hues of red and blue. She began to look around frantically. "It's a trap!"

"Eden what's wrong?" I asked.

She ran to the side of the roof and looked off the edge. "Shit!" she said.

I ran over to stand beside her and looked out into the parking lot. "Holy crap!" I yelled.

Out in the parking lot, all the way back to the road and as far around the building as I could tell, was a mass of small black and gray creatures. I knew what they were, as years of role-playing games had taught me exactly what it meant when you saw black and gray masses of creatures that seemed to move as one to the point that it looks like the earth itself is shifting.

"Rats," I said. Hundreds of rats were out there.

"Plague Rats," said Eden. "The ward uses the magical powers of whoever activated it to summon animals from the Fae Wilds. The stronger the magic, the more powerful and plentiful the creatures."

"So why are there so many? Why are there any?" I asked. "I don't have any magic powers."

"Well congratulations kid, it looks like you have a bit of magic in you," Eden said. "A lot of it, actually."

The rats started coming at the building with blinding speed. They swarmed the walls and began to enter through any openings they could find. That would have been fine because it would buy us time, but most of them decided just to scale the walls. Hundreds of them came scurrying up the sides of the building.

"What's the game plan?" I asked.

"Don't let them touch you," Eden said. She pointed her wand over the side of the building, and a powerful current of air surged from its tip. She began sweeping rats from the walls, but the more she sent falling to the ground the more climbed to take their place. After about a minute, she had pushed them back, but they were still steadily advancing. The hairs on the back of my neck stood on end. I whirled around to find them coming from the air conditioning unit and from the other sides of the roof.

I pulled out my new Silver Desert Eagle and fired three quick bursts into the AC unit. I had filled this magazine with silver, iron, and explosive shells, but I had forgotten the order. My second shot exploded, so the third was just a waste. Explosive rounds didn't cause large or even medium scale explosions, but they did make things go boom. The AC unit blew apart in the middle, warping and stressing the metal enough that it began to collapse in on itself. Rat guts and blood splattered out onto the roof.

"Are you crazy?" Eden asked.

"Yes, but not in the way you are thinking," I said.

"Don't blow them up! They're plague rats!" she said.

"Yeah, you said that," I said.

"As in the Bubonic plague," she yelled. "If they bite you, touch you, or you get their blood on us, we could be infected."

My mind raced. The Bubonic plague was all but eradicated — in the mortal world. In the Fae Wilds, the part of the world of the Fairies that is closest to our own world, it was still a very real thing. Most monsters were probably immune to it, but Eden and I were not. If we were infected it could kill us. To prevent that we would need to get to a doctor in order to be treated. Plague medicine would have to be flown in, and even if it were readily available, we would be under quarantine until we were fully cured or dead. Plus, anyone we encountered would be at risk. Even if it didn't kill us, we would be out of the way for an indefinite amount of time. I bet that would make an evil sorcerer really happy.

"Well if I can't shoot them, and I can't let them touch me, then what am I supposed to do?" I asked.

"You're a knight, right? Get medieval on them until I can figure this out. If I can reverse or cancel the summoning then all remnants of it including the plague will return to Second Earth," said Eden. She ran to the rune and started chanting.

"Sure, get medieval without touching them," I said under my breath.

I ejected my magazine and rifled though my pockets until I found my emergency magazine. This one had nothing but white phosphorous rounds. I slammed it in and turned to the side of the building. The rats were halfway up. I spun back around and found rats already on the roof in the other directions. I took aim and opened fire. My new gun roared as I began firing left and right. Fire erupted in plumes where I hit and rats began to burn.

When that magazine ran empty I slammed in a magazine without explosive rounds, but I holstered my gun. I ran at the nearest group of rats and started swinging my bat like a golf club. If I had my sword, I would have tried calling up white fire from the blade like my grandpa did. Since I had never been able to do that, it was pointless to wish I had my sword. My bat struck rats and sent them flying.

I kept backing as I hit them. There were just too many damned rats. For each one I knocked away a dozen took its place. I ran back and forth sweeping them out of the way as best I could. That's when I saw a square box on the side of the roof access shed. I ran to it and used my bat to break it open. I grabbed the lever and began to spin the wheel beside it. I ran back out to the middle of the roof, braced myself, and pulled the lever. The water hose blasted the nearest group of rats, and I swept it back across to stem the tide.

The plague rats were being held off but not stopped. "Any ideas Eden?" I asked.

The wizard stood up and whipped her hand at the nearest group of rats to her. She yelled and a gust of wind swept them from the roof. "The rune apparently can summon only one threat at a time. If someone else steps on it the rats will vanish and something else will take their place."

"Sounds good to me," I yelled. I swept back toward her and blasted rats away with my water hose. Eden turned her wand on me and shot gusts of wind at the rats behind me. "So step on it!"

"You stepped on it and this happened. Imagine what will happen if I step on it," she said.

I did. From what I had learned, Eden was pretty powerful for a wizard in most circles. We could end up with something far more terrifying. But the Bubonic plague needed to leave this word and now. "It's a risk we have to take! Do it!"

Eden whipped both wand and hockey stick staff around in a wide arc. Two circles of fire formed around us. Combined with the water I was spraying searing steam spread into the air. Eden kept spinning and the steam washed over the rats and pealed flesh from bone. Still they came.

"Do you really want to fight something worse than this?" she asked.

"I want to fight something I can hit without becoming a carrier of one of the worst plagues in human history," I yelled.

Eden turned and ran to the ward. She lifted her foot and stomped down on the symbol. Black fire roared from the bodies of the plague rats. Ash and smoke whirled into the air and vanished in sparks of gray light. I closed off the hose and looked around. The rats had come from me, and I half expected to see giants appearing around us when Eden stepped on the ward. Silence surrounded us.

I looked back at my wizard friend, and she was standing still. She had her hockey stick staff in her right hand and her wand in her left. I spun my bat around to get myself ready for whatever was going to happen. Side by side, we walked to the edge of the roof. Before we reached the lip, we heard a sound that froze us. There was growling coming from the parking lot.

CHAPTER 11

THERE WERE MONSTERS in the parking lot. I looked down at their grayish-blue fur and the jagged tuffs of hair on their backs. I watched the eight beasts prowl around the parking lot. Their bodies were like the bulldogs of old before all the purebred crap and pedigrees ruined their bodies. Their chests were massive and their torsos were sleek. Their legs were solid and thick with muscle. They were built for both speed and power. Their long tails were reptilian with spines running their length. Their canine muzzles were stunted, and their mouths were too big. They looked like they could fit truck tires into those jaws without straining. I could easily see their thick spike-like teeth and their hooked claws.

"Worgs," I said. "It had to be worgs."

They had been sniffing the parking lot, but their heads snapped up to my voice. One came running at the building and leapt. He made it about halfway up and crashed into the wall. His claws held, but when he tried to climb his weight dragged him down. He tumbled to the ground and began to prowl around. The pack of worgs began to prowl along the parking lot as one by one they attempted to reach us. Each attempt failed.

"They can't reach us," I said.

"But we can't get down," Eden said.

"Are you kidding? We can rain fire down on them," I said. I drew my gun and aimed at one of the worgs. It sprinted away in a zigzag pattern. "What the hell?"

"Worgs are smart, Church Boy. They know what guns are and how to fight people that have them. They also know how to fight wizards. I can shoot fire all day, and they will just keep their distance until we are too tired or out of ammo," she said. "But at least we are safe up here for the time being."

As if in response to our assumed safety, one of the worgs ran toward the building and crashed through the wall. The building shook. A moment later, another did the same. Then another.

"Well fuck," Eden said.

"Any suggestions?" I asked.

"Shoot them!" Eden pocketed her wand and took her hockey stick staff up in both hands. Fire sheathed the blade of the staff, and she scythed flames down at the worgs. Some backed off, but others kept crashing into the building. I started firing and emptied two magazines without scoring a single hit. That was the last of my ammo. I had more in my truck, but that was in the parking lot. I had something else in my truck as well.

"Can you get us to my truck?" I asked.

"How do you expect me to do that?" Eden asked. Another crash shook the building beneath us.

"You're the wizard—you tell me! Can you make us fly or something?" I asked.

Eden stared at me with her mouth wide. "If I could fly, do you think I would be stuck up here with you?" she asked.

"Well yeah," I said. "All for one and one for all!"

"I would have left as soon as the rats were summoned," Eden said.

One of the worgs leapt at the building again. It struck the wall halfway between us and the ground and its claws dug in. I knew it would fall so I ignored it. Another worg leapt at the wall as well. This one crashed into its friend and used it to leap frog the rest of the distance to the roof. I caught its accent out of the corner of my eye and dove at Eden. I got my arms around her and turned so that when we tumbled I took the brunt of the fall. We rolled, and I pushed her away so that she rolled further than I did. The worg hit the ground clawing and scraping so that it could turn on us.

I was back on my feet before the monster could turn on us, but when it finally managed to turn, it came at me in a powerful charge. I sprinted ahead and swung my bat at the beast's head. It skidded to a stop and reared back to dodge the attack. Eden said that the worgs were smart, but I never expected that. My swing left me off balance, and the worg came at me with snapping jaws. I fell backward and spun down to one knee to keep my balance. I sprang into a back pedal to avoid the beast's jaws once more and started parrying claws with my bat.

The span of the worg's shoulders was wider than my own. The beast came up to my stomach, and it was fast. Every time I managed a counter, I was thrown back on the defensive. I darted left and the beast followed me. It tried to claw at me, but I kept my distance. The worg leapt at me in an attempt to tackle me. I dropped to the ground as I swung my left hand up and across my body. I made contact with the worg and added my strength to its momentum. It went flying away from me.

The beast rebounded and came at me before I could recover. I rolled and swung for the fences. My bat connected with the worg's face, sending it tumbling backward in a hail of splinters. My bat had broken, and so had several of the worg's teeth. I looked down at my broken weapon and watched as the worg thrashed on the ground. It whined and whimpered with its jaw hanging awkwardly. I dashed over to it and slammed the remains of my weapon into its chest. The beast howled and thrashed, but then it fell silent. I watched as it melted into dirt and rocks.

I turned back to Eden as the building began to shake from the pounding it was taking below. I looked out at my truck and said, "I'll cause a diversion. You make for the truck and get out of here."

Eden shook her head. "If I get you to the truck can you end this fight?" I nodded. "When I tell you to go, start running and jump toward your truck."

I backed up. I figured I would give her all the help I could by pushing as hard as I could. Eden spun her hockey stick staff above her head and slammed the butt end down into the roof with her left hand as she lifted her right hand to the sky. The water on the roof began to run forward. I watched the trees in the parking lot sway away from me and I felt a cold breeze push against my back. Eden took her staff in both hands and began to spin it around her body with expert control. She chanted as she moved, and I heard the wind howl every time she raised her voice. The worgs kept slamming into the building, and I could hear parts of the wall fall away.

Eden kept rolling her staff around her body while chanting. I could feel the magical forces of nature rallying to her side. She spun her staff high above her head and shouted, "Go!"

I took off in a sprint toward the edge of the roof. I thought about all the battle cries I knew, and only one truly fit the situation. When I passed Eden, she spun fully around and brought the blade of her hockey stick staff out behind me as she summoned a deafening roar of wind.

I stepped on the lip of the roof and pushed off into the air while yelling the words from the Toxic Crusaders cartoon. "I HOPE I DON'T GET HURT!"

I wind-milled my arms as I ran through the open air. Just as I began to lose momentum, I felt a jet stream overtake me. The air current was so strong that it propelled me higher into the air and across the parking lot. Below me, the worgs watched as I soared over their heads. Some barked while others jumped and snapped at me. I passed them in short order and began to rapidly approach my truck.

As quickly as the wizardly wind had come it vanished, and I began to fall forward. I was at least seventy feet in the air and falling fast. Way too fast. "Crap!" I dropped from the air straight toward the bed of my truck. "Eden!" I yelled.

The little wizard wasn't done. The gravel in the parking lot around my truck began to shake, then swirl, and then it flew into the air as a tornado erupted around my truck. I passed into the air current of the tornado, and my descent slowed. But I wasn't out of the woods yet. Magic, real magic, still has to deal with the laws of reality. Those rocks didn't just disappear. The gravel was pelting me. Dozens of small rocks were slamming into me every second of my descent. To make matters worse I could hear the worgs coming at me.

I was over the bed of my truck. I pulled out my keys and prayed I would have enough time with the worgs coming at me. The tornado died, and I dropped the remaining twenty feet to the bed of my truck. One of the worgs leapt at me in mid fall. I whirled on it and brought a size fourteen steel-toed work boot across its jaw. The monster's head snapped to the side, and I continued my spin and planted my opposite foot in its throat. The worg fell away and crashed beside my truck. I landed in the truck bed in a crouched position with one hand in the air holding my keys.

I popped open my tool chest. My tool chest was a custom model— only two like it existed in the world. I lifted the lid, grabbed my safety goggles, and lifted the first panel filled with my work tools. The worgs were growling. I lifted the next panel that held a few specialty items for my chosen professions. I felt my truck shake. One of the worgs walked up the hood, over the windshield, and then over the roof of the cab. It stuck its snarling, drooling, mouth-foaming head over to look at me.

I shoved the barrel of my shotgun between its teeth and pulled the trigger. The worgs head exploded as iron buckshot tore through its brain. I grabbed it's shoulder and rolled it off The Rust Bucket. Shouldering my black and gray pistol-gripped shotgun, I slammed my tool chest shut. I looked around my truck at the remaining six worgs. I prowled around inside the bed of the truck as they growled and snarled.

"The lady told me you were intelligent, so I'm going to say this only once," I said to the worgs. "This…is…my…BOOMSTICK!"

I racked the action and unloaded a shell into two worgs that were standing together. Earlier, against Eden's fire and my pistol, the beasts had distance on their side. Now, no more than ten feet from me, the worgs didn't stand a chance. Iron balls tore through flesh, muscle, and bone easily. Worgs were not fairies, so it didn't matter what I shot them with. Typically, being shot with a shotgun will ruin your life. The magic that bound them to the summoning caused their bodies to break down into the elements of their power: earth and soil.

One came over my tailgate, and I spun on it. It reared up on me as I filled its chest and guts with my 12 gauge. I swung my right leg in a roundhouse kick, knocking the dying monster from my truck. "Do not touch my ride!" I yelled.

Two more worgs came at me, one from my left and one from my right. I charged the one on my right and shot it in the face. I dropped to the bed of the truck as its dead body collided with its partner. The two monsters crashed together, and their momentum stopped. I racked another round and sprang into the air. The other worg jumped at me, but I blasted it before its hind legs left the ground. I landed atop both dead beasts.

Eden screamed, and when I turned to her, the last worg slammed into my back. Its jaws wrapped around my shotgun as we tumbled from the bed of my truck. We hit the ground, and the beast rolled off me. It spit my shotgun out and put a massive paw on it. I stood up and pulled my spare knife from its sheath. The worg growled low as though it were laughing at me. I began to stalk to the side.

After two steps, I noticed that I was limping. Somewhere between the seventy-foot fall, the throw down in the bed of my truck, and the fall from my truck I had twisted my right ankle. The worg noticed it too. He came at me from my left, which forced me to balance on my right. I stabbed ahead to force the worg back. It darted to its left, and I couldn't pivot on my injured ankle in time. Jaws snapped tight around my forearm. I screamed in pain and terror as the monster barreled me over.

My back hit the rocky ground, and the monster began to worry my forearm. I started punching it in the head as my own blood began to drip from the worg's mouth onto my face. I panicked as I felt fangs ripping through my flesh and the bones of my forearm cracking. I grabbed at my knife in my closed fist. The shock of the initial bite had forced my hand into a vice grip, and it wasn't letting go. I pried at my own fingers, but they would not release my weapon. The worg slammed its paw down on my chest blasting the air from my lungs. It repeated the process. I gasped and gagged as the worg tore my arm apart, and I ripped my own skin from my fingers.

The worg took its back claws and raked them down my legs. I felt my muscles and flesh rip but had no breath to scream. The pain caused my body to jerk wildly, and my knife dropped from my unclenched hand. I took it by the blade and shoved it into the worgs throat. I pulled it across and covered myself in monster blood. As quickly as the light faded from the monsters eyes, it turned to stone and soil that fell atop me. My wounds were filthy, and I was covered in blood.

"Michael," Eden yelled as she ran to me.

Eden helped me crawl up to the side of my truck and propped me up. My pants and shirt were shredded, and I was losing a lot of blood. My vision was blurry and my breathing was shallow. I had shredded the skin on my right hand and slashed the fingers on my left when I killed the worg.

"Dammit, Church Boy, don't die on me," she said.

"Food," I coughed.

She climbed into the cab and pulled out the pie she had baked. She had silverware in her bag, so she started force-feeding me the pie. It was delicious! It would have been even better if each bite didn't come with a healthy portion of my own blood. The little wizard was a master at the art of baking. I ate every bite, and as I did the runic tattoos on my body converted the food and my life energy into healing magic. The bleeding stopped, my bones reset themselves, and the holes in my flesh sealed up. The pain did not go away; it stayed bright and new in my body as if it was all still happening. Magic would keep me alive, but it was going to remind me that it had saved my life.

By the time the pie was gone I was more or less okay. I could get up, I could fight, and I could keep moving. Every step would be painful; my body was still in need of healing, I was short a lot of blood, and the more I magically healed the more rest and food I was going to need. I could have used a month-long nap right now, but I had to keep going.

"Can you drive?" I asked.

"No," Eden said.

"Can't reach the pedals?" I joked as I got to my feet.

"I don't know how," she said in all seriousness. "My husband always insisted on driving me wherever I wanted to go."

"Your parents never showed you how?" I asked.

"No, they were dead before the Model T ever rolled off the assembly line" she said. "Why can't you drive?"

"I need to sleep like right now," I said. I reached into the truck and pulled out my cell phone. I pulled up a number and handed the phone to Eden. "Call this number and have them bring clothes. Then call Aaron. Get them here."

"What are you going to do," she asked as she took the phone. I answered by falling over in the parking lot. I managed to break my own fall, but as soon as I settled into the gravel I fell asleep.

CHAPTER 12

I WOKE UP on a soft bench of car seats. I was strapped into the middle seat, and my wounds had been patched up. The sun had gone down, or the window tint was just that dark. I unbuckled the belt around my waist and sat up. Then I did a quick assessment. My body ached, my muscles were on fire, and I was starving.

The door swung open, and a young man with spiked brown hair stuck his head in. He had blue eyes, a small hoop piercing in each ear, and a white smile that would make girls pay close attention to him. He was wearing a skintight shirt, jeans, and probably some awesome shoes. I had met him on several occasions, and he was always pleasant toward me. His name was Emory, and he was Aaron's boyfriend.

"Hi," he said.

"Hey," I replied.

"Feeling awake are we?" he asked me. I shook the last of the cobwebs from my thoughts and nodded. "Good. We have a problem out here, and I am going to need you to fix it."

I climbed out of the vehicle and realized it was Kerri's SUV. Great. That meant everyone had shown up. Things were finally working out for me. I followed Emory around to the other side of the vehicle. My truck was there with about two car lengths between the vehicles. Emory's car was on the other side of my truck. Standing there between my ride and Kerri's was Aaron with his hands in the air. Eden was leaning against my truck. Kerri was standing next to her truck with a wooden stake in one hand and a cross in the other. She had the cross extended like a shield toward Aaron and the stake poised for a strike.

"Michael!" Kerri yelled as I rounded the corner.

Aaron looked at me and said, "I told you not to move him!" Aaron was dressed for battle. He had his dark green sleeveless Under Armor shirt, his black ops pants with all the cool tactical pockets, and his black combat boots. There was a bag on the ground at his feet, and I was pretty sure it contained his scimitar, gun, and a ton of medical supplies.

Emory threw his hands up and said, "Well what was I supposed to do? Little Miss Top Heavy wants to put a wooden spike in your chest!"

"Hey!" Kerri said.

"Ignore him," Eden said. "He has vagina envy."

"Hey, Honey Half Witch, why don't you help out or shut up," Emory said. I laughed, and Eden cut me a look that told me to stop. I didn't, of course.

"I could rip your soul from your body," Eden threatened. She turned her head away from us, but I could feel her scowl fading just a bit.

Aaron smiled. "Michael, you really should be lying down."

"No time for that. I have demons to slay and a sorcerer to thwart."

"Who taught him that word?" Aaron asked. Everyone shrugged. "He's like a two-year-old. Teach him a new word, and it's all he says for weeks."

"Hey, bro, are you trying to thwart my vocabulary?" I asked.

"See," Aaron huffed. "He isn't going to stop."

"Because nothing can thwart me!" I chuckled as I walked over to Kerri. "Okay, Buffy, let's have the hardware." I held out my hand so she could hand me her medieval arsenal.

Kerri looked at me as if I had lost my mind. I get that look a lot actually. "Are you kidding? He is a V-A-M-P-I-R-E!" she said in a tone that was supposed to be a whisper but was filled with too much fear to be secretive.

"And he has a medical degree, so I am sure he can spell vampire," I chuckled.

"Several actually," Aaron corrected.

"You would think they would only give those to the living," Eden said.

"Eden, you are not helping! Keep it up and I am going to start making short jokes," I said.

"He is a vampire!" Eden snapped.

"Do you want to ride in the car seat?" I asked.

Eden fumed. I would pay for that short jab later, but she quieted down—because I thwarted her.

"Michael, aren't you supposed to kill him?" Kerri asked.

I sighed. "Aaron isn't a normal vampire. He has a soul," I said. As the words left my mouth, I heard her fan girl radar go off and knew that all she was thinking about was David Boreanaz. "It's not a curse or anything like that. It's more like a birth defect among vampires. Every once in a while one has a soul. Aaron even lives in the basement of a church." I flexed my fingers, and she handed over the stake and cross.

"So you aren't going to kill them?" she asked.

"Them? Aaron is the only vampire. Emory is human like us," I replied.

"I figured only a creature of the night would be caught dead in those shoes," she said as she folded her arms. "That or you."

"You know, on second though I like her. I still don't trust her, but I like her," Emory said.

I tossed the stake and cross into my truck. "Well, I guess it's a good thing you don't know how to kill a real vampire," I said.

"Stakes and crosses don't work?" she asked.

"Well, they work, but that's what the vampire-controlled media wants you to do. You could get the same results with a bullet to the head or chest," I said.

"That doesn't make sense," Kerri said. "Everyone back home carries crosses and stakes in their cars."

"Not my family. We carry guns," I said.

"Think about it this way: a person with a gun is a threat to anyone, but a person with a piece of wood trying to sneak up on a vampire is just a snack on the way," Aaron said.

"Alright, introductions and then we get to work," I said. "Kerri-Lynn, this is Eden, Emory, and Aaron. Everyone this is Kerri-Lynn, my—"

"Girlfriend," Kerri said, cutting me off. She walked straight over to Eden and extended her hand. The wizard shook hands with Kerri, and I got the strange feeling that there was a disturbance in the force.

Aaron walked up to me and whispered, "I really, really, thought you were in the closet." When I gnawed my bottom lip in frustration Aaron added, "Maybe you still are?"

"Plan time!" I yelled because I did not want to have this conversation again. I am not gay. I am not homophobic. I just have no idea how ANY relationship works.

We gathered and I explained the plan. Everyone, including Emory and Kerri, who were new to being involved in my plans, shook their heads and complained. I let them complain for about a minute. A good leader always considers the opinions of his team. A great leader encompasses those opinions into his plan. I played the Jeopardy song in my head.

"Hey!" I said. "Vampire, wizard, paramedic, and whatever Kerri-Lynn does for a living…what do you do for a living?"

"Stuff," she said quickly. Her tone had been strict and final. I didn't push the issue. She had thwarted my curiosity, blast her!

"And I am a doctor. You listed everyone else's profession, and I would like the same consideration," Aaron complained.

"I am listing everyone's super awesome skills! If we have a doctor what is the point of having a paramedic?" I said. Aaron conceded the point and I continued. "Vampire, wizard, paramedic, and stuff-doer. I'm making this call. We do it my way. If things go south we blame Eden, because she is the shortest, and we regroup with my Plan B."

"What's Plan B?" Emory asked.

Kerri raised her hand and said, "It's make a Disney movie and sell out. Make a Disney Movie. Sell out as much as possible until you can't sell out anymore. It's been Plan B since he was 9 years old."

There was a silence. Then everyone started staring at me. Eden was the first to speak up. She turned to Kerri and said, "You can keep him." Then the wizard climbed into my truck. Emory and Aaron exchanged goodbyes before Aaron climbed into my truck. Emory got into his car and waited for us all to pull out.

"So you are my girlfriend?" I asked Kerri when we were alone.

"You asked me four years ago, and I said yes. I don't remember you ever breaking up with me," she said.

"I texted you," I said.

"I don't date assholes, and that would be a pretty asshole-ish move, Hero," she said.

"So I'm still your boyfriend?" I asked.

"Yes, you stupid giant," she said.

"Cool," I said. I bent down to kiss her.

She put her hand up to my face. "You have a city to save and four years of anniversary, birthday, and Christmas presents to make up for before you get off the couch," she said.

"What?" I asked.

Kerri walked over to her SUV and climbed in. She started backing up but rolled down her window. "Get to work, Hero!" she said as she tossed me a tee shirt and pants. Then she drove off. Emory followed her.

I changed clothes and got into the Rust Bucket. My truck didn't have a back seat, so Eden had to sit in the middle. There was plenty of room, but she still brushed up against me. My wizard friend mumbled something under her breath and just glared at me when I said, "Beg your pardon." There were daggers in her eyes. Aaron just smiled.

I put the Rust Bucket in gear, and we headed out.

CHAPTER 13

THERE IS ALWAYS something about your city that you don't know. It can be something mundane or something grand. Kate's Bar is a little of both. It's a bar and grill. Nothing amazing about that. People go there all the time, but then so do magical beings. Kate's is in the middle of the artsy and trendy district for Baltimore, which is just outside the business district. Because of that, you would think more people would know about it. But as with most magical hangouts, it is a place that people avoid for some reason. I believe it is because their minds tell them that the saloon-style bar is tacky with its neon lights and honky-tonk music coming from inside. More than likely it's because their senses betray them due to *Ignorance Is Bliss*, and they ignore the place.

Detective Clay was standing in the parking lot next to an old red Mustang. He wore a brown jacket, a blue polo, jeans, and casual shoes. I parked right next to him and hopped out of the Rust Bucket with a wide smile on my face.

"Hey, Detective Clay! How are you doing? Give me my sword!" I said cheerfully. He stared at my crew and me. Aaron had gotten out and leapt into the bed of the truck to walk over to us. Eden had scooted out behind me and was lighting up one of those comically big cigars that she enjoyed.

Detective Clay just shook his head. "Do you have a monster to show me?" he asked.

"I have a vampire," I said as I pointed at Aaron. "And I have a witch, but they aren't really monsters," I said as I patted Eden's head. I could feel her eyes bulge out as I did so. She still had a few short jokes coming, though.

The right side of my face hit the hood of my truck. Both of my hands were pulled behind my back and I felt handcuffs being slapped on my wrists. Detective Clay kicked my legs apart, and I could hear both of my companions snickering.

"Well this could have gone better," I said.

"Why the hell did I ever think a clown like you could be on the up and up?" Clay asked.

"Up and up? Really? Dude, I'm the Knight of Innocence. If any knight is on the up and up, it's me," I argued.

"You said you were going to show me a monster. Instead, you bring me two of your punk friends! I'm hauling your ass in," he started frisking me. "What the hell? Another gun and a knife?"

"I can explain those, but if you would just look at my male friend he can prove he is a vampire," I said.

I saw Aaron walk in front of my truck. Detective Clay and I watched as he opened his mouth and pointed to his teeth. His fangs slowly grew to their full artery-piercing length. I always wondered how he managed to talk with his fangs out like that.

"Nice teeth. Did a dentist or plastic surgeon rig that for you?" Detective Clay asked. He started setting my weapons down on my hood. Shiny new gun. Knife. Back up knife. Brass knuckles. The nunchucks I had tucked into my belt.

"Nunchucks?" Aaron, Clay, and Eden asked in unison.

"I'm a martial arts enthusiast," I said. "I brought a witch!" Detective Clay looked over at Eden who was already in front of my truck. She took a long drag from her cigar but did nothing.

"Are you old enough to be smoking?" Detective Clay asked her.

"Maybe in ten years," I said. Eden rolled her eyes and blew out a long stream of smoke. "Eden, can you make with the magic now please?"

Eden's face brightened, and a wide smile overtook her features. Her voice was sugary when she said, "Golly gee whiz, I am sorry, mister, but my mommy told me not to help out assholes."

I gulped. "Seriously!"

"Yeppers. Besides, it's past my fucking bedtime," she said.

"Drats! Thwarted by a meddling kid and her vampire!" I said.

"No, no, no, you stop that right now!" Aaron said.

"Detective Clay, I brought them because they were the easy way out. This bar, take a look at it. Have you ever seen or heard of it? Did it show up on your GPS?" I asked.

"What the hell does that have to do with anything?" Detective Clay asked as he hauled me back up. He spun me around to face him.

"Inside this building you will find the answers you want. I asked you to meet me here so you could see for yourself how it works. Five minutes. That's all I am asking for. Then if you want to arrest me you can. I won't fight back," I said.

Detective Clay had every reason to throw me on the ground and call the cops to come get me. To his credit he seethed, he swore, and he did everything short of threatening me. In the end, he uncuffed me. He threw the rest of my gear into his trunk and slammed it shut. Then the four of us walked into Kate's for a drink.

Walking into Kate's is like walking into any other bar. There is a sudden change of temperature, the gravity of the world seems to shift, and the weight of the eyes of every other patron falls on you. Everyone reacts differently to such a shift in atmosphere. For me, it was just another day in the *real* real world. Aaron and Eden were regulars here. Some Dwarves that would look like bikers to anyone not in the know waved at Aaron. Some young magic users that knew Eden called her over but she declined. Most of the patrons flipped me off, so I smiled and waved.

Detective Clay was entering Kate's for the first time. I guessed it was a cop thing when he brushed his hand against his hip right where his gun should have been. His eyes shifted from left to right and never focused on anything in particular. He was obviously checking for any sign of abnormality. It was all around him, and his mind was probably telling him that the elves in the corner were just pretty college girls, or that the two bearded old men playing chess were just really fast players and that's why the pieces seemed to be moving on their own.

We went straight up to the bar, and the general staff scampered away. A woman with a sleeve of tattoos on her right arm and an eye patch over her left eye was behind the bar. She came over to us. She was tall, thin with a muscular tone, wore her long dark hair down, and was in her late forties. You could see from the lines on her face that she had lived a hard life that hadn't beaten her. She wore a plain red tee shirt while all the rest of the staff wore black.

"So a cop, a doctor, a knight, and a witch walk into my bar," she said.

"Hey Kate. This is Detective Clay, the guy I told you about over the phone," I said.

"Detective," she said with a nod.

"Ma'am," he said with a nod of his own.

Kate smiled at the two of us. "Now, I usually don't do this, but our chef has agreed to prepare a private dinner for the two of you. I won't ask you for your firearm, Detective, but I will need your word that you will not shoot him," Kate said as she set two bottles of beer down in front of Aaron and Eden.

"Why are you worried that I would shoot your cook?" Detective Clay asked.

Kate's eye hardened as she looked at him. "Because he is unlike anyone you have ever met. Also, just so you know, he is a chef; if you call him a cook, I will not be held responsible for what he does to you."

She motioned for us to come behind the bar and follow her into the back. There were a half dozen people running around. They were all wearing white chef's jackets and black baseball caps that they had turned backwards. On the front of the caps were the words "Orgoth's Crew." They ran around between stoves, ovens, freezers, and cutting stations. They were preparing this and plating that. All the while, there was a voice coming from the back with a thick, and completely fake, French accent.

"No, no, no! They are braised ribs. You sear them lightly. These are burnt, you fool!" said a deep voice. A tray of burnt meat flew down an aisle, and we had to duck out of the way.

"Shit! If they mess up too much this is going to end badly," Kate said. She quickened her step, and we followed suit.

"What is this? This cake tastes like it came from a box! Is that a box of cake mix in the waste bin? GET OUT OF MY SIGHT BEFORE I RIP YOUR BALLS OFF AND BEAT THEM INTO A REAL CAKE!"

A scared young man came running down the aisle, and a cake flew after him. Kate ducked, but I wasn't so quick. I was hit in the face by a flying devil's food cake with vanilla frosting. I didn't complain. Every once in a while, you have to take one for the team.

Kate handed me a towel to clean myself up as we reached the back of the cooking area. There was a stone wall with a wide and high opening to one side separating this area from the rest of the kitchen. Kate stepped inside the back area and said, "Orgoth, your private guests have arrived."

"Oui, oui," came a calm voice. "S'il vous plait venir et etre assis Messieurs."

Kate stepped out and motioned for us to enter. I turned to Detective Clay and said, "Look, this is going to make you lose your shit. I need you to swear that you will not shoot anyone! If you do you will only be hurting yourself." Detective clay rolled his eyes and pushed past me. I looked up at the ceiling and put my hands together in prayer. "I am trying. You can see me trying. This is not my fault!"

"MARY MOTHER OF GOD!" Detective Clay yelled. Then there was a crash and the sound of chairs and metal hitting the ground.

I licked some cake from the side of my face and continued to pray. "Alright, I'm clocking back in," I said. I turned around and went into the back of the kitchen.

Detective Clay was on the ground with his back to the wall near the entrance. There were two chairs overturned around him and two full sets of dinnerware on the floor. Detective Clay was fidgeting for his gun because he had lost his shit. The table in front of him was of old polished red wood. On the opposite side of that table stood a thirteen-foot tall ogre smoking a cigarette.

The ogre, Orgoth, was a giant. He had long wisps of grayish green hair that he pulled into a tight ponytail so that his tall and poufy chef hat could sit upon his head. The hat was a custom job made to fit around a head that was more the size of a large football helmet. Orgoth's eyes were yellow with dark centers. His nose was flat and his jaw was pronounced. He had tied his long chin hair into a braid and hand drawn a goatee on his face with a light green marker to match his hair. His shoulders were wide and broad with muscle. He wore a white XXXXL tee shirt that said "Head Chef" across the chest in black letters. The sleeves were ripped off. His black apron was one of those that you wear just around your waist. It was a custom job as well with a pocket on the side for his cigarettes and a pen. He had a belt of custom knives on his waist as well. He wore pants of some material that mortals no longer used for pants in America. His feet, however, were sporting a new pair of Lebron's size…wait…how the heck did he get sneakers that size when he couldn't find jeans?

Orgoth looked at me and said, "Monsieur Michael, your friend seems to want to shoot moi. Does he have the iron bullets?"

"Let's not find out," I said. I reached down and pinned Detective Clay's arm down. He immediately gained enough composure to punch me in the face. His knuckles cracked across my left eye. I winced but held my position and grabbed his other arm. "Detective!" I yelled. He looked at me, and I spoke clearly and annunciated every word. "I told you that you would lose your shit. This is Orgoth. He is the best chef in town, and he is going to make us dinner. Do not shoot him. If you do, he will cut off your arm and serve it for tomorrow's special."

Detective Clay looked up at me and then over at Orgoth. He started breathing in a way that could pass for normal. I pulled him to his feet as two attendants I had not noticed before ran over from the corner to set the chairs back up for us. They collected the dinnerware before we seated ourselves. Detective Clay seemed to have a problem finding a comfortable position as Orgoth watched him sit down. By the time the attendants finished resetting the table he had managed to stop squirming.

Orgoth took a final drag of his cigarette and then swallowed it. He clapped his hands together and said, "Salutations mes amis! I am your host, Orgoth, le Delicious!"

He bowed to us and I clapped. When Detective Clay did not clap, Orgoth did not rise from his bow. I elbowed Clay, and he began to clap. Orgoth rose back up to his full height with a huge grin on his face.

"Aucun, aucun, stop s'il vous ne plait, you will embarris me," the Ogre said in mock humility. He reached down to the table, and Detective Clay jumped back, a natural reaction. Orgoth picked up two menus and handed them to us. "Please make your selections, and I will personally prepare them."

I am a meat and potatoes kind of guy, so I picked the filet mignon. Detective Clay picked a rib meal, and Orgoth smiled at his selection. "It will be prepared tout de suite. Until then, I have made a wonderful wine selection for you tonight," Orgoth said.

"I'll just have a beer," Detective Clay said.

The smile left Orgoth's face. I saw his eyes narrow and begin to turn red along the edges. I grabbed Clay and started laughing. "HAHAHA, man you are a riot, Detective Clay! Everyone knows that you don't drink beer with fine French cuisine!" I said. Then under my breath and through gritted teeth I said, "You do not want to insult our host. He can bench press a bus. We do not turn down the wine selections of people that can bench press buses."

Orgoth caught the first part of what I said, and his eyes went back to their standard yellow. He began to laugh in a horribly bad French accent, "Wah ha haun! Detective Clay, tu are a very funny man. I like this."

Orgoth showed us a bottle of some very, *very* old wine. He pulled the cork out as easily as I would unscrew a soda cap. He smelled the cork, and it looked like he was having an orgasm. Then he poured himself a taste and lifted a pimp cup sized goblet to his lips. He lapped up some with his tongue. Then he sipped in some more and swished it around. Then he gurgled. After he was sure he had chosen the perfect wine, he poured for us, bowed, and turned to prepare our dishes. "Raphael! Francisco! Let us begin!" he yelled.

The two attendants ran past us to gather ingredients. I saw the names on their name tags—Ralph and Frank. Orgoth lived in his own little not-so-French world, and it didn't hurt anyone, so why should anyone correct him? They shouldn't.

"What the hell is going on?" Detective Clay asked me.

"There are more things in heaven and earth, Horatio, than are dreamt of in your philosophy," I said. "That's how a smarter man would start this conversation, so I am going to go with it."

"*You* quote Hamlet?" he asked.

"I am a bookworm that had to become a jock. You are a jock that picked up a gun and badge after failing English for four years in high school," I said.

Detective Clay looked at me with a cocked eyebrow. "How the hell did you know about that?" he asked.

I could have said that I had the magical ability to share the pain of every person that I met eyes with and that I magically gained understanding of every hardship they ever had. Instead, I came up with a clever cover up that no one would ever decipher. It was iron clad. "Uh, God stuff," I said.

"Anyway, if you are going to understand anything that is going to happen after this, you have to understand it from the beginning. Not the beginning of time or anything that big. You have to understand the beginning of my mission," I said.

As Orgoth began to cook, I told Detective Clay something that I had told only one other person. I told him how I got my sword.

Chapter 14

W HEN I WAS 18, I was racing home after asking out the girl of
my dreams. I had been so afraid to ask her that I almost missed
my chance. We had gone to the prom together as friends. It
never occurred to me that she would want to be my girlfriend. She did,
and she had been waiting on me to ask. When I did, she said yes.

I had waited until I was about to drop her off at home for the night,
and she started kissing me. That lasted a few hours, so I was late as heck
getting her home. Not to mention I was late getting home as well. I lived
with my grandparents and had a curfew. I was almost home—I just had
to cross the bridge and I would be a few miles away. When I got to the
bridge, I slammed on the brakes. It had collapsed. It was raining, but I
could see smoke coming from the remains like it had been burned. I
backed up to circle around to another crossing. I saw something on fire
in my mirror. It was a local halfway house. It was a place for kids that
couldn't stay with their parents. Some were little kids, some were teenagers,
but all of them were lost in some way. I knew what it was because I had
just helped my uncle install a jungle gym for them. I knew the fire department would have a time getting to them with the bridge out, so I
headed over there.

When I got there, I could hear people screaming inside. I grabbed
my sledgehammer out of the truck and ran up to the door. I was 6'2"
and 113 pounds soaking wet back then. It took me a while to bust down
the door. I ran in and started ushering people out. I knew there were
three adults and a bunch of kids there. I saw the three adults as they
helped the kids, but I heard more screams from upstairs. I ran up there
and started breaking down doors. More kids ran out.

I came to the last room. When I broke open the door, I froze. There
was a monster in the room. It was a demon, but I didn't know that at the
time. It was huge, at least as tall as Orgoth, with had huge black horns

on his head, bat wings, and a crocodile tail. It had dark, slimy skin and thick, corded muscles. There was a grotesque grin on its face; I will never forget that look. Its smile made my skin crawl, and just looking at it, I knew its smile meant despair for everything around it. It held out its hand, and its claws began to glow with fire. Slowly, it reached down so that it could begin burning whatever was in front of it. It was a little girl, and she screamed.

I yelled for it to stop, lifted my hammer, and charged in. I swung at its back with everything I had. It caught my hammer in its flaming hand. It ripped the hammer from my hand and hit me so hard that I went flying out of the room, through the baluster, and down to the first floor. I hit the ground so hard that the hardwood floor cracked. I had landed face down and everything hurt. The little girl screamed again and I got up.

Running back upstairs, I jumped at the demon's back. I put it in a choke hold, but that was just an annoyance to it. I must have looked like a little kid hanging on an adult's back. It got hold of my leg and pulled me so hard that it swung me through a dresser and part of the wall before it brought me around to face it.

It held me upside down in front of it. Then it spoke to me. Its voice was like the sound of a dying dog with the bass turned up to eleven. It said, 'What are you? Some would-be hero? A savior?'

I was bleeding from somewhere on my head or chest. Blood was running into my eyes. "Leave these people alone. Let the girl go. Please!"

It looked at the little girl. She was so scared that she could not scream anymore. It hadn't touched her yet. It looked back at me and said, "No. They will all die, and you will watch. Then you will die." That horrific grin grew even bigger.

"I won't let you hurt them!" I yelled. It started laughing. The sound was so sickening that it still haunts me. If you took a rake to a chalkboard, added a cement mixer filled with kittens, and then had it mate with a thousand car accidents it might sound like that laugh.

"Won't let me?" It said. Leaping into the air, it crashed through the roof. It flung me into the night, and I crashed through the cab of my truck.

I was hurt. My glasses were broken, and I felt like I had a piece of glass in my left eye. Everything felt broken. I tried to sit up but couldn't.

I was bleeding, it was hard to breath, and as I closed my eyes all the pain started to fade away. It felt so good.

Then they all screamed. My eyes popped open, and all that pain came rushing back into me. I screamed, forcing myself to sit up, and I saw the monster pushing everyone back into the burning home. It had landed between them and my truck. It had the little girl clutched in its claws. One claw was on her head as though he were threatening to rip it off. It breathed gouts of hellfire at them as it backed them up to the burning porch.

I still don't know how I got to my feet. All I know is that what happened next would change my life forever. I grabbed my sports bag out of the cab. All that was in it was a bat, a glove, and a baseball. I started limping toward the monster. My hands were bloody and broken, so it took me forever to unzip the bag. I pulled the wooden bat from the bag, the only weapon I had left, as I kept limping forward.

I prayed. I don't know why. I had prayed all my life. My prayers were never answered. In fact, I was pretty sure that when I prayed the opposite of what I asked happened. But I prayed. I prayed on the night that a demon tortured innocent people and expected me to watch.

"Please," I said. "Let me help them. Please! I'm not strong. I can barely see. All I need is a chance. Just let me help them!"

I limped up to the monster and raised my bat like I was going to swing for the fences. It whirled on me and held the little girl up like a shield. I saw her eyes, and all the strength that I had left in me washed away. My bat slumped in my grip, and the monster laughed again.

It leaned in until its face was barely an inch from my face. I could smell its rancid breath when it said, "I told you to watch. I want you to hear their screams. I want you to see their flesh burn. I want you to know that something like you, whatever you are, can never be a part of anything but the suffering of those around you. I will even let you live after this, so you can always remember this lesson."

It reached out to me with its clawed hand and touched my bat. It lifted it into position before my eyes. I was still gripping it. It squeezed the head of my bat and crushed it, and it didn't even grunt with effort. It was like crushing a grape.

The demon let my bat go and laughed again. It was hopeless. This thing was right. I couldn't stop it. But I could die trying. As it roared with laughter, I pulled back my broken bat and swung with all my strength. Through blood, fear, pain, and rain, I swung with everything I had.

"I won't let you hurt them!" I yelled.

I hadn't heard thunder or seen a single flash of lighting all night. Nevertheless, lightning struck at that moment. A single bolt of lightning struck my bat as I swung it at the monster's face. My swing flew past the demon's head as it was laughing. The top half of its head came flying off.

It dropped the girl, and I grabbed her as I crumbled to the ground. The monster fell sideways, and I watched its body begin to decompose so quickly that you would have thought that night a bad dream. It was no dream. I know that. I know because once I calmed down enough to look at my bat I found something very different in my hand. My bat was gone.

In my hand was a sword.

By the time I finished telling Detective Clay my little origin story, Orgoth was ready to serve us. The ogre chef placed a plate in front of each of us and said, "Bon appétit."

Detective Clay took one bite of his dish. He looked up at Orgoth and said, "You really are the best chef in the city."

CHAPTER 15

DETECTIVE CLAY OPENED his trunk and handed me my sports bag. I immediately opened it and grabbed the handle of my sword. I felt its power thrum through me. It was as if I was whole once more. I hadn't felt broken without it, but with it I just felt right. The rest of my gear was there, too. I pulled my black Desert Eagle out and hooked it on my right hip after slapping a new magazine in. Having twenty plus pounds of hand cannon on my waist was odd, but I would get used to it.

Detective Clay leaned against his car as I geared up. "So, what are you going to do about these murders?"

Eden was flicking her Zippo. "We find the sorcerer and kill him."

"Sorcerer? That's like a wizard, right? Human?" Detective Clay asked.

Eden threw up her hands and stalked away to stand over by my truck with Aaron. I couldn't help but laugh. "A mage that consorts with demons," I said.

Aaron's head snapped up. "Consort?"

I shrugged. "I have a three word a week calendar. I like expanding my vocabulary."

He narrowed his eyes. "Where did you get that?"

"Walmart," I said.

"What's the third word?" Aaron asked.

"If I told you, then it wouldn't be a surprise," I said.

Detective Clay had been shaking his head, but now he was waiving his hands. "Hold it! You can't just tell me that you are going to kill someone and not expect me to say something."

"Sure I can. He is a vampire. She is a wizard. I am a champion of God. That makes you the hard-boiled detective that bends the rules and keeps the law off our trail while we dish out the supernatural vigilante justice that the city needs but you can't provide," I said.

Detective Clay stared at me with his mouth hanging open. "Are you a fucking idiot?"

"Yes!" Eden yelled. "He is! I keep telling people this, but no one listens! He's a fucking idiot!"

"At least I can get on a bar stool without needing a stepladder!" I shot back.

Detective Clay grabbed me by the collar of my shirt. "I am not about to let you run around my city killing people."

"But what about vigilante justice?" I asked.

Aaron's hands clapped together. "It's vigilante, isn't it? That's your third word. What the hell kind calendar gives you 'thwart,' 'consort,' and 'vigilante'?" he asked.

"A good one," I said.

The detective shoved me back and slammed his trunk in frustration. "I don't care if everything you said is true. I am not about to let you run around my city doing whatever you feel like doing. You don't have any training, you don't have a badge, you don't have anything saying that you are the least bit qualified to deal with this!"

"I have a magical holy sword!" I lifted my sheathed blade above my head to emphasize my point.

There was a shriek, and something snatched my sword from my hand. I looked up to see a small winged creature flying off with my sword. Aaron broke into a run and leapt over me with superhuman strength and agility. The vampire flung himself through the air and tackled the winged creature to the ground. I rushed over as Aaron pinned the creature. He jerked his hand back, and there was a sound like a brick breaking. Aaron triumphantly held the head of a stone bird in his hand above his head.

I looked at the stone fowl and realized that it had to be the missing statue from the park. Had it been following me? I grabbed my sword and fastened it across my chest to prevent any further thefts.

"Michael, look out!" Eden yelled.

I started to turn around when something grabbed me by the arms. I was lifted into the air so fast that my neck snapped back violently. Pain ran down my spine and I screamed in rage. Without thinking, I rolled my hips back then forward. I used every muscle below my chest to rotate up and kick my would-be kidnapper in the face. I missed but struck its right shoulder hard enough to force it to let me go with just that claw. It refused to let go of me with its other claw, so its body tilted. We took a sharp left turn and smacked into the side of Kate's building.

My head smacked off the wall. I felt ribs break, and my vision went white with pain. We tumbled to the ground next to each other. The winged monster scrambled to its feet as I did the same. It leapt at me just as I got my legs under me. I rolled onto my back and raised my legs to my chest. When the monster landed on top of me, I let his momentum flip me and kicked him off with a monkey flip. I rolled up on to my feet and turned to face my attacker.

It was a stone creature like everything else that wanted me dead today. It was about four feet tall with bat wings and a muscular frame. Gray stone sculpted into the body of a man with the too-large head of a demon. It had clawed hands and feet to go with its stone fangs. To make it even creepier, it sported a pair of glowing red eyes. It was a gargoyle.

The gargoyle leapt at me again, and I drew my new silver Desert Eagle. I shot it twice in the face, and its head blew off on the second shot. The statue fell lifelessly to the ground. I turned around and started walking back to my friends. I noticed that I was limping a little. My stomach was full, so I would heal up pretty quickly, but darn if it wasn't going to be painful.

I saw everyone just standing around with their backs to me. "Hey guys, don't rush after me all at once. I'm good. I killed it. It was just a gargoyle," I said. No one looked at me, and I noticed they were all looking up at the sky. "Crap! There's a swarm of them, isn't there?" I looked up, and sure enough, a swarm of winged figures was banking around one of the buildings in the skyline.

"Jesus Christ," Detective Clay said.

"Michael, what's the call?" asked Aaron.

"They want my sword, so we let them try to take it," I said. I fished out my keys and tossed them to Aaron. "Gear up. Detective Clay, if you still want to help we are a little outnumbered by about six to one at first glance."

Aaron sprinted over to my truck and opened the door. He dropped back as Eden's hockey stick staff flew out of the cab into her hand. Aaron grabbed his gun and scimitar. Detective Clay ran to his car and opened his trunk. He pulled out an assault rifle that looked like something straight out of an action movie.

Eden lifted an eyebrow. "Is that police issued, Detective Clay?"

He didn't respond.

"Spread out! Let them come after me then pick them off," I said. "Eden, would you mind striking first and striking loudly?"

Everyone spread out and gave me room. I felt Eden gathering energy behind me. I looked over my shoulder, and the wizard angled her staff up at the coming swarm. She shouted, "Fire in the hole!"

A soccer ball-sized sphere of fire shot into the air. The swarm had begun its descent and was heading straight at us. The sphere flew past the first wave, and for a second I thought Eden had missed. There was a flash and burst of sound as the sphere exploded in the middle of the swarm. A shock wave of sound and heat hit the gargoyles, the surrounding buildings, and us. I was knocked back, but I held my footing on the gravel. Fire lit the sky, and I had to squint against it.

From the fire, a single gargoyle came out tumbling sideways to crash into a building down the street from us. I watched as it broke against the building. It was cool. Then I remembered that we were under attack. I looked back at the swarm and leapt to my left. A gargoyle crashed into the ground where I had been standing. There was nothing graceful or purposeful about it. The monster had been flung by the explosion.

I kept moving because more bodies came crashing to the ground. For the most part, they managed to hit the ground near me. I had to keep scrambling away if I wanted to live, and I could hear bodies hitting the ground around me and the sounds of battle that answered them. Moving out of the way of another falling gargoyle, I rolled over onto my butt to take in the battlefield. I had separated myself from my friends, and most of the gargoyles had landed between us. Good! They would come after me while Aaron, Detective Clay, and Eden picked them off from behind.

I got up and yelled over the commotion, "You bastards came for the knight, right? Well I am right here you rock-brained losers! Come get me!"

The sky was still filled with fire, and I saw a shadow pass over me. I dove forward, and something hit the ground so fast and hard that the gravel from the parking lot pelted me. The ground was shaking when I landed. I rolled to my feet and looked behind me.

This was no gargoyle standing behind me. A nine-foot-tall monster wrenched its fifty-pound tire-sized fist out of the hole it made in the spot where I had just been standing. Its body had the shape of a gorilla on steroids. Its rust brown skin was cloaked in flakes of ash-like fur. It had a gut that would make Santa look thin, but besides the bulk, it was lined with what looked like multiple six packs of abs stacked on multiple six packs of abs. Its hands and feet each had six fingers with four joints each. Between his knuckles were jags of hair that looked hard enough to break bones. Its face was clear of fur and ape-like except for the yellow-brown tusks pierced through its lower lip. It had a grotesque grin on its face. The bat wings were new, and he was a little bulkier than last time, but Anfalar, the Beast Bringer, looked just like he did when I faced him last.

"So, you are the knight," he said in a voice that sounded like thunder erupting from a zit.

"Yep," I said. "That would be me. The Knight of Foot in His Mouth."

His face scrunched up in a puzzled expression. He stalked forward. "I came for the fledgling knight. If you are not that, who are you?"

Really? He wanted to know who I was? I wanted to shout that my name was Nobody, but Odysseus might have taken offense. Besides, my sixth grade teacher's voice was screaming in my head, so I said, "To you? The Knight. The Hero. I am Bic Pentameter!"

"Bic Pentameter?" the demon asked.

"No, no, you have to say I am Bic Pentameter, or else it isn't funny."

The demon slammed his fists into the ground in a fit of rage. "I have come for your life and your sword. I will crush your bones, rip your limbs from your body, and swallow your heart before I break your sword."

"So you aren't going to say I am Bic Pentameter?" I asked.

In answer, a ton of angry gorilla-like demon came at me. I back-pedaled. The sounds of gunfire, wizardly magic, and screaming gargoyles filled the air behind me. My friends were tied up, which meant that this fight was strictly Michael versus Anfalar, Knight versus Demon, Good versus Evil.

"If you can hear me, I'm on the clock," I said to God and myself.

CHAPTER 16

I WAS NOT wearing armor, was still pretty beaten up from my earlier fights, and was going toe to toe with a demon that was almost twice my size. It looked bad, but that's part of the job.

The demon tried to run me over. He was bulky but not slow and came at me with the speed of a charging rhino. I slid to my left and drew both of my guns as he passed me. Anfalar tried to backhand me, and I ducked under his arm. I lifted my black Desert Eagle in my right hand and stuck it right up to his armpit. Then I started firing. My gun roared, and so did Anfalar. Demon or not, supernatural or natural, a bullet that big is going to hurt.

Dark ichor splattered on the ground and me. Anfalar spun away from me but brought his left fist around like a wrecking ball. I leapt back from the attack but not quickly enough. I was clipped by his spiked knuckles. He opened two jagged cuts across my chest. The force of the blow, glancing as it was, was enough to knock me twenty feet across the gravel. I skipped three times like a flat stone on a lake before I started rolling sidelong.

Lots of things were hurt. Some of my bones were fractured. I forced myself to my knees in time to see Anfalar pick up a car. "That's not fair!"

He threw the car, a sporty looking sedan, at me like a javelin. I was shocked and fell flat to the ground as it flew over me to crash into another vehicle. Then I watched as he lifted another car.

I scrambled to one knee and started firing. My guns were loaded with silver rounds. I figured that whatever I went up against would be vulnerable to them. Anfalar was big enough that all I had to do was keep my arms straight after each shot and aiming was easy. I emptied both magazines into the demon, and he dropped the car in front of himself. I scrambled for extra magazines, but I was out.

Anfalar beat his chest and roared. "Do you think your stings can hurt me?"

I shrugged and holstered my guns. "Well you did drop the car."

Anfalar kicked the car at me. It was a two-seater sports car, and it was skidding at me sidelong. I steadied myself and leapt in the air. I tucked my legs and let it pass harmlessly beneath me.

"Ha!" I barked triumphantly. "Like a freaking ninja!"

Before I could land, Anfalar came at me on all fours like an enraged gorilla. He planted his arms and swung his torso and legs between them. His feet hit me in a drop-kick style with the force of a speeding bus. I clipped the roof of the car that I had just leapt over and went careening through the air, crash landing in the street and rolling into a fire hydrant. I bounced off the yellow obstacle and hit the side of a building.

Nothing hurt anymore, and I was pretty sure I was dead. Then my spine and brain came back online. I realized that I had been hit so hard that each new instance of pain was registering on a time delay. The kick broke the remainder of my ribs and fractured my hip. I felt the small of my back hit the car and the upper part of my back slam into the asphalt. My left shoulder reported the shock of hitting the fire hydrant. Then my face reported that it valiantly cushioned the rest of my body before it hit the wall.

I peeled myself off the wall and looked back at Anfalar. "Is that all you've got, monkey boy?" I asked. I quickly prayed that the answer was yes and that he would give up.

Instead, he started convulsing. His stomach began to gyrate, and his chest started to pulse. His throat quivered while his cheeks puffed out. Then Anfalar belched. He let loose a belch that shook the ground. I could smell the rancid stench from across the street. I watched as dirt and stone rose into the air and began to take shape. It was then that I remembered that Anfalar was called "The Beast Bringer."

Two beasts the size of horses began to appear before him. I had to remember to change his entry in the monster manual from 'beast bringer' to 'beast belcher.' The magic he used felt like the magic that had flowed through me to create the rats earlier. These creatures looked a lot less threatening than the worgs, but I wasn't a sack of broken bones when I fought them.

The tattoos on my body were healing me. They were etched onto my body by a man I knew simply as Bigs. Bigs told me that I would need to eat my weight or more in food every day for them to work properly. I hadn't done that. I was always broke and always hungry. Tonight was an exception. Because of Orgoth, I was running on a full stomach, so I could use a special ability of my tattoos. I could call upon them to drain my physical and spiritual energy as well as the potential energy of the food I had eaten to heal faster.

There was a downside, a big one. Once I started, it was all or nothing. My body would heal until my tattoos felt I was in an acceptable condition. I would not be able to turn it off, and if my tattoos felt that weakening my body to the point where my heart stopped beating or my brain stopped functioning was necessary to repair the damage I had taken then I would die from over taxing my body's ability to heal. That was the worst-case scenario. The best-case scenario would be that I passed out from exhaustion in a few hours.

The creatures' features began to settle. Their legs were stubby and ended in cloven feet. Their bodies were thick with muscle. They had a strip of hair going from the top of their piggish heads to their tails. They were some kind of boar. I watched as the monster's tusks began to grow. They were four feet long from mouth to tip, thick jagged things with fang-like spikes jutting out from them in different direction with no discernible pattern. If one of those hit me, I wasn't just going to be impaled—I would be ripped apart from the inside out. I made my choice.

To do this, I needed to concentrate. I had never done it on such a large scale. The slightest loss of control would result in my death. I closed my eyes to focus on my healing. Well, I tried to close my eyes. My left eye closed, but my right wouldn't. That was when I noticed the flap of skin hanging off my face near the corner of my eye. I touched it and realized that it was my eyelid. My freaking eyelid was hanging off my face! It was just hanging there! That was just wrong!

I caught myself. The speed of thought is amazing. That little tantrum hadn't even cost me a second. That was good, because I didn't have one to spare. I winked and focused on my healing. My body temperature sky-rocketed. I could feel my stomach boiling, and I felt my heart as it pumped like the pistons of a Hemi engine. Sweat started gushing out of my pores so fast that it spurted like a backed-up water hose. Steam rolled off my body to create a thin fog. I began to pant. Then I started hyperventilating.

I watched as the warthogs finally came fully into the mortal world. They looked at me with hate in their eyes. Anfalar smiled to show me his mouth filled with ruptured and jagged teeth.

"I want to watch you shit out his entrails," was Anfalar's way of saying 'sick him.'

The beasts let out a high-pitched squeal as they charged. I watched through the steam with my right eye as their hooves cracked the asphalt of the street. I watched…then my healed eyelid slammed shut.

Drawing my legs beneath me, I vaulted into a crouched position by using my left hand and my hips. Pushing off with all of my strength, I emerged from the fog of steam in a forward flip. With my legs tucked and arms wide, I rolled once in the air, just barely avoiding the rush of the warthogs. They slammed into the building behind me as I landed on my hands and feet just past the curb of the sidewalk. I'm no gymnast, so of course I stumbled forward on all fours and fell over.

Anfalar looked at me in amusement. At least I think it was amusement. His smile had changed slightly; it wasn't as toothy or primal. He chuckled, which sounded more like a car backfiring.

"You prolong your suffering for my entertainment," the demon said.

I was covered in sweat and felt as if I had just run a 10k marathon. The pain from my injuries was still there, and the pain from my forced recovery was stacked on top of that. The warthogs had crashed through the building and were so focused on running something through that they had not noticed they missed me. I reached over my shoulder with my right hand and snapped my fingers closed around the handle of my sword as I stood up.

"Round two, asshole!" I said with steam shooting from my mouth with each word.

I drew my sword, and the night around me vanished. The Sword of Innocence, given to an apostle by the Son and blessed by God, filled the night with white light. I heard the gargoyles shriek in pain. I watched Anfalar, the Beast Belcher, cringe and back up a step even though he had a whole street and part of a parking lot between us.

"No!" Anfalar roared. "That sword cannot sing! It has no voice!" He covered his ears with his clawed hands as he screamed in pain.

I had no idea what he was talking about, and I didn't care. I sprinted forward but hadn't gone five steps when one of the warthogs came crashing through the wall of the building after me. I skidded as I spun to face it. My sword was in my right hand as I used my left to balance. The warthog was as big as a horse and as wide as a bull. It tucked its head as it charged and snapped it back up to skewer me. I turned sidelong so that I was between its tusks and arced my blade into a cleaving strike before it could realize that it hadn't killed me. My sword slammed down on the monster's skull, and I felt bone crunch and brains squish as I sliced its head in two.

I sprang up on the monster as it fell to the ground dead. Its momentum carried us halfway across the street. I used my own momentum to pull my sword free. I stood on top of the warthog as it began to melt into thick mud. I did not feel the pull of my sword's punishment for ending the mortal life of a soul, so I figured that either these creatures didn't have souls or their bodies were just physical constructs in the mortal world.

It didn't matter, because I didn't have time to ponder it. The second warthog came at me. It was shaking its head in a half crazed motion, so I couldn't just let its head come at my sword like before. I leaned to my left and braced my sword when the warthog snapped its neck from its right to its left. A tusk hit my sword, and I let the force of the blow push me out wide. The warthog started to round on me but found itself gimped by the pile of mud that had been its partner. It was turning, but it had to high step to do it. All the while, it swung its tusks at me as if it was insane. I kept blocking when the strikes got close, but I kept prowling around to its flank. The monster seemed to know what I was doing.

It took a moment, but once I was out of range of the tusks, I stepped up to the monster's torso. I brought my sword down on its spine and watched as it fell limp. It was still alive but completely paralyzed. I took two steps forward and shoved my sword into the warthog's head. I watched Anfalar's face as I cut down his minions.

That's when it occurred to me that the gargoyles weren't beasts. "So where is Alistair Dyhart? Is the all-powerful sorcerer too much of a coward to come himself? So he sends his lackey and some minions?"

Anfalar looked at me through squinting eyes. For the first time, he was looking at me like an enemy instead of as something that he would just scrape off his boots later.

"What did you call me?" the demon asked.

My sword had frightened him. My words stung him.

"A lackey," I said. "A fool, a jester, a gofer, a henchman. A demon that is *enslaved* to a mortal."

Anfalar leapt at me. He screamed with rage as he flew through the air.

"Let's do this!" I yelled as I charged. I really needed a better battle cry.

The Beast Belcher cracked the ground under his weight when he landed. He tried to drive me into the ground with a two-fisted hammer blow. I skidded to a stop just short of the blow, but the ground in front of me splintered into shards that slashed up my legs. I growled through the pain and stabbed ahead with my sword. Anfalar tried to back away from the blade, but he had committed too much to his initial strike. My sword caught his forearm as he tried to back away.

The Sword of Innocence flared as Anfalar howled in pain. It was a solid cut. His ichor steamed, and his skin bubbled from the touch of the holy blade. He swung a backhand at me in rage, but I dodged it. I retaliated with a slash to the gut, but Anfalar turned sideways. My sword grazed him but did no significant damage. Reflexively I kicked out at his leg, and I made a solid connection. That was like hitting a tree trunk with a twig.

Anfalar punched me. He didn't put his weight behind it, but his fist covered the area from the top of my face to the bottom of my sternum, so he didn't have to do much to make it hurt. His spiky knuckle hair cut open my cheek, collar, and chest, and I felt one of my lungs collapse. I stumbled backward, and he continued to swing at me as I dodged and fought the urge to pass out.

I danced back as I worked out his pattern. Left, left, right, left, left, right foot, left, left, left foot. When beings fight, they rely on training for the most part. Instinct is what governs us, and training quickly becomes instinct. You can't fight it. Anfalar's instinct was to fall into a rhythm and overpower me. My instinct was to learn how he moved. I'm not a great fighter, but I can outthink almost any opponent if given enough time.

Anfalar bore down on me with his full strength, and just when he was set up to throw two left-hand swipes again, I stepped into his attack. He compensated by trying to switch to his right hand, and that was when I darted forward under his left arm. He tried to follow me with his right fist and ended up throwing his full weight behind the attack. He flipped over onto his right side when he tripped over his own feet. He rolled up onto his hands and knees like a professional wrestler.

That's when I brought my left foot down as I sprinted in to swing my right leg forward and up. I kicked him right in the teeth. Anfalar grunted, and I saw his head snap up awkwardly as my boot was caught on one of his jagged teeth. He grabbed his mouth with both hands, so I jumped and kicked him in the throat. When he opened his mouth and roared without sound, I figured that I had crushed his windpipe.

Anfalar tried to attack me again, but his arms fell like wet noodles. Eighty pound wet noodles, but still wet noodles. I dodged them easily. I leveled my sword and asked, "Where is Alistair Dyhart?"

Anfalar's eyes softened, and he began to shake. I had crushed his windpipe, so I guess that was as close to laughing as he could manage right now. Gritting my teeth, I put my sword through his throat. I would have thrust right through the heart, but I didn't think he had one. Anfalar, the Beast Belcher, a true demon from Hell, a servant of chaos, and a child of Lucifer, died by my hand.

Somewhere behind my eyes a storm rolled in. I felt lightning strike my soul, and thunder burst within the tiny scar made by the lighting. I felt empty, alone, scared, and discarded.

Fourteen.

Aaron, Eden, and Detective Clay had finished with the gargoyles and were running over to me. I waved them back. I wasn't in danger. I withdrew my sword and watched as the demon burned in holy fire.

CHAPTER 17

I CLEANED MY sword and walked over to meet up with my team. We had been outnumbered and unprepared for anything like that fight, so I took a mental inventory of them. Eden seemed all right, except for the fact her shirt was ripped up to expose her left breast and arm. She was smoking again so she was fine. Aaron didn't have a single hair out of place. He looked like a model ready for the runway. Detective Clay was covered in dirt, and he had a few scratches here and there. For his first supernatural throw down, I say he came out looking like a pro!

"Is everyone alright?" I asked. I still wanted to make sure my people were okay.

"I think the detective is going to need a minute," Eden said.

I looked closely at Detective Clay and noticed he had hung back a bit. He was gripping his rifle a little too tightly. I walked over to him slowly and made it a point to show him that I was sheathing my sword.

"Detective Clay," I said in a friendly tone. "How does it feel to shoot a monster that was planning to do harm to law-abiding citizens?"

Detective Clay backed away from me defensively. "They were made of rock. The girl…she was throwing fire at them…real fire. And him…the vampire! I watched him rip one of them in two. Then he did it again."

He was obviously shocked by what he had seen. Eden can be scary, and I can understand being unnerved by magic. He said that Aaron had ripped two stone gargoyles in half. I knew that Aaron was strong, but not that strong.

"Yes, but you have to remember they are the good guys," I said.

"The demon!" Detective Clay shouted. "I saw you fight a demon. It knocked you across the road. I thought you were dead. Then you just got up as if nothing happened. You should be dead. Why aren't you dead?"

If some supernatural creature had asked that, I would have shrugged and walked away like a boss. Keeping your enemies and the people you protect ignorant of what you are capable of is pretty important. You don't want your enemies collecting information on how to beat you. But Detective Clay needed answers.

"Do you see the tattoos on my arms?" I asked to get his attention. When Detective Clay looked at me, I pointed to my tattoos. Then I pointed to the wounds on my neck and chest. I was already going to be paying for it, so I might as well do a little more good. "They're magical. I'm not magical. They allow me to heal at an accelerated rate and from just about anything."

I focused on the two wounds, and Detective Clay watched as they scabbed, crusted over, broke apart, and the skin regrew. He touched my collar where my new skin was pink and still tender. I flinched but he just poked me again.

"Well holy shit," he said in a breathy voice.

"Detective, I can't explain the world to you. I barely understand it myself, but I can help you if you are willing to help me," I said. I held my hand out to him. I was going to need all the help I could get.

The grip he had on his rifle finally relaxed. He took my hand in a grip that let me know I had found a strong and sure ally. We shook, and he said, "Call me Garrett."

I nodded and returned the grip. "And you can call me Michael. Michael White, Knight of the Crucifixion, and the Knight of Innocence."

Garrett yanked me forward and stepped ahead so he covered my back with his body. I heard tires squeal and turned to see a black sedan speeding away. It was Alistair Dyhart's car. I snarled and started to chase it, but then I stopped. Garrett lay on the ground with a bullet hole in his chest.

Aaron was there in a second. He pushed me out of the way and started checking for a pulse. I just stood there like a big idiot. "He's alive, but I need to get him stable and to a hospital. Michael, you get the hell out of here."

I snapped out of my trance. "What?"

"A police officer has just been shot. You have a bunch of guns and have littered this place with bullets. I, on the other hand, am a doctor that was out getting a drink with a friend. Get out of here! Go!" Aaron yelled as he handed me his weapons "Take Eden and go. Get moving!"

I did as I was told. I may have called the shots when it came to fighting, but this was where Aaron was the expert. Eden and I jumped into the Rust

Bucket and took off after the gunman. I rooster-tailed out of the parking lot and jumped the curb to save time. I caught sight of the sedan rounding a bin a few blocks down. Flooring the gas, I shot down the road, taking the turn at 70 mph. They weaved through the traffic ahead of us. I managed to gain on them, but with the heavy traffic, I could not get within range to run them off the road.

Eden took her wand and held it toward the roof. She chanted something under her breath, and suddenly blue swirls of light were flashing across my windshield. Cars started pulling over and letting us through. I smiled at her.

"No more short jokes for the rest of the night," I said.

"I could just as easily put a ball of fire up your ass," she said to me.

I grinned as I pumped the accelerator. I was almost behind the sedan when they opened fire on us. They had shot Clay with a pistol, but now they were using an automatic rifle. Bullets struck my truck and ricocheted out into the night. Eden ducked.

"Bulletproof glass," I said.

"This thing doesn't have heat, but it has bulletproof glass?" she yelled.

"It has heat!" I shot back.

I swerved around to the driver's side of the sedan and started to match their speed. "Can you take out the tires with a spell?"

"You just saw me create a small sun in the sky not ten minutes ago. I'm a little tapped on magic right now," Eden growled.

"Then take the wheel." I rolled down my window and had to brace as the sedan slammed into us. I straightened and hit them right back.

"Are you crazy, Church Boy?"

"Nope, just ticked off!" I said.

Eden grabbed my leg. "I really can't drive!"

I pulled her onto my lap. Then I positioned her leg and jammed her foot down on the gas. I slid from under her and out the window. "Keep it straight and keep up with them." She held the wheel like it was about to attack her, arms stiff and with her full weight behind her grip. They rammed us again, and I had to slam my right foot on the back of the seat and my left foot on the AC vent on the driver's side of the dash. I heard the vent crack open and felt it cave beneath my weight. There went my last working vent.

The gunman started firing into the passenger's side window. Bulletproof or not, the glass would not hold up to a prolonged assault.

"What do I do?" Eden screamed.

"Turn right and ram them off of us!" I yelled.

The wizard may have been small, but in a battle I would rather have her than a dozen giants. She reminded me why when she spun the wheel of my truck. The Rust Bucket does not have power steering, so you have to put some muscle behind it. Eden spun my wheel and hit them with enough force to run them up on the curb. I rolled onto the roof and into a crouching position. When they came back at us, I leapt out at them just before we collided.

I hit the roof and managed to secure myself atop the moving sedan. A split second later bullets came flying through the roof at me. Before any of them could ventilate me, I heard the magazine click on empty. I didn't have time for anything dramatic, but that's what I did anyway. Drawing my sword, I rolled down to the hood of the sedan. I rotated my blade so that the tip pointed toward the ground. Then using both hands I thrust the blade down into the engine.

I took my anger at Clay being shot. I combined it with my anger over the loss of the vent in my truck. On top of that, I added the loss of another day of my life. I combined them with my will and slammed all of that into my sword. White light erupted from the blade. The engine roared, howled, and suddenly stopped making any noise at all. The driver swerved and slammed on the brakes. I tried to hold on, but the momentum was too great. After the third round of side-to-side, I was flung from the vehicle, sword and all.

The sedan crashed into a guardrail, bounced off, and flipped over once onto its roof. We were on a bridge overlooking highway traffic. Eden just barely managed not to run me over. I stood up. There was no time to sluggishly clamber to my feet. I gritted my teeth and felt blood flowing freely from my gums. I pushed up and realized that the left side of my shirt was gone along with an unhealthy amount of flesh. I could smell the blood running from my scalp down across my nose. My pants and boots were soaked with blood. So it may have taken me three or four minutes to actually make it all the way up to a standing position, but I did not sluggishly clamber to my feet!

I stood there in the street with my sword in my right hand and my left arm hanging limply. Looking down at my arm, I growled, "You don't get to slack off!" I clenched my left hand into a fist and slowly flexed my wrist. I flexed and tensed my muscles until I bent my fist up to parallel my shoulder. Then using a substantial amount of strength I pumped my fist into the air, pointed a finger, and leveled it at the flipped sedan as I yelled, "YOU BASTARDS HAD BETTER BE ALIVE SO I CAN KILL YOU!"

Eden grabbed me from behind. "Michael, the cops are on the way. We have to go."

I pulled away from her. "No. I need to finish this."

I limped forward a step and then stumbled into a running motion. Then I fell on my face. I got back up with Eden's help. I wanted to rush ahead at the sedan, but she ushered me back to the truck.

"Please tell me you can drive," she said. "I really can't do it."

"I have possible brain damage and a severe loss of blood. I'm better off than most drivers on a Friday night," I said.

We got into the Rust Bucket. I had to crank the engine to the tune of Inspector Gadget before it turned over. Once it did, we made a dramatic get away. I saw blue and red lights in my rearview. They were off in the distance, but I decided that blending into highway traffic was the best thing to do. I pulled onto the freeway and drove off into the night.

"What did you do to their engine?"

I grunted and had to swallow some blood before I could talk. "A few months ago I couldn't pay my electric bill. They cut my power. It's weird—they usually give you two or three extra months and a couple of notices, but the day after mine was due they cut it. Anyway, it was cold, and I had a box of Pop-Tarts in the cabinet. It was the only food I had, and I figured I could use the sword to power my toaster. I hooked my jumper cables up to the sword and toaster, and I put a little will into the sword. My toaster spat white fire, the Pop-Tarts were vaporized, and I learned that science and religion don't mix. Not easily at least."

"You used a holy relic, a conduit of mystical power, to run a toaster?" Eden asked.

"I really wanted Pop-Tarts," I said.

"God can't be real. At least not your god. What god would put that kind of power into the hands of an idiot!"

I was mostly silent for the rest of the ride. Eden called me many things, and at times she slipped into another language—possibly one of the many African languages—and repeatedly called me a child. When we reached Eden's house, I offered to help her with her bags.

"I can carry my own shit. Go home and get some rest, kid," she said as she walked up to her porch. "I'll have another pie for you tomorrow. Just call before you come get me."

I watched Eden enter her home before I drove off. I drove home with the radio off and a rage building in my chest. Garrett had taken a bullet that was meant for me. He could be dying or dead right now. He was hurt while I was still standing. This night could not get any worse.

CHAPTER 18

ERRI'S SUV WAS parked outside my apartment. I parked next to it and stowed all my gear except for my guns and sword in my tool chest. I texted my cousin Drey to tell him I needed emergency repair work done on my truck. Drey did all my repair work. When it came to fixing my truck, he was pure magic with a wrench. It may have helped that he was half fae.

I walked up to my door and saw the hole had been patched with a board and nails. When I opened the door, the smell of food overtook me. *There was food in my home.* Kerri had laid out a piping hot dinner on the table. I looked around and noticed that everything had been cleaned. I wasn't a slob, because my daily routine was get up, get beat up, limp home, pass out, and repeat. I left my gear, bandages, and sometimes my blood everywhere. Now my place was spotless.

"Dad, I can't talk right now," I heard Kerri say as I walked in the door. "I am fine, Daddy. I told you I wanted to see the country and explore my options." There was a pause, and I could hear a man's voice screaming over the phone but couldn't make out what was being said. "Daddy, I am grateful that you helped me pay for college, and I always will be, but I am a grown woman with three college degrees. I can make my own decisions on where I live and work. We can talk later. I love you."

She hung up the phone and turned toward me. There were tears in her eyes. "You're home!" Kerri yelled. She ran over from my couch and hugged me. My ribs screamed in pain.

"Let go," I said a little more harshly than I should have.

"Thank God you are alive. I thought they had killed you," she said.

"Kerri, please let go," I said again.

She let me go and looked at me. "How did you get away?"

"I killed the demon," I said.

"Good!" She paused. Kerri looked me up and down. Then she went pale. "You look like you were in a train wreck."

"That good? I thought I would look a lot worse," I chuckled.

That's when I fell down to my knees. Kerri dropped down to help me balance. I had reached my limit. I needed food and rest.

"I got hurt pretty bad. I had to do something stupid to survive. I need food," I told her.

Kerri helped me over to my table and took care of me. She fed me pot roast, mashed potatoes, collard greens, and homemade sweet tea mixed with lemonade. Yes, she made both sweet tea and lemonade and then mixed them in front of me. When I was done with my fifth plate, she went into my kitchen and brought me an apple pie that she made from scratch. I looked back at my kitchen, because until that moment I was sure the creation of food in my home was a dead dream. The only thing that passed for food in my house was those darn protein bars.

I ate the whole pie. Then I ate the second one she brought me. I am not ashamed that I asked if there was a third one. There was! When I was done, I told her I needed to rest.

"Not until you take a shower," she said.

"Kerri, I can barely sit up in my chair. I don't mean that I am tired. I mean my body is refusing to respond to my attempts to maintain balance," I informed her.

"I could help you shower," she said. "Or I could run you a bath."

I thought about being in the shower with her. It would be wonderful. I shook my head. "No. A bath will do," I said.

She ran a bath for me while I sat with my head on the table. I had to ask her to help me out of my clothing and into the tub.

"Your skin," she said when she started to undress me. "It's raw!"

I looked down at my naked body and saw that most of the skin on the front of my body was indeed raw. It had been regrown in a hurry. Much of it was still bright pink and hairless. When I turned around to get in the tub, Kerri gasped at the sight of my back. I didn't want to know how bad it was. I was pretty sure most of the skin on my back if not all of it had been regrown.

I wanted to scream when I put my foot into the water. Kerri somehow managed to support most of my weight as she helped me sit down in the tub. Once I was settled, I reached for my washcloth and Kerri popped my hand. She took my soap and washcloth from me.

"Sit still. Relax," she told me. "I will be back in twenty minutes. Just relax." She left me there with nothing to do but sit in the tub as if I had all the time in the world. She came back with her phone, set it on the sink counter, and hit a button and it played soft music. "Twenty minutes," she said before she left again.

Time passed as I sat in the tub. I couldn't remember the last time I had taken a bath. The hot water felt harsh on my new skin, but it was heaven on my muscles. I let myself drift between being asleep and awake. One time I closed my eyes, and when I opened them Kerri was there cleaning my feet.

I opened my mouth to say something but stopped. She was singing to herself. It was a song I did not know, but the song didn't matter. Her voice, though. I had forgotten how much I loved to hear her sing. I used to go to church with my family just because she was going to be singing. Our church had banned me from attending when I was six. They lifted the ban when my Grandpa told them he would no longer attend a church that would not allow his grandson in their house of worship. Shortly after that, they told us that I would never be allowed to become a member of the church when I came of age. I stopped going to church then, except when Kerri was going to sing.

She bathed me and rinsed me off with warm water. Then she helped me into my shorts. I had to lean on her all the way across the hall to my bed. She had put my sword next to the bed with my baseball cap resting atop the handle. Then she climbed into bed with me.

"How did you do it?" she asked me.

"Do what?" I asked.

"Kill the demon," she said.

"You really want to hear how I killed a demon?" I asked. I wasn't annoyed or angry, but it was as strange thing to talk about.

"Yeah. I mean, when it disappeared I thought it escaped," she said.

Alarms went off in my head. "What?" I asked. "What do you mean it disappeared?"

Kerri sat up and frowned at me. She looked at me hard for a moment before her features showed a hint of panic. Getting out of bed, she left the room, came back with her laptop, and set it on the bed. She pulled up several YouTube pages, and all of them had very blurry, very violent, and very loud videos of a monstrous humanoid slaughtering people. All of them were posted just hours ago.

Kerri brought up video from several local stations. Each one was reporting on a disaster that they had dubbed the "Slaughter Party." A rave here in Baltimore ended in the deaths of thirty-seven young people. Bodies were still being identified, and several people were injured. All of this had happened while I was fighting Anfalar. He laughed when I asked where Alistair Dyhart was. He had been a distraction. Thirty-seven people had died.

I watched the videos two or three times each. I had really messed up. Anfalar and his goons had me pinned down so I wouldn't be able to interfere with this killing spree. I slammed the laptop closed and screamed in a fit of rage. Then I slammed the side of my fist against the wall, sending cracks along the point of impact. I threw my pillow off the bed and thrashed like a mad man.

I moved to get up, and that was when my body gave out. My rage had used up the last of my reserves of physical energy. I fell onto my back and could not move. I willed myself to sit up, to smash my bed apart, or to do something to express my anger. All I could do was lay on my back, unmoving and useless.

Kerri had moved up against the wall farthest from my bed. She had her laptop pulled to her chest. Her eyes were wide in shock. The look on her face was a stark reminder to me that I was not the boy she knew before. I was no longer docile or weak. No. The look on her face, in her eyes, reminded me that humans could be monsters just like any other being.

I couldn't turn my head, so I moved my eyes to look at the wall that I had hit. I thought I had only cracked it, but I had actually put a hole in the wall. "You should leave," I said.

There was a silence in the room. I heard my door close after a minute. I closed my eyes in utter defeat. I had allowed thirty-seven people to die. I had allowed a good man to take a bullet for me. Worse than anything else, I had scared away the woman I loved. I did not even have the ability to tremble in grief.

A warm hand touched my face. I opened my eyes to see Kerri standing over me smiling. She was wearing an over-sized Autobots tee shirt, her glasses, and nothing else. She leaned over and kissed me on the lips. When she pulled away, she looked me in the eyes.

"I will never leave you," she said.

I still wanted to scream and thrash everything. "Kerri, all that follows me is evil. You saw the videos. There's no reason you should be around me."

Kerri was shaking her head. She crossed her arms and pulled her shirt halfway up. "Let's see if I remember everything you told me when you came home. You traveled across the world," she said. She pulled her shirt all the way over her head. She was wearing a dark blue bra and matching panties. "You trained under great men in the art of combat."

Kerri climbed atop me and placed her hands on my chest. She leaned down so that I could look at her eyes behind those fire engine red glasses. "You got a college education. Two degrees. You actively try to learn something new every day," she said. "How can you be so stupid?"

"Your family hates me. Hell, your dad would disown you for being with me!" I argued.

"So what? I am a grown fucking woman. Who I love, who I care about, and who I choose to spend my time with are my decisions to make," she said in challenge.

Kerri kissed me. She parted her lips so that mine followed suit, and she guided me in a dance that I knew but had not practiced. Biting my lower lip, she sat up on her knees. She did not smile at me, instead looking at me as though we were supposed to be right here and nothing I said to the contrary would matter.

She took off my shorts and threw them onto the floor. Her bra and panties joined them. Kerri-Lynn gripped my penis in her right hand and guided it into herself while astride me. "You are too weak to move, but you have enough strength to be hard? Men are strange things," she said. "Or do they just have strange things?"

"Kerri," I started to say, but she covered my mouth with her right hand and placed her left index finger upon her lips.

She shushed me and said, "You don't get to talk. You told me to leave, remember?" She clenched, and I felt a wave of pleasure wash over my body. "For four long years I waited for you. I kept a crappy job all through college just to keep my phone bill paid so my number would not change. I checked my email every day, I checked my phone every time it rang, I called your mother and grandmother every day, and I prayed for you every morning, at every meal, and every night. My every prayer to God had your name attached to it."

Her body moved to the rhythm of a silent drum. She sat tall atop me as she swayed forward and back. Her hips moved her up and down while she clenched and stroked my manhood. "You do not get to send me away Michael Franklin White! You do not get to dump me! You do not get to shield me from your life!"

Kerri bucked up and slammed down on my lap. She began to ride me as though I were some wild horse. I couldn't move, but I could feel everything. She put one hand behind her and placed one on the bed beside my shoulder. She leaned forward and began to gyrate back and forth. Her breath was labored, but she moaned out a small symphony. I gritted my teeth as every muscle in my body strained to move. I was frozen, bound by weakness and gravity as though I were shackled to the bed. A grunt escaped my lips just before I roared in frustration and ecstasy.

Both of her hands slammed onto my chest, and she began lifting herself up and down rapidly. I felt the heat in the room build, and with every rise in degree, her vagina tightened around me.

"You do not get to send me away! You are going to be mine until I tell you otherwise!" she said. She slapped me and then kissed me. Her nails dug into my shoulders as she rode me into the sunset. Kerri screamed atop me when she came, and that sound brought me to climax.

All the rage began to leak out of me when she fell atop me. I was a fool for trying to send her away. My heart was pounding, and I was filled with a feeling of great satisfaction. I still could not move, but it did not matter. I was perfectly fine right where I was.

I heard Kerri breathing quiet and slow. "Good night, Kerri," I said.

She sat up and looked into my eyes. "Who said that we were done?" she asked me.

Kerri rode me for the next two hours. I did not complain, and I did not dream of changing anything about it. When we finally went to sleep, I could just about move my pinky toe if I used all of my strength. Kerri covered us up and laid her head on my chest. The last thing I remember was her saying, "You belong to me, Michael. I belong to you. I love you. I always have and I always will."

CHAPTER 19

WHEN I WOKE up, Kerri had already started her day. The sun wasn't up, but she was cooking. I could smell bacon, eggs, pancakes, and several other things that still could not possibly exist in my kitchen. Either Kerri was a wish granting genie with a sweet disposition, or she was the most powerful being on earth. My kitchen could not possibly have food in it!

The smell of food temporarily numbed the pain of my body, but it all came back to me. Every cut, scrape, bruise, and break came rushing into my body in a symphony of pain. A lesser man would have screamed out loud. A lesser man would have passed out. I, however, am a Knight! So I won't tell you that I covered my face with both my pillows and screamed like a child that scrapped their knee because that would not be becoming of my station. I totally just manned up. I even did some push-ups. Bare-knuckle push-ups. On gravel...that I keep in my room.

My phone rang. I reached over my head and grabbed it off the little stand I keep above my bed. A hard voice yelled at me. "What did you do to my truck?"

"Drey, it's *my* truck," I said.

"Not if you keep fucking it up like this! Hell Little Cousin, how do you manage to always find something with claws to rip up the paneling? Why is there duct tape in my engine?" he asked.

"I may have made some minor repairs," I groaned.

There was a long silence. I then heard a crashing sound like a lot of metal slamming into even more metal. "Look Little Cuz. You stick to fighting vampires and demons or whatever. Do. Not. Touch. The. Engine. Next time I am going to tell Gramps and my dad," Drey said.

I thought about what Gramps would say to my mistreatment of the Rust Bucket. Then I thought about what my uncle would say. Neither would be happy with me, and both could easily kick my butt.

113

"Okay, okay. I will call you first next time. How long until you can have it fixed?" I asked.

"I will have it back to you tonight at the latest. I am going to go ahead and overhaul the engine and do your inspection; it's due anyway," he said. "I saw Kerri's truck in your lot. She visiting?"

"Yeah," I said.

"Does her father know she is there?" he asked.

"I'm not sure," I said.

Drey grunted. "Don't mess it up with her," he said. Then he hung up on me.

So I wasn't the only one that thought I was going to do that. *Great.*

I got up and stretched. My body was moving just fine, so there was no use worrying about the pain. I walked out to the kitchen and found Kerri in nothing but a Wonder Woman tee shirt, boy shorts, and an apron. The apron was pink, frilly, and had an inscription across the chest in white letters that said 'I can cook, I can clean, and I can kick your ass.' She had her braids tied up into some crazy bun, and of course her glasses made her look like the nerdiest homemaker in the world.

She was on her phone again. "Chester, I don't care what you or Daddy think of him. He is a good man, a kind man. He has never done anything to hurt me and treats me better than Daddy ever treated Mama." There was a pause, and then she continued. "When Mama left I helped raise you, the twins, and took care of Daddy. I kept my grades up. I kept our home and you brats clean, and kept Daddy sober as much as I could without shooting him. I love you all, but its time you learned to fend for yourselves. I'm going to live my life the way I want to from now on. Love you little brother, but I have to go."

I let her hang up before I stepped into view. "So when did you start cooking like this?" I asked.

She never looked up from the stove, but I could see her quirk her lips up. "I have spent a lot of time over your house over the years. I never knew why your grandmother fixed so much food. Until this year, when you told me you were a Knight," she said. "After you left again I asked your grandma if I could come over and cook with her. Apparently keeping a knight fed is a full time job."

"She makes it look easy," I said.

Kerri looked up at me with a sly smile. "How do I make it look?"

"Sexy," I said.

She smiled all the wider. "There is some cash on the table. Can you go get some orange juice? Four gallons," she instructed. "Oh, have you seen the big chef's knife? It's missing from the block I bought."

"You bought me a knife set?" I asked.

"I bought you a kitchen. What did you do before I came here? Eat roman noodles?" she asked.

"I wish! I can't afford roman. I pretty much fix things in restaurants, and they pay me in meals," I told her.

"Oh lord. Have you seen the knife?" she asked again.

"I didn't even know there was a knife," I said.

"Okay" she sighed. "Orange juice. Four gallons. Go!"

I went to get dressed. My phone beeped. It was a text from Aaron. Detective Clay was going to live. He had been wearing Kevlar, and that alone had saved his life, but he might never walk again. The bullet's impact had damaged his lower spine. If I had taken the shot, I might have possibly been able to heal from it. More than likely it would have killed me outright, magical healing be damned, if the impact alone had done so much to a man more muscular than me who was also wearing Kevlar. He had saved my life.

The sun was about to come up, so Aaron was going to be stuck in the hospital. He would find a nice place in the basement or the morgue to hide from the sun. At least he was in a place that had a steady supply of refrigerated blood for when he woke up.

I got dressed in some sweat pants and a tank top. I could run to the store to clear my head. It would give Kerri a chance to finish cooking, and it was good exercise. I grabbed my keys, my phone, and the cash off the living room table. Looking on the couch, I noticed Horace was gone. I spotted him on the bookshelf. Kerri must have put him there.

"Back in a few minutes," I said over my shoulder.

I opened my front door, and something crashed into my chest so hard my vision went white. I went flying back into my house and landed hard on the floor. My ribs cracked, again. All the air was blasted out of me, and all I could think about was that the third demon was here. Kerri screamed, and I heard a stampede moving through my house.

I was slipping from consciousness, but I dug deep to fight it. Multiple screaming voices filled my ears, sending my adrenaline through the roof. Most were so muffled they would be nearly impossible to understand under normal circumstances. Each voice was drowning out the next and merging into a storm of incoherent babble. The sound pounded against me as I struggled into a sitting position. My vision came back just as the butt of an assault rifle slammed across my forehead. I went back down, but I flipped my legs so that the momentum rolled me onto my feet in a crouched position.

I saw men in tactical gear swarming into my house. They all had assault rifles, and most of them were trained on me. I heard Kerri scream again, and my mind started plotting a course to get to her. A dozen or more people were all screaming different orders at me in different pitches and registers. They were assaulting me with a wall of indecipherable sound. From my crouched position, I saw a metal battering ram sitting in my doorway. That's how they had started their attack.

Two men came at me from either side. I was outnumbered and outgunned. The best thing to do would be to try to reason with my attackers. Kerri screamed again and all reason left me. The two men that approached me tried to force me to the ground. I snapped my elbow up into one's groin causing him to go limp. I grabbed him by his collar and leg and threw him across my body into his friend. The assailants yelled more words at me that became even more garbled by their rise of excitement.

I sprang up to my right and grabbed the rifle of the closest man. I don't think they expected a guy that had been hit with a battering ram to move like I did. Then again, I don't think they were expecting me to put up a fight at all. Michael Combat Rule number 3: Always put up a fight! I pushed his rifle up and into his chest. I turned behind him and grabbed the butt of the weapon to pin it to his throat and him to my chest. His buddies spun on us, but I backpedaled into a wall to use him as a shield.

"Michael!" Kerri screamed. I could see her in the kitchen, on the ground with guns all around her.

I also saw the back of one of the attackers. The tactical vest he wore said in large white letters, 'POLICE'.

"You guys are cops?" I asked. "Why didn't you just say so?" More unintelligent screaming came at me.

There was my answer. We like to find fault in our heroes. The police are human, and a common human mistake in any dangerous situation is screaming. When you scream, you inspire confusion. Even if you are screaming 'police' or 'freeze' or 'duck' it doesn't matter. A suddenly raised voice inspires fear. We all know that. Think about what you instinctively felt when you were a child and an adult approached you screaming. You did one of three things: you froze, cried out, or ran. Freezing is Darwin in action. Those that cannot adapt are weeded out. Crying out or running is fight or flight. Simple choices right?

Now imagine almost two dozen people all yelling something at you in a different tone. Imagine each one repeating themselves because they think you can't hear them even though they are the only one speaking. Well their friend just said the exact same thing, but they added an accent and three words. But it's okay because their other two buddies are repeating them verbatim just with a few more words and a slightly different demand. Dammit, you must be thick or ignorant if you don't understand what the fifth person is saying by now. They are saying the exact same thing people seven through seventeen are saying. They are even more helpful because, without informing anyone else, they shortened the dialog from three sentences to two words that they have been repeatedly screaming like a mad person since the first person began to open his mouth. Now people eighteen through twenty-four are spectacularly efficient. They all know what they are supposed to be doing and saying, but their voices are all being muffled by everyone else's screaming.

Perfect communication!

I whispered to the guy that I was using as a shield, "I'm sorry man. If I knew you were a cop, I wouldn't have done this. Maybe you should talk to your boss and get the word "Police" put on the front where people can see it."

I let him go. He spun on me with wide eyes. That's all I could see, considering his full-face cover of ski mask, helmet, and goggles. As I put my hands up, two of his buddies pushed him out of the way and started hitting me with their batons. I tried to protest, but the first strike was across my face. I went down, and a heavy boot hit me in the head. Then a few more boots and a few more baton blows. Then I passed out.

I woke up in the back of a police wagon. Not a car but one of the armored transports. I was handcuffed and strapped to a wall. Lots of things hurt more now. Some of my teeth had been knocked out. I only knew because I felt new teeth growing in. Yay, new pain.

The door opened. People with badges and other visible declarations that they were the police hauled me out of the wagon. They escorted me by gunpoint into a building filled with more people that I could easily identify as police officers and into a ten by twelve room. The room had one table, three chairs, and a two-way mirror. Both of my hands were handcuffed to the one chair on the far side of the desk. My ankles were cuffed together as well.

The armed escort left. I had to sit in the room alone until someone came to talk to me. It is a standard tactic for softening a hostile prisoner. It does not work on someone that has spent the majority of their life alone. I counted the tiles on the ceiling. I counted the intersections of the squares and then divided them by random numbers to see which equations would present me with answers containing multiple prime numbers. When I got bored with that, I considered the structure of the room and what I had seen beyond it. I created a mental layout for the floor and backtracked my way through the structural design. There was no way to be accurate about it, but I liked to build things.

Forty minutes later two detectives walked in. One was a woman with a large file in her hand, and the other was a man with a box full of files. They both set their items on the desk and stared at me. I smiled at them.

"Mr. White my name is Detective Banks. This is my partner Detective Wilson. I am going to make this simple," the woman said. "You are going to be arrested for four counts of assaulting a police officer, but only after we book you for the attempted murder of Detective Garrett Clay."

The smile melted from my face. "What?"

The man chimed in. "Detective Garrett Clay, the man who caught you with a bag of illegal weapons yesterday. You shot him last night, you little prick."

"No I didn't!" I yelled. I was panicked. Every synapse of my brain was firing a warning that I was being set up and that it would stick.

"Mr. White, we have witnesses that put you at the scene and a mountain of evidence, but you have a chance to make this go a lot easier on yourself," the woman said.

"It's more than you deserve, you little piece of shit. Banks, I still say we let him hang for what he did," said the man.

"Wilson!" the woman snapped. "We don't want to answer a murder with an execution. Mr. White, if you confess we are prepared to offer you leniency."

I listened to their words. Then my shock fell away and my brain started functioning. "You're cops. You can't offer me leniency," I said.

Detective Wilson snapped around to look at me. "What the hell did you just say?"

"You haven't read me my rights. You aren't even trying to interrogate me. You're just trying to get me to confess to a crime," I said.

Detectives Banks and Wilson looked at each other with a puzzled expression. They temporarily dropped their good cop bad cop routine. It came back a moment later when Detective Wilson stormed over to me and got in my face.

He leaned down and put his head right up to mine. "You tried to kill a cop, you fucking asshole. You assaulted three officers while resisting arrest. You are lucky to…"

I spit out some of my broken teeth onto the desk. My new teeth had been forcing them out, and the timing was just perfect. They landed on the desk. "I have broken ribs too," I said. Wilson was about to say something, but I spit out another tooth. I looked at Detective Banks and said, "So, are you willing to arrest me after I defended myself against an assault team of unidentified officers? Officers that didn't knock on my door, say 'this is the police,' or even wear their badges in plain sight?"

Detective Wilson backed off. Detective Banks sat down and looked me squarely in the eye. I looked her in the nose. "You shot Garrett Clay," she said.

"No, I didn't. I can show you my gun. Your bullet won't match it."

"We have witnesses," she said.

"No, you don't. If you had even one witness, you wouldn't tell me about it. You think I attempted to kill a cop. If I had a lawyer you would be trying to hide the existence of a witness from them, not telling me that you have one," I said.

"Fucking thugs always think they're so smart," said Wilson.

Something turned my stomach. I was with Detective Clay last night, but the majority of the city would have just driven past Kate's Bar unless they had seen the battle in the parking lot first hand. I was sure that some, if not all, of the patrons had watched the fight. So why was I a suspect?

"Detectives, who told you that I shot Detective Clay? How did you even know where I lived?" I asked.

They both looked at me and then back to each other. Before either could answer, another cop stuck his head in the door.

"Detectives, we have a situation out here that needs your immediate attention," the newcomer said.

"Don't move, asshole," Wilson said as he and Banks left. I was handcuffed to a chair, so where was I going to go? Some people are just jerks.

A few minutes passed, and I started singing *The Song That Doesn't End*. I was on my seventeenth verse when the door opened again. My eyes narrowed with rage as Alistair Dyhart walked in wearing a tailored gray suit with a pink shirt. He adjusted his tie as he shut the door behind him. Then he sauntered over with the confidence of a murderer that had a victim locked in a dungeon. Calmly he pulled out a chair and sat down.

"Hello, Mr. White. How is your day going?" he asked.

I did not reply. I flexed my wrists. The cops had wrapped the handcuffs around the arms of the chair and put both cuffs on a single wrist. Both of my wrists were like this, and my legs were cuffed together. I started pulling against those cuffs so hard that I began cutting my skin.

"Well I imagine your day is not going so well," Dyhart laughed. A sadistic smile appeared on his face. "My day, however, is going wonderfully. Last night I was able to bind my associate, Ophalistis, to this world permanently. All it took was a few young fools...or rather, their blood. Girls that could have been saved if some young idiot had given me his sword."

I felt myself growling. Through clenched teeth I said, "I am going to make you pay for every person that you harmed."

"That's a lot of people, Mr. White. I have been running raves and killing young fools for years. It was only recently that anyone started to connect the dots. Even your precious Church was clueless," he said.

"You know about the Church?" I asked.

He chuckled. "Of course I know about the Church. I know about you knights, monsters, and the fae. Were you foolish enough to think that your precious Church was a secret?"

I pulled harder at my restraints. "Why are you here?" I asked. Then I listened to the words that had come from my mouth. I was asking the wrong question. "How did you know I was here?"

The sorcerer chuckled. "Why Mr. White, I am a district attorney. Specifically, I am the prosecuting attorney in your impending trial. I, along with Mr. Ophalistis as my assistant, will be prosecuting you to the full extent of the law."

I tilted my head to the side as the gravity of his words settled on my shoulder. He was going to railroad me. He would blame me for all his murders. With Ophalistis helping him, he could enthrall the judge and the jury. He wouldn't even have to present a case. The jury would find me guilty on his orders alone.

Dyhart sighed. "I can see your tiny mind is having a hard time processing this," he said. "I am going to send you to jail for the rest of your natural life. Why kill you when I can make you suffer for my wrongdoings?"

I tried to break free of the handcuffs, but they held fast. Dyhart watched my frustration and laughed. "Did you really think that some muscle-bound thug could win against a man of my intelligence and power?"

"When I get out of here," I started to say, but he cut me off.

"You won't be getting out of here. I will be making sure that you are booked and that bail is set to some amount that you cannot count to on your fingers and toes," he said as he stood up. "Ophalistis is already interviewing witnesses for the prosecution. I am sure they will be very willing to place you at the scene with intent to kill in your eyes."

He started to leave and I growled at him. He stopped just as he reached the door. Alistair Dyhart turned to me with a wry grin on his face. "Perhaps I am doing this incorrectly. Why prolong things when I can just be rid of you here and now?"

He leaned forward and opened his mouth as though he were about to say something. Instead, he belched. It wasn't loud, but it was foul enough to make me wish there was an open window nearby. His breath before had been pleasant, almost wintry fresh, but not now. I wondered what could have changed. He looked at me once more, laughed, and left the room.

"Well that was just rude," I said. Then I remembered that I had just been in a fight with a demon that belched to summon monsters to kill me. "I need to stop getting hit in the head!"

I looked around the room and saw nothing, so I looked under the table. There was something on the floor that resembled a bungee cord. It was blue with purple stripes in a checkerboard pattern. Well it wasn't a giant boar, a swarm of plague-infected rats, or a worg, so I felt relieved. Until its head rose up from its coiled body…along with its other two heads.

I tracked the three-headed snake as it rose up. Its heads lifted above the table with ease. It kept rising. I watched as it revealed itself to be at least seven feet in length. Three pairs of reptilian eyes looked back at me. Forked tongues flicked out to take in the scents of their prey: me. Slowly they reached out to the table and began to slither across it.

I stood up with the chair bending me over awkwardly. I shuffled backward to get away from the snake. It sped up. I shuffled faster. It sped up. I started hopping backwards. Then I hit the wall. It took every ounce of balance that I could muster not to fall forward on to my face. Once I was steady, I looked at the snake. It was coiled atop the desk. All three heads hissed an instant before it sprang at me.

I tried to turn my body, but I was severely limited in my range of motion. I managed to turn myself enough so that the head that was going for my neck missed. Instead it bit my right shoulder. Its fangs pierced my flesh and burned like hot grease. Another head wrapped around my right arm and the arm of the chair. It secured its hold by biting me in my chest. The final head wrapped around my waist and bit me in the side of my torso near my liver. The rest of the snakes body wound around my legs. That is when I fell on the floor. I turned as I fell so that I took the brunt of the fall with my right shoulder, landing with the snake's head beneath me. I felt the snake's bite relax, but the creature did not let go.

The landing hurt, but the scream I let out had nothing to do with my fall. The three heads had latched on, and all three bites were on fire. The snake pumped burning venom into my body. It felt like I was being injected with battery acid. I bucked and kicked wildly, smacking my shoulder repeatedly against the floor, but couldn't dislodge the super-natural serpent. My lungs started to strain from screaming. In my mind I called for help, but all that came out of my mouth was garbled unintelligible sounds more akin to an insane hillbilly in a cartoon rather than a college educated knight.

I kept thrashing and yelling. In the back of my mind, I knew that it was useless, but if I gave in, I would just die. It's better to die fighting than to just die, right? My mind raced for a solution, a plan, anything to fight back. When the chips were down the human body could perform superhuman feats of strength, and right now all of my chips were on the floor. I clenched my fists and focused my thoughts on the handcuffs on my wrists. If I wanted to live then I had to break free. All of my anger and all of my fear strengthened my muscles as I locked my arms and pulled with everything I had. Poison was running through my veins alongside adrenaline. The cold steel of the handcuffs bit into my flesh as I desperately pulled against the restraints.

Blood ran freely from my wrists. My body felt like it was boiling on the inside. My teeth clenched as I grunted through the pain. I kept pulling and began to growl like an animal. The snake around my bicep released its hold and rose up to face me. Its tongue shot out then it opened its mouth and hissed. It surged down to my neck and bit my throat.

The chair arm snapped, and my right arm came free. Desperately my fingers gripped the snake at my throat and started to pry it free. The serpent hissed at me when it came loose. I held it away from my face, but it was strong. It started to force itself back down to my throat, and my strength was dwindling. The poison felt like it was melting me from the inside out. The snake gained ground, and my vision began to blur as my grip loosened.

The snake forced my arm closer to my throat. My fear took full control and I panicked. I opened my mouth and chomped down on the snakes head. My teeth bit into reptilian flesh. Blood filled my mouth as the snake began to spasm. I could hear it hissing inside my mouth. Its jaws snapped closed over and over again in my mouth. Fangs stabbed my cheeks, gums, and tongue. I jerked my neck back and forth, ripping the snakes head off. Then I turned to spit out the offending serpent's head.

My body was on fire, the poison eating through me and warping my body with infection. I could hardly breathe as my lips, tongue, and throat began to swell. Dark spots began to form in my vision. Between the splotches of darkness, I saw the third head rise up. It hissed as it kept rising into the air. There was a pop as the first snake head fell free of my skin. It was flat and bloody. The initial fall must have crushed it.

The third snake head swayed from side to side as it dangled its dead counterparts. It flicked its tongue and then struck at me. Just like the other two snakes, it went for my throat. Still not wanting to die, I rolled to my left, just barely avoiding the strike. Snake head number three hit the ground, and I knew it was still tangled with the chair as much as I was. I used the last of my strength to fling the chair up and over my body. The snake was caught up in the chair, so when I slammed the chair down, I slammed the snake down beneath it. My adrenaline had been outpaced by the poison. There was no strength behind that blow other than gravity. The snake took the hit and slowly slithered from underneath the chair.

Now I was laying on my stomach. All of my strength was gone. My insides were on fire. Around came the snake. From my prone position, I could just barely see it out of the corner of my eye. The snake head unhinged its jaw to an impossible size. Its mouth grew to the size of a large garbage bag. I tried to move, to scream, to do anything, but my body would not respond. On came the snake, its dark eyes intent on swallowing me.

I heard someone yell, "What the hell?" Then Detective Wilson came into view behind the snake. He picked up a chair and slammed it down on the snakes head. He repeated the process several times until the snake stopped moving. When it finally succumbed to the beating, he called out for help. He looked at me and asked me, "How the hell did you get a snake in here?"

I rolled my eyes. They kept rolling into the back of my head.

Chapter 20

I WASN'T PASSED out—I just couldn't respond. I couldn't move, I couldn't blink, I couldn't scream! The poison had shut down most of my motor functions. Worse, it was still burning the inside of my body. I wanted to scream so badly. My tattoos were meant to help me recover from physical injury and trauma. Poison might distort my body, but since it was a reaction to natural chemicals, my tattoos did nothing to aid me. It was the same story with my allergies. When you have to fight evil with a runny nose, it is somewhat embarrassing.

Detective Banks ran into the room. "What the hell happened to him?"

Detective Wilson threw the chair off to the side of the room. "He had a fucking snake."

Banks looked over to the door then around the room. She looked down at me in confusion and asked, "How the hell could he get a snake in here while he was handcuffed to the chair?"

Wilson kicked my chair as he stomped around my body. "He broke the fucking chair. The little shit breaks the chair then gets hold of a snake so he can sic it on us, but it attacks him instead. Serves him right."

I felt more people moving around me. Some were running. Others were poking and prodding me. Whatever the hell they were doing did not really matter to me. I was going to die here surrounded by cops that wanted my head and poisoned by a magical snake. This was it.

"Get out of my way!" a voice said. "Michael! Michael! What the hell did you do to him?"

It was Kerri's voice. She knelt over me and pulled me into her lap. I saw she was wearing one of my flannel shirts. It was way too big, but it looked good on her. Kerri pulled out a cell phone and screamed at the surrounding police. "If he dies, I am going to have every one of your badges on a fucking chain around my neck at his funeral!"

Wilson flipped her off. "Fuck you, lady, he brought the snake in here."

Kerri looked around frantically. "What snake? Where is it, and how do you think a handcuffed man being escorted at gun point snuck a snake into an interrogation room, asshole?"

Wilson made a gesture to where the dead snake had been. That's when his eyes bulged out. Looks like he didn't know how construct magic worked. The moment that magically-created snake died, its body had wasted away into the basic elements used to create it. I heard him sputter over an answer, and would have laughed if I could. In that moment of triumph, I almost forgot that I was dying. Almost.

Kerri was on the phone now. She was crying. There was so much confusion and noise now that I could not make out what she was saying. I caught a few words: hurry, please, and dying. I wanted to tell her so many things. I wanted to apologize for being the idiot that I was. I wanted to thank her for being there when I needed her. Just like now. I wouldn't get the chance to do anything now. When she hung up the phone, I passed out from the poison.

Chapter 21

S LEEP IS MAGICAL. Seriously! Sleep equals magic. When you sleep, your body and mind can do amazing things. There is a reason that every person in the world, since the dawn of time, and in any theory of creation that you can think of, must sleep. Magic exists in everything. When we go to sleep, even those of us that have no magical power of their own, like myself, can experience magic.

Sleep gave my body the power to ignore the pain I was in. In addition to the poison coursing through my body, I had bones to fuse together, muscles to mend, and skin to fully regrow. My earlier expedient healing had put me at the bare minimum of fighting condition. Now my tattoos were working to get me back to my peak, and as miraculous as they were they did not inhibit pain in any way. Sleep inhibited pain. Sleep took my pain, boxed it up, and put it into the attic of my mind.

Then, of course, there was the mental magic of sleep. I found myself standing in the sky. That may seem controversial, but I was standing in the sky. Not falling, floating, or flying. I was standing in the night sky above Baltimore. Just to test things to see if I needed to start screaming or not, I lifted my foot and stomped on the air beneath me. It felt solid.

I looked down on the lights of the city. They were beautiful. From that angle, I could easily imagine this as the view God must have when he looks down at my city. I felt a chill wind all around me, but I did not feel cold. The thought occurred to me that I could be having an out-of-body experience. It wouldn't be my first, but it would be the first one I had while asleep.

"It's beautiful, isn't it?" Bill Fred said as he walked up to me.

I wasn't in the mood for small talk, so I said, "Yeah, I screwed up."

The angel shook his head. "I asked if it was beautiful, not if you screwed up."

There was something about his voice. I looked to Bill Fred, and the look on his face was not one I was used to seeing. Bill Fred, the angel and my divine adviser, looked confused.

"You honestly don't know, do you?" I asked.

"No," he said.

That rocked me back on my heels. Not only had he given me a direct answer, but I was shocked to hear that he did not know if the scene beneath us was beautiful or not. I studied him for a moment to see if he showed a grin or smile. Surely, it had to be a joke.

"Do you know the difference between us?" he asked while he stared down at the city below us.

I rolled my eyes as sarcastically as possible. "You're an angel, and I'm a human. That's a big duh."

He grinned for just an instant. "No. The difference between us is smaller than the smallest particle that man has identified. When God creates anything, he gives them a small piece of himself. It is why all things are connected. When he created me, he gave me a small piece of himself and called it Grace."

I watched as a thin line appeared on his lips. It grew into a wide smile. "Grace," he went on, "is what lets me watch you battle evil. It is what lets me know when you need a friendly word. Grace is what allows me to stand before True Evil and say *no more*."

I nodded. "So…I'm sorry, but what am I supposed to be learning? I was in the middle of dying from poison."

Bill Fred looked up at me. "Do you know what God named the piece of himself that resides in you?"

I shook my head.

The angel chuckled. "He named it Free Will. It is the most beautiful and most dangerous gift there is. Do you know why?"

Again I shook my head.

"Because Alistair Dyhart used his free will to invite demons into your world. Because Garrett Clay used his free will to pull you aside and shield you from a bullet. Because you used your free will to risk your life yesterday not once but four times fighting against powers that were designed to be greater than you. Because, Michael Franklin Joshua White, you can see beauty."

I looked down at the city below us. The lights, the buildings that reached into the sky, the swaths of trees, the lakes, and the roads. I realized that together they created something far greater than anything they could be individually. I realized that, like my friends, the battles we had fought, and me, the city was stronger when I saw it as a whole. This insight, like this view, was a rare gift.

"Thank you, Bill Fred," I said. I looked at him and scrunched up my face. "Are you going to help me with the whole dying from poison thing?"

He laughed and said, "No, Aaron is doing that. I just wanted to have a talk with you before you got back to protecting Garret Clay. Also, you may not want to thank me. There is only one way back to your body from here."

"Okay. So how do I get back to my body?" I asked.

Suddenly the air beneath me was not so solid. I fell from the sky. The press of the air as I fell was so strong I could not breathe. My eyes felt like they were being scraped apart. Every time I tried to control my fall, I found myself spinning and flipping. The sound of my body exceeding terminal velocity was maddening. I could see my city below me and I realized that I was heading for it like a guided missile.

With nothing within my power beyond my own voice, I screamed, "Angels are assholes!"

Then I crashed into a building.

CHAPTER 22

I WOKE UP in a hospital. How did I know it was a hospital? Because with all the tubes shoved into me, I was either in a hospital or on a spaceship being probed by aliens. There are just too many non-human, extra-human, and meta-human beings on earth for me to deal with aliens at this point in my life. There was a tube shoved down my throat, and I immediately pulled it out. I started coughing and sputtering as soon as it was out. Then I started pulling out sensors and tubes.

"Michael, don't," I heard Kerri say. She was on a chair in the corner with a blanket covering her. She dashed up to my side and pushed a button on the headboard of the medical bed.

"Nope. I hate hospitals. I cannot be in a hospital. You know what happened the last time I was in one," I said, ripping an IV out of my arm.

"That was a long time ago," she said.

"Yeah, well you don't really get over a doctor treating your fractured leg with a lobotomy or the procedure being stopped by your uncle punching the doctor in the middle of the operating room," I said.

I swung my legs down to the floor just as the door to the room opened. Aaron, wearing the white coat of his profession, walked in with a nurse in tow. He stormed over and started to shove me back into bed.

"I don't care how indestructible you think you are. You are in no condition to get out of that bed. So sit your ass back down."

I grabbed my friend's wrist. Aaron may have superhuman strength, but I had fear backing my muscles. "I am not staying in here, Aaron."

He met my eyes. Doctor Aaron Drake snarled at me, his patient. That faded away in an instant when Aaron Drake, my best friend, softened his features and withdrew his hand. He patted my shoulder.

"Just sit here for a minute," he told me. "I will get you discharged, but let me get you some meds for the poison."

Aaron turned to the nurse who had followed him into the room.

He asked her to get my discharge papers. He also took out a prescription pad and asked her to fill several prescriptions for me. Once she was gone, he walked over and slumped down in a chair. Kerri stood next to me with her hands on my shoulders.

"You do not make life easy, Michael," he said. "Demons and fake gargoyles I can deal with. But magical poison and cops swarming my hospital are too much for me."

"Well you fixed me up anyway, doc. Thanks. How did you handle the poison?" I asked.

"I didn't. I drank your blood," he said dryly.

I swallowed hard. If I had a mirror to look at, I am sure I would have seen myself go pale. Gently I reached up and touched my neck. Kerri started feeling it as well. We both knew what happened when a vampire sucked your blood. Either you died or you turned into a vampire.

"You did what?" Maybe I had misheard him. I prayed that I had.

"I. Drank. Your. Blood," he said.

There was silence. There always is when you get bad news, that point where the mind must adjust to the information that it had taken in. As humans, we are designed to adapt, but adaptation takes time. Physically centuries. Mentally it could take centuries as well, but that is why the mind does it in stages. Generally, for most people, the first stage of adjustment to most information is anger. I am not most people. I'm just not typical. For me the first stage is curiosity. I started wondering if vampires had allergies—I spend a LOT of money on allergy medicine.

Kerri, however, is typical. She is also a lot faster than Aaron or I suspected. In an instant, she had crossed the room and thrown herself down on Aaron. She landed with her knee in his gut, and at the same time she struck him with a right cross.

"You son of a bitch!" she screamed.

I saw her rear back for another punch, but Aaron caught her hand. So she hit him with her other hand. Kerri was a lot tougher than she looked. There was blood where she had split open Aaron's lip and more coming from his nose. I sparred with Aaron, and I admit that I have attacked a little harder than I should have during those sessions. I have never punched him hard enough to draw blood. Kerri had, and it looked like she was just warming up.

Aaron grabbed her left arm quickly and pushed her back. "I didn't turn him!" he yelled. "It takes a lot more than just drinking his blood. I would have to give him mine. Instead, I gave him blood from our stores at the hospital. You just had to be O negative, didn't you? We only had four quarts in stock. Luckily you can live with that."

Silence fell again. Kerri stopped shaking with rage. She was calming. I watched her unclench her fists and decided that, no matter what I did from now on, I was going to stay on her good side. Her non-face-punching and dinner-making good side.

"The poison was resistant to every antivenom we had, and with no snake to identify I couldn't request anything be flown in. Considering the shape you were in, we didn't have time. I enthralled everyone around, drank you dry, and then pumped you full of fresh blood. I was two pints into you before I realized that the poison was magical. There is still poison in your system, but not enough to kill you," he said.

"Will the poison hurt you?" I asked.

"I threw it all up. Most poisons wouldn't bother me, but you never know with magic," he said. "How did a magical snake get in there with you anyway?"

"Alistair Dyhart. Turns out he's a D.A. and is in charge of the case they are building against me for shooting Garret Clay," I told them.

"Well that won't fly. Clay is two floors down from here. He has been stirring in and out of consciousness since before you were taken in for questioning. Once he gets some rest, he will be fine. His biggest problem is the shock of finding out that the world is a whole lot bigger than he thought. He will set them straight when he wakes up," Aaron said.

"They won't come after you with the lawsuit I am going to file," Kerri said. "Those assholes beat you like you were a criminal."

"They thought I was. Being me didn't help. Every one of them probably wanted to shoot me, but thankfully they showed restraint," I said. Everyone that met me disliked me unless they knew about the world beyond the normal human perspective. It had always been that way ever since I was a little kid. I wanted to change the subject, so I said, "Hey, Aaron, you are bleeding."

The vampire touched his face and looked at the blood on his fingertips. Aaron pulled a paper towel from a dispenser on the wall and cleaned the blood from his face. He grumbled as he cleaned himself up. Kerri shot me a look, and when our eyes met, she seemed lost. Aaron, as human as he seemed, was what she had been taught to fear. First by the media, and then by those around her. Here was a living nightmare patching up her boyfriend. I could not tell her how to handle it. This would be her call, and it would set the pace for their relationship.

Kerri walked over to Aaron and took the paper towel in her hand. "For a doctor, you are really bad at that," she said. She pulled some more paper towels off the wall and began to clean him up. "I'm sorry. I just don't like it when people hurt him."

Aaron nodded. "I'm not going to hurt him. I'm not going to let anyone else do it either, not if I have a choice in the matter."

Kerri shrugged. "You also scare the hell out of me."

Again, Aaron nodded. "I tend to do that. The first time he met me he almost peed himself."

"No I didn't!" I yelled.

Kerri laughed.

"Yes you did," Aaron insisted. "Your little pecker started sputtering. Either you were going to pee or you were really excited to see me."

"I…I…what?" I sputtered.

Kerri laughed all the louder. She finished cleaning up Aaron's face and looked between us. "You found a gay vampire that likes making you question your sexuality? This is just too good!" she said as she walked back over to me.

"My dick did not sputter," I said to her.

She took on a cooing tone as she said, "Oh, I know it didn't baby. It's not little either, just in case you missed that part." I had missed that part. I felt embarrassed, but that washed away when Kerri leaned forward and kissed me.

"She's right, I have no business calling that thing little," Aaron said.

I was back to being confused, embarrassed, and speechless. Thank God that was when the nurse came back with the discharge papers and the medicine. Aaron took them from her and asked her to leave us alone. She retreated from the room, and I started signing the discharge papers.

Aaron began handing me medicines and explaining them to me. I half listened to him. Whenever he handed me a bottle I looked at the label with all of its instructions and warnings. I did not read them; I just committed them to memory.

Kerri smacked me in the head. I grabbed the spot where her hand had struck, and she stuck her finger in my face before saying, "Stop that right now! It was fine in school, but these things could kill you."

"What was he doing?" Aaron asked.

"He can remember any sequence of words or numbers that he sees. It drove our teachers crazy. He would flip through the pages of a text book on the first day of class and then ask questions about topics that we were months away from studying," she said. She grabbed my ear and yelled, "Pay attention to your doctor!"

"Okay, okay," I said. I listened as Aaron explained what the medicines did and how to use them properly. He did tell me a few things that weren't on the labels.

After Aaron had gone over all the medications, nine in total, Kerri asked him a few questions. I felt like a small child as they went over how they would proceed with my healthcare as though I were not even there. It did not help that I was wearing a backless hospital gown with teddy bears on it.

"Can I have my clothes now?" I asked.

"Shh. Shh. In a second, sweetie," Kerri said absently.

When I started to protest Aaron shushed me as well. Again, instead of getting angry, I wondered if being shushed by people that were concerned for you was normal. As I pondered the mysteries of having loved ones, the lights went out. The room was filled with the soft hum of absent electricity.

"The generators should kick on in a second," said Aaron.

We waited but nothing happened. Light finally surged into the room, but it was from Kerri's cell phone flashlight app. The hairs on the back of my neck began to stand up. I closed my eyes and began to awaken my senses to the supernatural. I immediately felt a rush of power in the air. Looking over at Aaron, I saw him calmly shift his weight onto his toes. Kerri, who had just punched a vampire without a thought, pulled her arms close to her body in an attempt to make herself a smaller target. There was something very powerful and very dangerous in the area.

Someone screamed in the hallway.

"Can I have my clothes now?"

CHAPTER 23

ARON CHECKED THE hallway. The scream had come from a nurse that a patient had felt up in the darkness. Aaron punched the guy and knocked some of his teeth out. When he came back into the room, Kerri pulled out a large gym bag from the closet. She set it on the bed and handed me underwear, socks, blue jeans, a brown tee shirt, and my work boots. I quickly got dressed, but I still felt naked without my weapons and my hat.

Kerri-Lynn Briscoe proved how awesome she was when she reached into the bag and pulled my sword out. I smiled at her and she shrugged. "The cops went through the entire apartment. They tore it apart. But every time one of them went near your swords or guns they just ignored them. Even the crates of ammo were ignored. I figured I could smuggle it into you since no one could see it."

She handed me the sword, and I strapped it around my waist. "Oh, they saw them. Tools of the trade tend to be ignored by anyone not in the know. I never noticed my grandpa's sword sitting around the house until I got mine." As I was threading the sword belt, she pulled out my Desert Eagles and my knife. I took the knife and fixed it on my right hip opposite my sword. "Stow the guns. There are too many things in here that could explode. Plus, the walls aren't thick. If I miss, someone could die."

Kerri put my guns away and pulled out my cell phone. She downloaded the same flashlight app she had onto it and handed it to me.

Aaron cracked the door again and sniffed the air. "I don't smell anything on this floor, but there is definitely something in the building. Dyhart has to know you're here. You think he came for you?"

"No. He's a coward and won't risk himself. He only approached me before to gloat about being smarter and more powerful than I am. He might send a henchman or use one of his new powers, but it won't be him. Besides, if it's really as powerful as it feels it has to be Ophalistis."

"What if it isn't? What if it's something else that's just as strong as a demon?" Kerri asked.

I shrugged. "Then I kill it."

Kerri shoved me. "Can't you just leave? If it wants to hurt you, all you have to do to protect people is not be here. You keep fighting and keep getting beaten up. Sooner or later aren't those tattoos going to run out of power or something?" Her voice was quivering.

I pulled her into a hug. "I'm sorry, Kerri, but I can't run. It isn't after me. It's trying to kill Garrett. I have to protect him. In addition, there are people here that need machines to keep them alive right now. This thing cut the power and the backup power. It has probably killed a number of people just by doing that. I have to kill it now," I said. "You ready, Aaron?"

"Michael, I can't fight here. If anyone sees me, they're going to ask questions. It's already weird enough that I only work at night and look like I just turned 25."

"Good point. Kerri, hand me my hat," I said.

"I didn't bring it," she said.

I shook my head because my hearing must have gone bad. "What?"

Kerri flipped the bag over her shoulder. "I didn't bring it."

"You snuck two guns and a sword in here, but you forgot my hat?"

"It's just a hat," she said.

Aaron stepped back. I leaned in so that I was nose to nose with Kerri and had to bend down a lot to face her that closely. I spoke softly and more seriously than I believed I ever had before. "It is not just a hat. It is a Baltimore Orioles Baseball Cap. If we are ever in a burning building, and you have to carry me out, I want you to remember that hat. If you can't save the hat, you leave me to die with it. If you have to make a choice between saving that hat and saving a suitcase full of hundred dollar bills, you had better save the hat. That hat is every ounce of my faith in God and humankind."

She nodded slowly, all the while looking at me as if I was off my rocker. I kissed her forehead and gave her another hug. I may have hugged her a little tighter than normal.

"Kerri, kill your light and let Aaron get you outside. He can see in the dark. Get out, get clear, head for the church, and stay there," I said. "I will catch up when this is over."

Kerri hugged me again. Aaron patted my back. Then they disappeared into the darkness of the hall. I secured my cell phone on my belt so that it would shine straight ahead. I tried to tell myself the radiation from my phone would not affect my penis in any negative manner, but I couldn't help but worry. Opening my mind, I focused my senses. As Aaron said, there was nothing on this floor. I headed out into the hallway. Except for my light, there was nothing but darkness. Nurses and orderlies were moving around, but they were hugging the walls. I had to ignore my instinct to guide them to safety. The patients would need their help once the power came back on. I rushed past them and offered a kind word where I could. They probably couldn't really see me past the nimbus of my light, so they didn't notice the sword and dagger on my hip.

I asked one nurse for directions to the fire stairs. She pointed me down another hallway, and I hurried in that direction. I hit the fire stairs and started down them with my hand on the rail. I wanted to go halfway down and vault the rail to drop to the next flight of stairs, but I was already work-ing up a sweat just getting to the stairs. I walked down four flights and was breathing as if I had just pushed all my limits at the gym. The poison in my body combined with the blood loss was making me weak. Maybe taking on a demon alone wasn't the best idea, but it had to be done.

The door to Garrett's floor read ICU. Aaron said he would be okay, but I had seen the mental responses people had to learning about the magical world. Garrett had handled it well, but that combined with being shot would look like a need for intensive care. I eased the door open and peered into the hallway. I saw flashlights and people moving in a semi orderly fashion. Just as the nurses could not see me beyond my light, I could not make out all the figures in the hallway. I cut my light and stepped through the door. I let my senses guide my motions. Nothing looked out of the ordinary. Nurses and orderlies moved to assist doctors and patients. I smelled blood, but this was a hospital. I didn't smell fresh blood, so that was good, but I didn't hear yelling. In fact, I didn't hear anything more than footsteps.

I should have heard conversations and people stumbling around, but I didn't hear anything. I tried to run over to the first set of people I could reach but had to settle for a brisk walk. Finally, I caught up with a nurse and a police officer. Worried the officer would try to arrest or detain me, the closer I got the more I felt that being arrested would be the least of my problems. I reached them just before they ducked into a room on the left side of the hall. I tapped the officer on the shoulder. He stopped and so did the nurse. They turned around simultaneously and stared at me.

Their eyes were wider than they should have been. They looked glazed over and devoid of emotion. I waved my hands in front of both of their eyes, but they did not react.

"Can you guys hear me?" I asked.

"Return to your room. All is well," they said in zombie-like unison.

"So yes on hearing me, and a big fat no on all being well," I said. Either they were in thrall, or this place had the best morphine on the planet.

The nurse, a tall and lean woman the same height as me, gently took my shoulder and tried to turn me around. The officer, an average sized man with a linebackers build, prodded me with his flashlight. In my weakened state, the minor gestures moved me back quite a bit. I pushed back and started past them. The officer's hand clenched my shoulder, and he shoved me harshly back the way I had come. I stumbled backwards for several feet before I caught my balance.

"Return to your room. All is well." he said.

"Okay," I said. "Looks like we do things the hard way."

No sooner had I spoken than the nurse darted forward throwing a punch and forcing me to dodge to my right. She dropped low then came at me with a rising uppercut. Skipping back out of the way of her attack, I discovered that they must have offered martial arts training in nursing school, because this registered nurse transitioned into a spinning sidekick that would have made Bruce Lee proud. The soul of her sneaker hit my forehead and slammed my head into the wall. Sound vanished from around me, and all I heard was the ringing of my ears accompanied by the sound of my skull cracking the wall. Pain enveloped my head. My vision shifted. Up became down, right became left. Down and left retreated to somewhere in the distance behind me. I slumped to the floor and tried to remember how to sit up without falling over.

"If you will not return to your room then I must insist that you stop living," she said.

She was too fast. I don't know if I could have matched that speed when

I was at my best, but I couldn't even follow her movements enough to block right now. She towered over me as her officer companion pulled out a semiautomatic pistol. As he slowly lifted the weapon, I began to stammer incoherently.

People who are enthralled tend to be weak-willed, but that isn't always the case. It is true that a weak will can play a part in enthrallment, but even strong-willed people can be enthralled. Typically, when someone is enthralled, their free will is muted and overshadowed by the will of another. This can be a very fast process, such as with magic, or a slow process, such as with Stockholm syndrome. The results of the enthrallment can vary, but power and experience make up for time. A powerful being can create a Stockholm level thrall in a few seconds, but it is far easier to create thralls like the zombie twins here.

It's a general rule for good guys that we do not kill thralls. They are victims. So saving them is what we try to do, even if they are about to put a bullet in your head. A demonic enthrallment is best countered by a priest, but in a pinch I can do it. I reached down to my sword and put my hand upon its hilt as I stammered.

"Hear me!" I said. My voice was not loud. It was calm, steady, and free of judgment. I lifted my eyes to look at the nurse and officer. They had stopped moving at my words. My voice was backed by the power of the sword. I spoke with the power of Absolute Truth. "Children of creation. Son of Adam. Daughter of Eve. You have within you a piece of God himself. A darkness has shrouded it. It has tainted you. Hear my words and be free of this evil. You are loved. Let nothing other than your own desires and dreams fill your soul. Praised be he who gave his life for our sins and blessed be you, his children."

The officer dropped his gun to the ground. He fell to his knees before me with tears in his eyes. He wept. It was a silent thing. He just stared at me in disbelief as his shoulders bobbed up and down. He looked down at his hands and slowly lifted one to his chest to touch his heart. Many people touched their hearts after being touched by the power of their God. I guess that is where they felt their soul resided. He started to say something. He probably wanted to ask me a question, but I spoke first.

"Sleep child," I said.

He slowly slumped down on the floor and closed his eyes. The rest would do him good. I didn't get to relax because the nurse kicked me across my mouth. Rolling down the hall with the blow, I was laid out flat on my back and spit out blood.

"Crap, she isn't a Christian," I said.

Absolute Truth or not, it doesn't work if someone doesn't believe you. Yay for free freaking will! That's the thing about powers related to the divine. You can always use them to help someone, but they must be willing to accept it. I reflexively spoke to them both as though they worshiped God or Jesus. The officer was Christian, or some variant, but the nurse was not, so there was no reason for her to be empowered by my words.

She dropped with her legs to either side of me. Both of her hands took hold of my throat, and she began to choke me. I grabbed her wrists and managed to pry them off, but she was strong. I was not going to be able to hold her back for long, so I searched her body for anything to signify what she would believe. A tattoo, a necklace, anything! I came up with zilch.

I got desperate. I started to put little things together. She was strong. She had no jewelry, symbols of religion, or worship on her. I decided to go with the one religion that seems to serve the majority of people in the world besides Christianity. The one religion that has no symbol.

I threw her hand back so I could grab the hilt of my sword. The power of Truth rang again in my voice when I said, "Hear me, Daughter of Creation. Child of Evolution. One seeks to control you. One seeks to force his way, his belief, upon you. I tell you now that you are stronger than this. That you are a child of the universe. You are strong, you are powerful, and you are wise. Be free child and continue your path. Prove to all that you are master of your own fate and slave to no one."

She blinked at me. She kept blinking. Tears formed in her eyes and she stopped trying to choke me. She believed in science, and even that is a religion. I only needed to tell her that her belief was valid and that her will was stronger than the will of one who would harm her. It was still the word of God, but it was also the words of her belief. No God is right or wrong. They are all one and the same. Science is just another part of every other religion and vice versa. We just haven't figured out the whole jigsaw puzzle yet. We probably aren't even close.

She began to cry openly, and I told her to sleep. I shouldn't have done that. She fell atop me in a very intimate way. I controlled myself when she did. I kept my breathing steady and tried to slide her off me without her girl parts touching my boy parts. It didn't quite work, but we were both wearing clothes thank goodness.

I maneuvered her off me and made sure she was comfortable before I stood back up. Grabbing the officer's flashlight, I continued down the hallway. I decided that freeing the enthralled and ushering them to sleep would be better than being attacked again. Touching my sword, I began to address everyone I approached. I cycled through reminding them of God's love, the surety of science, the absolute power of The One God to three Jewish folks, and for one guy I cited the wisdom of Xenu. This little trek reminded me how hard it was to be a knight. Fighting I could do, sort of, but even with my ability to memorize everything I read it is hard to keep track of what inspires faith, hope, and love to thousands of people. Just reciting verse won't work unless you and those you seek to help believe the verse. For Truth to work you usually have to speak from your heart.

I made my way further down the hall without incident. Just as I finished easing a male nurse down to the ground a door swung open ahead of me. I whirled my borrowed flashlight toward the open door. Out stepped a man in a well-fitted red business suit. He was taller and leaner than I was. He was not muscular. In fact, I would have called him skinny if skinny people weren't meatier than him. He had long, dark hair that he let hang to his shoulders. He had a thin mustache but no beard or even a sign of stubble. I watched him carefully as he straightened his black tie. When he was done, he turned to me absently and gave me a lazy smile.

I looked him over from head to toe. Something was wrong. His skin was too white. Not pale but white, almost like milk in a fridge with the light blown. His dark hair was too dark, he was too thin, and his features too angular. He seemed to combine the most beautiful features from several races into one frame. Features such as full lips, strong cheekbones, broad shoulders, long fingers, and bright eyes all existed on him. If it had been a consequence of birth, then his body would carry those features better. As it was, he had an exotic beauty more akin to an abstract painting than a portrait.

"Ah," he said in a soft but firm voice. "The Knight has arrived."

I shifted the flashlight to my left hand and put my right hand on my sword. "Hello. Do I know you?" I asked.

"Yes and no. We have met, but we have not had the pleasure of introductions," he said. He bent at the waist and bowed. "I am Ophalistis, Lord of Thralls."

I dropped the flashlight as I stood. I drew my sword before my flashlight hit the ground. White light filled the hallway as my sword awoke to the demon before me. I turned my body so that I led with my left foot. My back was close to the wall as I stood on the left side of the hallway. I kept my sword ahead of me with my arms extended toward the right side of the hallway. This way I could sweep my sword from right to left with ease.

The demon had taken human form, and with any luck it would limit him to something approaching human limitations. I was injured, but if I struck fast and hard I could take him. I resolved myself to take the fight to Ophalistis, but before my body could react, another figure stepped through the doorway. Detective Banks stood between Ophalistis and me with her right side to me. Slowly she turned to her right to face me. She had her gun pointed to her own head. The hammer was cocked, and her finger was on the trigger. As the blood drained from my face, Ophalistis smiled with teeth that were far too white to be real.

"Child of God," I said with the power of Truth.

Ophalistis hissed and closed his hand around Detective Banks' throat. I could see his nails digging into her skin. Blood began to well up in beads along her jugular. Ophalistis looked over her shoulder at me and placed a finger to his lips as he made a shushing sound.

"None of that, Knight of Innocence. If you speak with the power of the sword, I will kill her. If you call upon its power, I will kill her. If you want her to live, then I suggest that you calm yourself."

"What do you want, monster?"

The demon smiled. "I want to talk to you. That is all."

I eased my sword down and took a nonlethal stance. "Then talk."

Ophalistis let go of the detective's throat and once again straightened his tie. He looked me over from head to toe. His smile faded and he frowned at me. "You do not look so formidable."

"No, I don't. I look like a nerd that took a bunch of steroids and got some bad tattoos. That's been pointed out by several assholes, so one more isn't exactly going to matter," I said.

"*Spiritually* you do not look formidable," he said.

That one was new. I watched as his eyes roamed across my body. He specifically kept his eyes away from my sword, and that tipped me off to what he was doing. He was looking at me in the magical spectrum. It was an ability akin to my ability to perceive the supernatural and unusual. My ability relied on context clues, gut feelings, and intuition. It was not magical. I just stopped letting myself explain away the world around me as mundane and safe. What Ophalistis was doing was magical. He was seeing more than my flesh and clothing. I had no idea what he saw or what I would look like magically. I did, however, know what would come next. He would look at me for a moment and then smile and laugh to himself like every other magical being did when they took a good long look at me magically.

As if on cue Ophalistis raise his chin, smiled, and chuckled. "You are an interesting one. What magic do you have?"

I shook my head. "None."

He arched an eyebrow. Then he squinted at me. "You are lying."

"I have a holy sword, allergies, and a superhero complex. If I had magic I would have used it in our last fight," I said. "You remember that fight, right? The one where I hit you in the face with the hammer?"

"You have no idea how ignorant you are, mortal. Your kind is known to be incompetent and foolish, but you go far above and beyond. How did you kill two of my brethren without magic?"

"Four," I said.

"I beg your pardon."

I held up four fingers. "Four. Four of your brethren. I've killed four demons to date. It's like a hobby. One more and I get a new blender."

The demon glared at me. "You are in no position to make threats."

"I'm not making a threat. I am just stating a fact. I, a mortal, have killed four demons. Three had souls. I did not use magic. I did not trick them. I fought each one in single combat and defeated them. I'm kind of awesome," I said.

"Arrogant," spat the demon.

"Nope. I suck at just about everything, but I am good at my job. I was given a holy sword to protect the world against evil, so that's what I do," I said.

Ophalistis didn't answer. He just stared at me for a long time. Then he nodded. "You say you are good at your job. Does that mean you kill anything that you consider to be evil?" he asked.

I eyed the demon. "I kill anything that decides to hurt others."

"Ah, a true hero," the demon said. "I have seen your elk before, knight. I do not doubt that you will do whatever it takes to ensure that those under your protection are unharmed and unmolested. To that end, you would kill me without a thought."

"Darn right I would," I growled.

"Then what if I were no longer a threat to those you protect?" Ophalistis asked.

"What?" I asked in return.

"I want you to end your contract with Alistair Dyhart and enter into a deal with me."

I blinked at the demon. "I am not in a contract with that lunatic!"

I guess it was Ophalistis' turn to blink because that is what he did. "More lies!" he roared. "*You* are his assassin. He sent you to kill my brethren and me so that he can collect our powers, per our bargain."

"Bargain? What bargain," I asked.

"Are you truly so simple, mortal? We do not just rise to the summons of any practitioner. We were enticed. He offered us not only freedom, but also his power upon his death. He is not an extraordinarily powerful mage, but he has enough strength to make a bargain worthwhile. When he dies, we will receive his power. When one of us dies, he will receive our power. Here in the mortal world there is little that can kill us, so we had nothing to lose and everything to gain." He looked at my sword and hissed, "But then, as soon as we came to this plane, one of The Twelve is there to steal our lives."

I'm not sure when or why I began shaking. Maybe it was because this demon was using a woman as a shield. Maybe it was because an evil sorcerer had been using me to do his dirty work. Maybe it was because a demon that required innocent people to die so that he could walk the earth was upset that someone might try to *steal* his life. Maybe it was a combination of all three. I don't know the answer. I knew that killing a demon and a sorcerer would make the shaking stop. I lifted my sword.

"Woman, shoot yourself in the leg," Ophalistis snarled.

Detective Banks snapped her arm down and fired a round into her own thigh. Blood spattered over her gun, her hand, the floor, and the walls. She fell to the ground without a word. There was no scream of pain or rage. She just fell over, her features expressionless as she hit the ground. Then she quickly put the barrel of the gun back up to her head.

"A warning," snapped the demon. "You do understand that the next time you advance she will die, don't you?"

I was already frozen before he spoke. Now I didn't even dare to breathe. My eyes moved from the detective to the demon and I gritted my teeth. "I understand."

"Good. I will make this simple for you, knight. I want you to kill Alistair Dyhart."

Some of the tension that was building inside me fell away and was replaced with confusion. "What?"

"I want to hire you to kill the sorcerer Alistair Dyhart. He would have you kill me, but I prefer to live."

"What?" I asked again. My razor sharp intellect was in rare form.

He straightened his tie. "I simply want you to do your job. You consider yourself a guardian of humanity, do you not? Simply rid humanity of a thorn in its side."

I glared at him and snarled, "I'm not your henchman."

That must have annoyed him. His whole demeanor changed. He scowled at me and held out his hands in frustration.

"Of course, how could I forget?" he asked himself. "You are a pretend hero. You want to play good mortals versus bad monsters. Did you know that the sorcerer was going to start summoning more demons? In fact, he has decided that summoning them in small amounts is a waste of time. He is going to rip open a portal to Hell right here in this city."

I felt the blood drain from my face. I tried to find the words to respond but couldn't. Alistair Dyhart, that second-rate sorcerer and first-rate jerk, was going to open a portal to Hell in my city. He was going to sentence 620,000 people to death. Men, women, and children would all die just so he could gain a little more magical power.

"I can tell you when and where he will attempt this. Of course, for that information you must agree to kill him for me," said Ophalistis.

"Why don't you kill him yourself?" I said. It was more of a reflex than anything else. I was scared, so I asked questions.

"Per our contract, neither of us can kill the other. If he kills me, he loses the powers he has gained. If I kill him, I will be banished back to Hell without his powers. So you, Sir Knight, are my best *hope*."

I blinked at how close he had been to Star Wars-ing my help. I doubt he had ever seen the movies, but he had been real close.

"Honestly, Sir Knight, I do not want a portal to Hell opened. I do not want the competition. I would prefer to have the sorcerer dead and to leave this city," the demon said.

"You want to leave?" I asked.

"Why yes. I certainly do not want to be in a city where one of those swords resides."

"And you will leave peacefully without any tricks?"

"Of course."

"No. I can't trust you."

"Keep in mind, Sir Knight, that without this deal you have no idea when or where this ritual will take place. You need me. You need my deal!"

I shook my head. Maybe that nurse had hit me harder than I thought, because there was no way this demon was offering me a deal. A deal that would spare Baltimore from becoming a playground for all the denizens of Hell. My options were limited. Make a deal with a demon or take my chances. Looking down at my sword didn't inspire any sort of divine guidance or wisdom, so I guess that meant I had to make my own decision on this one. Stupid free will.

"You will release everyone in the hospital from your thrall and leave them in peace," I said. "Give me that on good faith, and you will have your deal."

Ophalistis smiled and nodded. "Done!" he said. He told me when and where the ritual would take place. Then he released his hold on the hospital occupants except for the Detective. The light of my sword died as the hospital's lights came on.

"When I am gone, the woman will regain her conscious mind. If you pursue me, she will kill herself," the demon said. Then he turned on his feet and walked down the hall. I heard the elevator ding, and he vanished into the car.

No sooner had he gone than Detective Banks dropped her gun and began screaming. Medical staff would come running from every direction as soon as their wits came back. That meant it was time for me to go. I ran up to Garrett's room and saw that he was alive. Detective Banks would be getting help in just a few seconds, so I bolted before her partner, Detective Wilson, came back to his senses and got a good look at me.

As nurses swarmed the scene, I ran back down the hall to the stairway. My body argued with every stride I took, but I didn't have time to listen to every ache and pain I had. I had to get clear of the building. There was nothing left for me to do here. If I was kept in the hospital to survey the damage of the poison or locked in jail, then the bad guys would win. The city was in danger, and I was the only one who could save it.

Baltimore was screwed.

CHAPTER 24

I
T WAS RAINING when I left the hospital. I didn't have a coat or umbrella to keep me dry. Heck, I didn't have anything to hide my sword, but that didn't matter. The rain was coming down hard enough to obstruct the view of the sword on my hip. Still, the other poor pedestrians on the street shied away from me on reflex.

The storm came down upon my head and shoulders like a cold shower. I had just made a deal with a demon, and I thought on the demon's words. Ophalistis said I was nothing more than a pretend knight. He said I was a murderer masquerading as a hero. It's nothing I haven't thought about in the past, but to hear it from a fiend from Hell is a wake-up call. I had spent my whole life in the dark about the supernatural world. My eyes were still closed. Angels, demons, Heaven, and Hell. They were the players of the game, and we mortals were just pieces being moved along by the roll of their dice. I was a Knight of the Crucifixion, and that meant nothing. I didn't have power or magic. I was a mortal pawn for angelic beings.

I was a pawn for other mortals as well. Had Dyhart really been using me as an assassin? Had all of this, the murders, the binding of Ophalistis to the mortal world, and the injury of that poor detective all been because of me? All because I was arrogant enough to play hero? The head of my order once said I was nothing more than a monster waiting in the shadows. Come to think of it, there were only four other Knights of the Crucifixion in the world right now, and only one of them thought I was worthy of the title. I didn't believe I deserved to be one of them most of the time.

I hadn't been paying attention to where I was going. Somehow, I found myself on a bridge. Lights from the traffic below surged past the railing. To any onlooker it must have looked like I was considering suicide, but as depressed as I was it never crossed my mind. It was just fun to watch the cars race by. The trucks were my favorite. Lighting danced across the sky and thunder rumbled above. My head tilted back, and I frowned at the sky. I left the bridge behind as I continued to walk in the rain. I'm not sure how long I was in the rain or how far I walked, but when I stopped, I found myself in front of Kate's bar.

Confused, depressed, and soaking wet I stepped up to the door and pushed it open. The jukebox was playing *The Gambler* to an empty bar. No one was inside except for Kate. She looked up at me when I walked in. There was a stack of cash on the counter, a bottle of booze, and a sawed-off shotgun. Kate didn't stop counting the stack of cash she had in her hands, but she did look down at the shotgun. She finished counting, picked up the gun, and set it under the counter.

Kate looked down at the floor under my feet and sighed. "I just mopped, Sir Knight."

I looked down at the puddle I was making, having walked past the welcome mat like an idiot. "Sorry."

She shook her head. "It's okay. Come have a seat." I walked over, and she threw a towel down on a stool so I could sit down. "Who do I call to give you a ride?"

I looked up at her but didn't answer. Anyone except Eden could come get me, but I didn't want anyone to see me like this. I didn't want anyone to know what I had done.

When I didn't answer, Kate asked me a different question. "Which of your friends do you not want to walk through that door right now?"

"Kerri-Lynn," I said without hesitation.

She pulled out her cell phone. "What's her number?"

I was already shaking my head. "You can't call her."

"Yes, I can. Give me her number, Sir Knight."

I don't know why, but I did what she said and recited Kerri-Lynn's number. Kate called her. They exchanged pleasantries, and Kate gave her the address. When Kate hung up, she turned around to grab a bottle from under the counter. It was a dark bottle with no label. She set down two shot glasses and filled them both. One she pushed over to me, and then she took up the other for herself. When she lifted her glass, I followed suit. We clinked glasses and both tossed back our shots.

I shot to my feet. My head bowed, and I coughed so hard that I almost threw up. In fact, the only reason I didn't throw up was because I coughed up smoke! Kate slid me a glass of crushed ice with enough water in it to help it go down. I drank the ice water and blew air out in puffs until my throat and mouth stopped burning.

"What the heck was that?" I asked.

Kate was laughing and bent over just like I was. "Fire water! Dwarf wine. Humans shouldn't drink it, but it's fun as hell once you get past the burning."

We both took deep breaths to cool down our throats. It took us a few minutes. When we were cooled off, Kate pulled out a different bottle and poured two more shots. I looked at her warily, but she smiled at me. "It's just rum. Real human rum."

We clinked glasses once more and drank. I like rum. When I drink it I feel like a pirate.

"Hard day, Sir Knight?" she asked me.

"You could say it's been a hard couple of days," I said. She nodded and poured me another shot of rum. "Kate I really can't afford…"

"We are closed, Sir Knight. Anything I pour now is paid for with your tale. What has you so defeated? I watched your battle last night. You should be proud that you vanquished your foe."

I drank the shot. "I beat him. I killed him. I took a life. It's not something I'm proud of."

Kate poured me another. "A demon attacked you and your friends. It singled you out and tried to kill you. What options did you have?"

"I could have banished it back to Hell. I didn't need to kill it."

"Demons are not fallen angels. They are not wayward souls. They are created from death, sin, and suffering. They cannot create anything other than suffering. You did the world a favor," she told me.

I drank another shot. "I just made a deal with a demon."

Kate arched her eyebrow. She drank a shot of rum and blew out a long breath. "A deal or a pact?"

I looked up at her. "Is there a difference?"

"A pact connects you magically to another being. Deals don't…unless you make one with a fairy, but the fair folk are always different," she said. "So you made a deal. So what? People make deals all the time. If it fixes a problem, then does it matter?"

"I made a deal with a demon!" I yelled.

"But not with the devil!" she yelled back. "Did you trade your soul? The soul of your firstborn child?"

"No," I said.

"Then who cares. You are a knight. You answer to God and your order. That sword on your hip gives you options. You made a deal. You can always back out of it or move forward. Yes, people will judge you, yes they will talk about you behind your back, but in the end you keep this city safe."

Kate poured me another shot. "When you first came to town, I thought you would be dead in a week. Here we are almost a year later, and you are still alive and kicking. So tell me, Sir Knight—is this deal that you made going to end in your fall or your triumph?"

I looked up at Kate. The smile on her face reminded me of a shark. Her one eye gleamed with a light that I had not seen before, and I got the impression that her gaze was not something I wanted to focus on me for too long. I did not look her in the eye for fear of Insight showing me whatever had created such a person.

"Kate, what are you?" I asked.

That shark-like smile widened. "I'm just a bartender," she said.

"No. *What* are you? You aren't human," I said.

She reached under the table and pulled out a jar. It was filled with money. "Five dollars gets you a guess. Ten dollars gets you a hint and a guess," she said.

I dug through my pockets. I found a wad of ones and counted out ten. Kate took the cash and stuffed it into the jar. "I have seen the rise and fall of nations throughout the east," she said.

I thought about her words. Lots of creatures could claim that. Might as well go with the obvious answer. "Are you a god?" I asked.

"No," she said. "You can try again next time. Your ride is here."

The door to the bar opened, and Kerri walked in. She offered me a smile, and I stood to walk over to her. I took a glance back at Kate. I was going to need a lot of five-dollar bills.

CHAPTER 25

KERRI DROVE ME home. I told her about what happened at the hospital. She listened quietly and let me get everything off my chest. I told her about making a deal with a demon. I told her about being used to kill both Anfalar and Jezzepus. Then I told her about the rave tomorrow night and how everyone there was to be sacrificed. I did not pay attention to the road or anything else. At that point, my whole world was the passenger seat in Kerri's SUV.

"So this sorcerer is going to summon more demons and try to get you to kill them so he can steal their powers?" she asked.

"Pretty much," I said.

"He is a fucking idiot. He actually has magical powers, but that's not enough for him? He has to steal from demons, and to do that he has to sacrifice innocent people. I say you go along with the demon and kill him," Kerri said.

"What?" I asked.

"Kill him. The asshole deserves it. He kills people without a second thought, so why shouldn't you dish out the same justice?"

I thought about it for a moment. She wasn't wrong, but she wasn't right. I held the Sword of Innocence. I was supposed to protect mortal lives. Here I was contemplating using my sword to take a mortal life instead of saving it. I looked down at the hilt resting between my legs and sighed.

"Look, maybe I don't know what I am talking about. I guess in the end this is between you and your boss, right?" she asked.

I nodded.

"Then you should ask him what he wants to be done."

We drove in silence the rest of the way home. The Rust Bucket was in the lot when we pulled in. It had a fresh paint job, new tires, and a new air freshener. As usual, there was a note attached to the housing of the front left tire. It said, 'Heat and AC working. I also changed the upholstery that was soaked with your blood and burned it. Love you Cuz.' I patted my mighty steed and thanked the gods of gremlins that I had it back.

Kerri slept in my arms that night. We didn't get much sleep since it was already so late, but I rested. My body was still and able to heal. It was quiet. My mind needed the break. I was exhausted. Thank goodness Sundays were for sleeping.

"Wake up, honey," Kerri said.

I opened my eyes. Kerri was dressed in a pink and white sundress with a white shawl on her shoulders. She was holding one of my suits and a pair of dress shoes. "Get cleaned up and dressed. Church starts in two hours," she said.

I sat up and glared at her. "I don't do church," I said.

"You do today. You almost died twice in the past two days. You are going to church. It won't hurt to have God on your side tonight," she said. Then she did something that showed me how the rest of our lives would be if we stayed together. She reached down and yanked the covers off the bed. She tossed them aside, and when I protested she snatched my pillow. Then she threw it to the side of the room as well.

"Get up. Get clean. Get dressed," she said.

I followed orders and hit the shower. The hot water eased the tension from my muscles. As I showered, I surveyed my body and found that I had some nicks and scratches that hadn't healed. My tattoos only cared about injuries that would prevent me from fighting, so the mundane stuff was left to nature. I shaved and got dressed, and when I looked in the mirror, I saw an idiot in a suit. Kerri came over to me, and on sheer reflex she straightened my tie.

Before we left, I called Eden and let her know about tonight. The wizard would be ready. I could tell Aaron after church. Aaron and Eden were great, but what I really wanted to do was call my grandpa. Having him by my side would make tonight easy, but I decided not to. This was my city, my fight, and my problem. Not his.

Kerri made me drive. "If you try to get lost, I'll punch you in the throat," she told me. Apparently, she knew me too well.

The Rust Bucket started on the first turn of the key. In fact, my truck ran like it just came off the factory line. I looked over at Kerri. She looked like someone's favorite babysitter. Kerri had that girl-next-door quality that some women never lose. Even my truck was better with her around.

I managed to get us to the church in one piece and even found decent parking. We still had a good hike up to the church. I saw Priest Greyshadow spot us from atop the steps. He crossed himself upon seeing me. People gave us a wide berth as we ascended the steps. Deacon Darrel and another deacon I did not know moved to intercept me. I gritted my teeth and considered flipping them both down the steps.

Kerri quick stepped in front of me. She halted them both with a smile. Taking my hand in hers, she walked past them as she said, "No, thank you, gentlemen, we can find our own seats." We reached the top of the steps, and Priest Greyshadow ushered us in. We sat in the front row. No one sat to my left, but with Kerri on my right the pew filled with children and older patrons that just seemed to want to be close to her.

The service started, and I was worried. We weren't Catholic, but apparently a celebration of faith is easy to fall into and to follow. Priest Greyshadow was a man of God through and through. His sermon was not just fire and brimstone. It was faith, love, purity, and triumph.

"I look out among those that have gathered today, and I see children of God," he said. "I see generations of hardships, generations of belief, and generations of victory in the eyes of our Father."

A cheer of 'amen' went up at his words.

"God has blessed us with something intangible—something that we barely understand. He has blessed us with innocence."

My eyebrows shot up at that.

"The Father entrusted innocence to the Son, and he in turn entrusted it to us. It is not a weakness as some would believe. To be innocent is not to be helpless or ignorant or immature. To be innocent is to be without fault, repentant of sin, and to have the willingness to move forward. To be innocent is to accept one's limitations and not to fault another for theirs. Innocence is love for your brother regardless of aspects of his creation that you do not agree with. In this building right now there is innocence, and we must all remember that it is a strength, not a weakness," he preached.

There were shouts of 'amen' and 'hallelujah.' Kerri clutched my hand and gave me a thankful smile. We read bible verses, and Priest

Greyshadow delivered unto us a broader interpretation of the events surrounding The Crucifixion. Amazingly, he never mentioned Judas. It was somewhat disturbing to have the story told without the mention of the betrayer. Not having an obvious person to blame as the bad guy turned the tale of Christ's death from a simple betrayal to an all-out terrorist plot that ended in a public assassination.

As the priest preached, the back of my head began to ache. I knew there was more to Christ's death than what was in our book. For one thing, I knew about the Apostle Knights. The twelve swords were present, and eleven of them in the hands of capable men. Why hadn't they intervened? Because Jesus asked them not to? No, it was more than that. Other powers were in play. Major powers. Powers that wanted to take advantage of the fact that the Son of God was a mortal man. Powers as vile as or worse than the ones gathered in my town.

My head started pounding. The more Priest Greyshadow preached, the more the back of my head tried to break loose from the rest of my skull. Maybe it was the people. Large groups of people scare me. I turned to see hundreds of sets of eyes focused not on the pulpit but on me. I saw anger and disgust in those eyes and felt the weight of pure hatred on my shoulders. Priest Greyshadow may not have been preaching about Judas, but his flock could sense that I was walking the same path.

The pressure in my head was unbearable when Priest Greyshadow said, "And now a special treat. We have a visitor among us that is regarded as one of the best voices in Virginia. She has agreed to lead us in song today. Please welcome Kerri-Lynn Briscoe."

Kerri stood up and walked beyond the pulpit to ascend the stage. Obviously, she and Aaron had done more than sit quietly in the Church last night. She spoke with the conductor for a moment, and then the music started. When Kerri began to sing, the entire room gave her their full attention. Her voice carried so perfectly that the microphone seemed a formality. Her pitch and tone mixed with the music as though her voice was creating every note. I stopped looking at the faithful behind me and looked up at her. I remembered her voice. I loved her voice.

The pain in my head started to grow. I didn't want to, but I had to leave. I got up, marched out of the chapel, went down to the basement, and then down another level. There were only three rooms here. One was

Aaron's, and it was locked for the day. The room across from his was for me when I was injured. I went to the room at the end of the hallway.

I walked in and sat down in a small room set aside for private worship. Aaron often used this room. It was an eight by five box with a portrait of Christ watching over a world of children on the far wall. In the corner was a mini fridge. There was a sign on the fridge that read "Partake of His bounty. Give back when you can. Even Jesus sat down to supper." There was plenty of bottled water in the fridge, along with a couple of roast beast sandwiches—I haven't said roast beef since I was old enough to read Dr. Seuss, and no one has ever corrected me. I took a sandwich and a couple of bottles of water. There were candles around the room and a box of matches. I lit a few and sat down on the small bench in the center of the room.

I ate and drank in silence for a moment. Then I looked up at the picture of Christ. My mouth was full of food when I said, "What should I do?" There was no answer. I swallowed and tried being more specific. "What should I do about Dyhart and Ophalistis? To kill one is to empower the other. To kill either is to break a commandment...not that I haven't already done that. I have never taken a human life, and any nonhuman life has always been in defense of another or me. I don't know what to do, and I could use some guidance."

Silence followed. I took another bite of my sandwich. I waited and drank some more water. Still I heard nothing.

"Alright," I said. "Maybe I didn't identify myself. This is Michael Franklin White. I won't use my full name, because we both know that can get you killed. I am the Knight of Innocence and the guy that keeps getting his butt kicked in your name. The one that keeps finding some dumb reason not to die. I could use some advice if you don't mind. My back's against a wall here, and a single word from you could help."

Silence.

"Anything?" I asked.

Silence.

I threw my water at the wall and stood up screaming, "God, Jesus, anyone sitting on a cloud watching over the human race! I need some advice! I need to know what to do!"

Still there was silence.

"WHY DON'T YOU ANSWER ME? I FIGHT FOR YOU! I FIGHT IN YOUR NAME! I AM WILLING TO DIE FOR YOU! I DO ALL THAT YOU ASK OF ME, AND YOU CAN'T EVEN GIVE ME ONE STINKING MINUTE OF YOUR INFINITE TIME?"

I ran over to the wall and started punching it with my right hand. The first punch cracked the wall, and the second busted one of my knuckles, but I kept punching. When my hand hurt too much, I started kicking the wall with my left foot. I nearly broke my foot on the fourth kick. I stumbled back and got ready to charge the wall in pure rage.

"You might heal fast, but the pain should still tell you that the actions you take are stupid," Aaron said. I turned and found him standing in the entrance. He was wearing nothing but a pair of boxers. His hair was mussed as though he had just gotten out of bed. Aaron wore tight fitting clothing sometimes, but they did not do his body justice. His muscles were toned to the point they looked like they had been sculpted from marble. As he stood there in the doorway as if he had all the time in the world, I felt oddly intimidated by the sheer power of his form. Aaron may have been a doctor, but his body, attitude, and presence were always that of a predator.

"Hey man, sorry to wake you," I said sheepishly. "I was just praying."

"You didn't wake me. That whole sleeping during the day thing isn't accurate, and you weren't praying. You were throwing a temper tantrum," Aaron said as he walked in and sat down on the bench.

I blinked at him and looked down at my bloody hand. "I was having a private conversation."

"No. You were having a temper tantrum. It's nothing to be ashamed of. All you humans do it when you think God isn't listening, or he doesn't jump right in and fix your problems," he preached.

I started to argue, but Aaron cut me off. "See that painting of Jesus? He is looking down on a world of children. Babies. That's you. That's Kerri-Lynn. That's Emory. That's everyone. The Father sees us. He cares for us," he said.

"He sure has a hell of a way of showing it," I said. "I need his help."

"Great! So he helped you," Aaron said. He clapped his hands and smiled at me.

"Umm, no. He didn't help," I argued.

"So he took away your legs?" Aaron said.

I looked at him with a puzzled expression on my face. I looked down at my legs and gestured to them.

"I guess he didn't," Aaron said. "How about your arms?" When I didn't answer, he just kept going. "Your eyes? Your ears? Your sword? Your free will? Did he take anything from you?"

"No," I said.

"See Michael, this is what mankind in general does not understand. God loves you. Every god. Every rendition, every incarnation, every personification of God loves mankind. But love and favor are not the same thing. Every living being in this vast reality was created in some way by the All Mighty. So why should he tell you how to harm his own creations? You want an answer, well here it is: you are a human, and your greatest gift is free will. You have the ability to decide for yourself what the best course of action is. It doesn't have to be right for everyone in the end as long as you do what you believe is best. You don't have fangs or claws, so he gave you a sword that repels evil. So you tell me right now what else he needs to do for you?"

I stood there facing the wall in silence. Aaron, the vampire, was a preacher by action if not by profession. He had been a Catholic longer than the United States had been around. He was devout, righteous, and honest. He was also a damned creature that had a better understanding of faith and hope than I ever would.

"I made a deal with a demon to kill a mortal," I said.

Aaron got up and walked over to me. He put a gentle hand on my shoulder and turned me to face him. There was a kind smile on his face. He hugged me and patted my back in a manly fashion. Aaron pulled back to look me in the eyes as he shook his head. Then he punched me in the gut. Vampires are strong. Aaron was strong for a Harlequin Vampire. I doubled over his fist, and he held me there while I struggled for air. When I finally managed to get a breath into me, he lowered me to the ground.

"I hit you hard enough to knock you off your feet. I didn't try to catch you; I just stopped moving. The fact that you didn't fall to the floor and crack your skull open may or may not be a sign that God is all right with your decision. Take it as you will. Clean up my chapel," the vampire said as he walked out of the room. As an afterthought, he looked back at me and said, "Will you need me tonight? I always have your back, bro."

I looked up at him from the floor. Weakly I gave him a thumbs up. He nodded and left. I heard his door close. I waited for my lungs to reflate. Once I could take a deep breath again, I got up and cleaned up the little chapel. Making my way back to the service, I stayed in the back. Kerri was still singing with the choir, and her voice was still radiating the room. I listened for a while, but my head was still hurting, so I decided to go outside and wait for the service to let out.

I sat in my truck and waited for Kerri to come out. A half hour later, she emerged from the church doors. An hour later, she made it halfway down the stairs, and another half hour after that she made it to the truck. I watched her as just about every single patron of the service wanted to shake her hand. Even the deacons seemed to forget that she had arrived with me. Children gathered around her and joyfully asked her questions. We were a contrast. I could walk into a room full of pacifists and they would beat me with chairs. If Kerri walked into a room full of terrorists, they would all hold hands before skipping off to build homes for orphans.

She made it to the truck with a procession of children following her. She got inside and locked the door. When I pulled out of the parking lot she asked, "Why did you leave?"

"Headache," I said.

"Father Greyshadow was nice enough to let me sing. You never leave when I sing," she said.

"It was a terrible headache." I zipped around a car that was going ten miles under the speed limit.

"Did you at least pray about what you should do?" she asked.

"Yeah," I said.

Her voice was weak, almost trembling, when she said, "And?"

I sighed. "Free will is amazing, and I am lucky to have it."

A soft smile touched her lips. "Are you going to fight?"

"Of course."

The smile left her face. "You could die."

"Of course."

"Want to have 'you might die sex'?"

I nearly hit a building.

CHAPTER 26

YOU MIGHT DIE sex is awesome! There is a lot of kissing, a lot of trying things that you probably shouldn't, and a hell of a lot of sex. Animalistic, brutal, clothes ripping sex. After that, you get a sandwich! Then you get more sex!

I woke up at 5 pm. Kerri-Lynn was asleep next to me, her golden skin shining with sweat. That beautiful hair of hers was a mess, she was still wearing her glasses, and her lips were parted just enough to look like she was waiting to be kissed. She was sleeping on her stomach with her breasts propping her up just a bit. Her butt was in the air and slightly covered with a swath of the bed sheet. One of her legs was hanging off the bed.

My hand slid between her legs, and I let my fingers dance along her lips. She moaned and I pressed harder. When her hips lifted, I kissed her back. I kept fingering her until she spread her legs. Then I slid behind her, taking her hips into my hands. Her warmth overtook me as I entered her. As she clenched around me, a soft moan escaped her lips. Kerri-Lynn groaned with excitement as I slid slowly back and forth. She tried to push up with her arms, but I put a hand on her back just below her neck.

"Don't move," I told her.

"No Sir," she said in a weak voice.

I saw her fingers dig into the covers. She groaned in pain and pleasure. At one point, I put an arm around her waist and lifted her so that I could lay her across the width of the bed. I stood up but I never left her body. She screamed as I began to rock harder into her. She pushed up onto her hands and knees when she came the first time. Then she collapsed when she came the second time. The third time she came all she could do was moan and cry.

When we were done, I held her in my arms. She sat on my lap in silence for a while. She rubbed my chest. Her fingers traced along a fresh scar across my right pectoral. Every once in a while she would press her head against my chest and kiss me over my heart.

"Do you have to go? Can't you call the police, or the army, or your grandfather?"

I wanted to tell her I could call someone. I wanted to tell her not to worry. I just wanted her to be happy. Instead, I kissed her forehead. We hugged, and I lifted her into the air as I stood. For just an instance my fears and troubles faded away beneath the touch of her skin and the smell of her hair.

When I set her down on my bed, I looked her in her eyes. "When something goes bump in the night, someone must stand up and bump back. When a single person cries out in fear, a capable person must come to their call. When shadows rise around the innocent, a knight must rise to face them. I am someone, I am capable, and I am a knight."

She looked at me with wide eyes, and in those eyes I saw fear, lust, and wonder. It was hard to turn away from her, but it was time to get ready for work. There was a secret compartment under the floor of my closet. I opened it to reveal the three storage bins hidden there—a red one, a blue one, and a black one. The red one was the one I needed for tonight.

"I have to get ready," I told her. Kerri followed me to the living room where I set the storage bin on the floor. I opened it so she could see what was inside. As Kerri stared in awe at the contents of the bin, I went about gathering my weapons.

"This is armor! Actual freaking armor!"

"Yep. Did I mention that I'm a knight?"

"Oh shut up."

I set my weapons out on the table and then reached into the bin so I could start getting ready. Before my hand touched anything in the bin, Kerri grabbed my wrist. "Let me." She looked at all the gear around her, and a smile quirked across her lips. "Just tell me where to start and what to do."

We started with plain clothing. She helped me into a pair of dark blue carpenter jeans. Before zipping them, she gave me a good luck kiss…below the belt. Then she put on my belt. After that was a black long-sleeved athletic Under Armor shirt. Kerri had to stand on the couch to get it over my head, and when she did, she took her time running her hands down my chest and torso to smooth it out. Once my shirt was tucked into my jeans, she fastened my belt.

My footwear of choice is typically sneakers or work boots. For a throw down like this, I went with a brand-new pair of black steel-toed work boots. I hadn't laced them, so Kerri relieved a pair of her running sneakers of their neon laces. She double threaded plain black laces with the green neon laces as one would a child's shoe and double knotted them.

Next came the armor. Kerri helped me into a dark blue Kevlar vest. Some people look at me strangely when they see me fighting monsters while wearing Kevlar, but one day a troll is going to pull out a gun. Then who is going to be crazy? Not the 200-pound guy in Kevlar with a sword fighting the 600-pound troll with a semiautomatic! To add to my modern day gear I had steel knee and elbow pads. Kerri tightened them on my joints. When she pulled the next item out of the bin, her jaw dropped.

"This is just awesome!" she squealed.

Kerri pulled a sleeved shirt of titanium rings from the bin. I had to put it on myself since she couldn't lift it that high without it being awkward. She slid black bracers on me that closed with adjustable crank buckles rather than being laced. The iron plates on the bracers were emblazoned with a red cross. Next, she helped me into a set of greaves with the same design as the bracers. Finally, she slid my hands into a pair of fitted work gloves with ridged iron plates padding the knuckles.

"What's next?" she asked.

"Weapons," I said.

Kerri strapped a hunting knife to my left calf. Next, she took a modified tool belt and strapped it tight across my waist. This was my version of a tactical vest or web belt. It was a model that clasped around both thighs. Into the pouches and slips went conventional and nonconventional tools of the trade. A hammer road my right hip, and a hand axe paired it on my left. Chalk, vials of holy water, extra ammo, a heavy-duty flashlight, and my lucky gaming dice all went into a sealed pocket. Say what you want, but every little bit helps in a fight. Next were my guns. We loaded them with iron and silver. I loaded one magazine with eight explosive rounds. My black Desert eagle was strapped to my right hip, and my silver one was on my left. The weight was still awkward, but I was going to need all the firepower I could carry. Finally, Kerri slipped my sword belt around my waist. This placed my silver dagger on my right hip and The Sword of Innocence on my left hip. If you looked at my waist from front to back you would see gun, dagger, and hammer on my right, and on my left you would see gun, sword, and axe.

"You look…" Kerri started.

I cut her off. "We aren't done."

I reached down on the table and picked up a tee shirt. She helped me into it. It was a black tee shirt with a picture of Darkwing Duck on it. It said in purple letters 'I Am The Terror That Flaps In The Night!' Over that went a short-sleeved black and red flannel work shirt, and of course the jean jacket that Kerri had given me the last time I visited my grandparent's in Virginia. It was that visit that brought us back together, and subsequently it was the reason she was here now.

I walked back to my room and came back with two items. The first was my cloak. It was red with gold trim. On the back was a picture of the Crucifixion in gold thread. I hated my cloak because it reminded me of the Templar Knights, and I hated those guys. However, I figured I needed every inch today. She swung the cloak over my shoulders and fastened it to the pockets of my jacket as if it was meant to be there. I pulled my crucifix out on its long chain to rest atop the cloak. On the table was one last item. Kerri handed it to me, and I fixed a triangular titanium shield to my left arm. I couldn't decide on a logo when my armor smith forged it, so I asked him to put several small logos on it. Among them were Captain America's shield, the Hyrule shield, and Lion-o's claw shield.

Finally, I handed her the most important item of my gear…besides my sword. I knelt down so that she could put it on me. Kerri-Lynn, the girl that had been my playmate, the young lady that had been my girlfriend, and the woman that was my lover, placed my Baltimore Orioles baseball cap on my head. When she did, I stood up before her and let her take a good look at me.

She stepped back. I was a hodgepodge of medieval and modern battle gear. Her eyes were wide, and her arms seemed to be looking for something to balance her. She had been fine a moment ago, but now with my cloak and all the symbols of my faith it must have been a sight to see.

"God in Heaven, you really are a knight. I mean, I knew you were. I saw you fight, I saw your grandfather, I saw it all. But looking at you…"

She scanned me from head to toe once more. "Michael Franklin Joshua White, you are really a Knight!"

"Did you doubt me?"

She shrugged. "No. Not once. But…wow. A real Knight Templar."

"I am not a Knight Templar. I'm part of the church, but I am not one of them."

"Right. The Crucifixion. You are a Knight of the Crucifixion, a Knight of the First Order."

I nodded and put a hand on her shoulder as I looked her in the eyes. "I need you. I need a wheel man…er…woman. If things get bad, I need you to get Aaron and Eden out of there."

"Aaron and Eden? What about you?"

"I am being honest with you Kerri. If one of us is going to go down, it will probably be me. I am a vanilla mortal with a magic sword. Aaron is a vampire with supernatural endurance, reflexes, and strength. Eden is a wizard that throws around real magic. Besides that, if something tries to kill one of them, you know I am putting myself between them and it."

"That's stupid. Don't get me wrong, I don't want your friends to die, but don't you trust them to defend themselves? To actually fight?"

"I sure do. I know they can defend themselves, but in the end, I asked for their help. I'm responsible for them. Anyone that is willing to fight beside me gets to come home. They come home. Got it?"

She looked at me for an instant as if she wanted to strike me. A smile flashed across her face but shifted into a grimace. She shrugged her shoulders and shook her head in resignation.

"They come home. I will be your wheel woman. What else do you need me to do?"

CHAPTER 27

THERE ARE TIMES when being a knight is absolutely amazing. I have felt the power of faith in many forms. I have seen the beauty of the world of the faeries. Heck, I have had moonshine made by hillbilly werewolves. Being a knight has filled my life with fantastical experiences. So it is a real bummer when you have to carpool in order to battle evil. We had to pick up Aaron and Eden.

We got Eden first. The little wizard was dressed to the nines in black jeans, a black tee shirt, and black sneakers. Around her waist was a thick belt with three pouches on each side. There was a small pistol on her right hip and a set of wands on her left. She wore a long leather coat with a bunch of pockets and a dark purple cloak over it. On her hands were red fingerless gloves. The time for hiding and blending in was over, so instead of a hockey stick Eden carried a straight staff carved from some dark red wood. The staff was a few inches taller than she was.

Aaron was dressed as he always was—dark pants, dark shirt, dark chain shirt, and $200.00 sunglasses at night. He had added a black leather jacket to cover up a shoulder rig that sported what looked like a mini Uzi.

We took Kerri's SUV. It had room and cup holders, both of which I put to use. As I drank my large soda, I looked around at my team. Eden flicked her lighter and gnawed on an unlit cigar. Aaron lounged across the back seat where my shield was. He thought I couldn't see him writing '+4 dork cover' on it in black marker, but I could.

Kerri had put on one of my spare Kevlar vests. It was big on her, but she had thrown on one of my tee shirts and a baseball jersey to cover it. Inside the jersey, she had a shoulder rig for her gun. With form fitting jeans and running shoes, she looked like a woman going to drop kids off at the pool.

"Is this the place?" Kerri asked.

"Yep. Find a parking spot away from everyone. Don't drive up," I said.

Kerri found a parking spot across the street from the building. We all piled out and got our gear on. Aaron was the last one out of the SUV. When he looked over and up at the structure he whistled. This was going to be the sight of the biggest rave that the murdering bastard had thrown. Hundreds of people would be sacrificed, and a gate to Hell would be opened right in the middle of my city if I didn't kill a human being. Good or evil, it didn't matter. He was human, like me, like Kerri, and like everyone else that I loved.

I looked up at the structure and wondered how the acoustics were in an eight-story parking deck. We stood in front of the Central Parking Garage on East Lombard Street. I had been by the building a few times in passing, but I had never been inside. The bottom floor of the garage was brick and glass. The higher levels of the structure had open paneling for better ventilation and sound management. Could you imagine the sound of a hundred engines roaring in an enclosed building? It would be deafening. Like most buildings of its type, this one had a few convenience stores attached to the building. The stores were all closed.

The sun was already down, but I could not hear music. I opened my senses and focused on the building. I could feel a hum of subtle energy coming from the building. Still I heard nothing. I kept focusing and realized that I could feel the vibrations of intense sound in my feet. I knelt down to touch the ground. Sure enough, I could make out the pulse of rhythmic sound. The ground was shaking all around us.

"Does anyone hear anything?" I asked.

"Nope," said Aaron.

"No," said Kerri.

"You won't hear anything. Somehow they are keeping sound from escaping the building. Light too. The sorcerer has been practicing," Eden said.

"So he upped his game?" I asked.

Eden nodded.

"Can you shut him down, Eden?" Aaron asked.

"No. There is too much energy flowing around in there. He is using it to hide, and the little weasel is good at it. We need to get in, and I'll have to be able to see him before I can counter him."

"So what's the plan?" Kerri asked.

"We go in and try to evacuate the place," I said.

"Michael, that isn't an option," Eden said. I looked at her over my shoulder. "The ritual has already started. I can feel it from here. It's kind of like a magic circle. Everything in there is trapped. Unless we can disrupt the energy, every living creature in there is part of the ritual. If one person leaves, nothing will happen except to that person. Some supernaturals and even some humans could survive it. If two dozen leave, the backlash could rip the building apart. If a hundred tried to leave all at once…"

Aaron whistled.

"That means we have to get to Dyhart and stop him in a building full of people. We can't fight in there," I said.

I looked the building up and down. My mind raced for a solution. We couldn't fight in a building full of innocent bystanders. I could kill someone with an errant swing of my sword. Heck, I could kill half a dozen with a missed shot of my gun. I knew Aaron would be all right in a fight with his reflexes, but Eden would be like me. She wouldn't be able to bring magic to bear without endangering others.

"So once you are inside you are trapped?" Kerri asked.

"No," Eden said. "The backlash from leaving could kill you if you aren't prepared. Aaron or I could probably walk out. You could with the sword, maybe, but that's not a guarantee. A normal mortal might die on the spot, or best case scenario end up having a seizure or something else that might kill them."

Kerri pulled out her gun and chambered a round. "Then there is no point in me being the wheel woman."

"Hold on. What do you think you're doing?" I asked.

"Watching your back," she said in a matter-of-fact tone.

"They're watching my back. You are staying with the car."

"No, I'm not. They're going to have goons, grunts, or whatever you call henchmen. You shoot like a noob. I can shoot the hairs off a cat's ass. Now are we going to stand here and argue, or are you going to give me something I can swing with if I lose my gun?"

I wanted to tell her no. I wanted to shove her in the SUV and tell her to leave. I wanted to leave with her. But I knew how this was going to go. Two decades of friendship had told me how this was going to go. The girl still had all the blue, pink, and purple crayons from every box I ever had.

Why? Because she told me she wanted them. I pulled out my hammer and handed it to her. She shoved it into her belt and then went to her SUV. She returned with a pair of purple mechanics gloves on her hands.

"Okay people, here is the plan," I said. "We go in. We neutralize every threat we find. Do not kill any mortals. Wound them. Cripple them if you have to, I don't care. If they fight us, we hurt them. When we find the demon and the sorcerer, I kill one of them. I just don't know which one yet. Eden, if you can stop the ritual you tell us how we can help. If anyone gets hurt, I need you on it Aaron. If Aaron gets hurt, we give him blood. Everyone got it?"

They all nodded.

"One last thing. We all come out of this alive. Got it?"

They all nodded again.

"Alright my fellow vigilantes, let's go thwart a sorcerer that is consorting with demons!" I said.

"Damn it!" Aaron said.

We had parked in the garage across the street from the one the sorcerer decided to use as the staging ground for his ritual. The bad guys had blocked off all the entrances and were admitting people into the rave in an efficient and orderly fashion. No one was being turned away. Step one was to stop anyone else from entering.

We had no idea if the people working the rave would be in the know about what was going on, so we had to assume that they were. If you do not know who your enemy is, then assume everyone is an enemy. Aaron sprinted toward the door with superhuman speed. He dashed past the first doorman and hit the second in the gut with as much force as he had hit me earlier. The first doorman turned on him and reached behind his back to grab the gun he had in his pants. I was a few seconds behind Aaron, and I hit the doorman turned gunman in the back of the head with a two-handed hammer blow. He went down and people started screaming.

Aaron tried to calm down the crowd. I reached down and took the gun from the guy I had just knocked out. I pointed it skyward and fired four shots into the air. The crowd outside went running. Eden and Kerri caught up just as everyone else broke camp.

"Why did you do that? Won't they call the cops?" Kerri asked.

"Probably not. Statistically speaking, most people willing to participate in a blatantly illegal activity don't call the cops when they should. If they do we will deal with it, but right now we go inside and get to work," I said. I handed Kerri the gun, and she slipped it into the back of her pants. Collecting the one from the man Aaron had dropped, I gave it to her.

I also took their wallets, relieved them of their cash, and got some mixed looks from my friends. I shrugged at them and continued to empty the wallets of cash.

"This is ill-gotten money. I need to help these men by converting it to something not evil. Something like food and rent." They didn't buy it.

"I'm broke, and we just dropped some bad guys. I'm taking their loot."

I took a sack out of a pouch on my belt and unfolded it. I attached metal clips to it so I could attach it to my belt for easy access. In big black letters on the side of the sack it read 'LOOT'.

Eden had stepped up to the entrance. She had her hands extended and her head bowed. I could already feel the magic in there. It felt like the steam from a pot of boiling water. As my senses focused on the entrance to the parking garage, something strange happened. Something flashed across my vision. There was fire—dark orange and gold flames engulfed the building. The ground was split open as if someone had taken a jackhammer to it. People were burning to the point that I could see their bones as they desperately tried to smother the flames that were upon them. Then the scene was gone, and I was standing in front of the parking garage again with no idea as to what was going on.

Eden looked at me with wide eyes. "You just saw the ritual taking effect, didn't you?" she asked.

I shook my head. Not in answer—I was trying to clear my thoughts. I can't see magic like a wizard can, unless there was a fireball flying at me or a bolt of lightning, I was pretty much just like every vanilla mortal. My perception of the presence of magic was based around paying attention to what I couldn't see. As cool as it would be to finally see magic and power, I didn't have time to deal with anything new.

"Yeah maybe," I said. "Can we go in?"

"The ritual is going well for Dyhart. Once we enter the building, we may as well be in another dimension. We will be completely cut off from the world beyond this building," Eden told us.

"Meaning?" Kerri asked.

"Meaning that we won't be able to interact with anything outside. Just as we cannot hear them inside right now, they cannot hear us. Pretty much the only reason we can still see the building is that it's so rooted into the structure of the city. If it hadn't been here for years and used by so many people it would be all but invisible," said Eden.

"So nothing we weren't already prepared for," said Aaron.

I stepped past Eden. "I would say ladies first, but I think I should take point," I said. I pulled my shield from my back and stepped into the building cautiously. Eden came next with Kerri behind her and Aaron bringing up the rear. Together we waded into the beginnings of a gate to Hell.

CHAPTER 28

H AVE YOU EVER been to a rave? It was nothing like what I expected. I'm an introvert. Give me my room, some books, and a mini-fridge, and you can have the rest of my apartment. I don't go to any social gathering that has more than five people in the room unless I am being provided with: a) anime, books, comics, or science-fiction memorabilia, b) games and gaming accessories, or c) an interview with someone that writes or creates anime, books, comics, games and gaming accessories, or science-fiction memorabilia. I'm a nerd. So when I imagined this rave, I thought I would be walking into the middle of a loud party. I could not have been more wrong.

What I walked into was beyond my scoop of understanding for the word 'party.' I had my shield in front of me just in case someone started shooting. My shield could not have protected me from what happened when I entered the site of the ritual. Absolute darkness blanketed me. Then purple light streaked across everything, then blue, then yellow, then red. It was the equivalent of magical gunfire. In those flashes, I saw dozens of people participating in acts that could only technically pass for dancing and easily be mistaken for high impact pornography. Music louder than thunder hit me hard enough to rattle my bones. A base beat from a speaker I couldn't see shook the ground and physically pounded against my shield. A haze of smoke from the combination of a fog machine and more legal and illegal substances than I knew existed hit my nostrils. That was the break down as far as my senses could take it. What I actually felt in the first few seconds of entering the rave was a concussive blast of light and sound. My body reacted to the primal fears of flashing light like lightning, loud noises like the roar of a predator, and the loss of air as if being drowned. I panicked.

My heart began to pound louder and faster than the base beat. I had to get out of that place. Every instinct I had told me that this place was evil. It was wrong, and I was in the middle of it. I turned to run away, and it saved my life.

I turned to my right, and that brought my shield around to the gunman with the machine gun leveled at me. The sound of the shots didn't register right away, but the magical gunfire of the strobing light was accented by the fire orange flash of actual gunfire. Rapid hammer blows rang off my shield, and I heard the mechanical click of an automatic rifle along with the ring of metal hitting my shield. I ducked my head behind my shield and screamed in fear.

That scream lasted only a second. My instincts may have wanted me to leave, but some nut had just opened fire in a room full of people. I had to put him down now before anyone was hurt or killed. My feet dug in until I was balanced, and then I bulled ahead at the shooter. Bullets bombarded my shield and streaked by as the gunman filled the air with hot lead.

The assault abruptly stopped, and the report of the gun was an empty clicking sound. I looked over the rim of my shield and saw the gunman lift the butt of the rifle to strike me. Up came my shield to knock the blow aside as my free hand came around in an iron-knuckled right hook. My punch hit the man right in his temple like all my teachers had told me to do. The poor bastard might have stood a chance if I hadn't put all of my fear from being in that place into my punch. That punch landed with the force of a sledgehammer. The gunman spun in the air head-over-heel to land in a heap on the dance floor. He was sprawled out at an odd position with his right arm behind his back at an impossible angle. I couldn't tell if he was breathing or not.

My head was back in the game now. Fear was still racing through my body, but I didn't need to run from this place. I felt like doing a small victory dance, and had just started to move, when Eden hit my shield with her staff. My eyes locked on her in alarm at the little witch's action.

"Don't dance!" she yelled. "Look around you. Don't you feel it?"

I turned my attention to the room. Everyone was still dancing. An assault rifle had just opened up in the middle of a parking garage filled with hundreds of people, and none of them were phased by it. I took a deep breath. It was supposed to be settling, but the gunpowder mixed with the drug-laced air didn't settle anything. My mind opened to the room. I felt it before I heard it. There was a strange beat playing alongside the rave music. Its base was deep, and my spine thrummed with it. I wanted to dance. More urgently in my mind was the thought of taking Kerri and Eden into the smoke, bending them both over around me, and doing things to them that I had never imagined. It would be so easy to rip their clothes and weapons off, force them to the ground beneath me, and fuck them until they were raw and bloody. I wanted to hear them and every other woman in this place moan and scream as I fucked them so hard that I ripped the civility from them. It wouldn't take much to break every woman in this building down to their base instincts of eating and fucking while having my way with each and every one of them.

I shut my mind. This wasn't how I thought about sex or women. Every thought that had just run through my mind became my focus for a moment as I locked them away. Even blocking those thoughts still left me with a hunger to devour everything with a set of x chromosomes in the building. The only way I could think of to counter this lust was to go to my happy place. My mind tracked back to the one thing I wanted more than anything that flesh could offer. I thought about Wild West Mars. Magic was real. There were realms of fairies, elves, dwarves, and all sorts of mythological beings. So logically, Wild West Mars had to exist. One day I was going to find it, and then I was going to say 'screw this knight business.' I was going to be a space cowboy!

I was back in control. Aaron walked over holding Kerri in his arms. When he got closer, I noticed that he wasn't holding Kerri at all. She had her arms around his neck and her legs around his torso. Her lips were plastered on his neck, and she kept biting him.

"Have you ever been with a woman? I know you are pretty much taken, but does it count as cheating if it's for a good cause? You really should explore how a dead vampire and a living woman get along. How they fit together," she purred.

"Can you do something about this?" Aaron asked as he pointed at Kerri with both hands.

I drew my sword and said, "Child of God. Daughter of Eve. Get off of him!"

Kerri yelped and jumped off Aaron. She backed away from him and covered her face so we couldn't see her blush. When a black girl blushes, it's a rare and beautiful thing. I knew what had come over her. If I hadn't been so scared for my life, it would have come over me, too. In fact, my jeans were now a few sizes too small.

I turned to Eden. "How did you overcome that compulsion?"

She blushed as well and turned away from me. "I am a wizard. Some second-rate compulsion could never overcome my mental defenses."

I nodded. Both Eden and Kerri had fallen prey to the magic of the ritual. I could smell their sex. They were like bitches in heat, and I wanted to take Eden by the hair and…WILD WEST MARS! This place was driving us to debauchery. Now don't get me wrong. Sex is great. Sex is awesome. When it isn't our choice, then we have a problem.

"I hate to worry you guys, but we have incoming," Aaron said.

My eyes darted through the parking garage, and I saw five men moving through the crowd. They were dressed in plain clothing, but they didn't blend in. They were too big and too focused. I didn't see assault weapons in their hands, and they weren't together.

"Spread out and take them down. Try not to kill them, but don't hurt the bystanders," I said.

Aaron darted left, back toward the entrance. One of the thugs went after him. Eden went right, and of course a thug went after her. That left me with three to myself. At least that is what I thought.

Kerri ducked low and hustled into the throng of enchanted ravers. I waded in as well, but I did not follow her. I heard a gut-wrenching scream and saw one of the three thugs go down. At that moment, a sense of nausea overtook me and I froze, and so did the other two thugs. We traded gazes as the three of us stood unmoving. Even through the fog and insane lighting, they looked a little green, too.

"You guys don't have to do this," I yelled above the music. "When this ritual goes down you'll be killed. You do know that, right?"

In response, they both drew small pistols. Then they opened fire right into the crowd. Bullets flew into the crowd of enthralled dancers. No one moved, and no one shouted in fear. They were going to die because these dick heads wanted to shoot me.

It's not often that I get to flaunt my toys, but this was one of those times. I jumped forward at the sight of the guns, brought my shield to bear, and whipped out the magic. "Anziehen!" I yelled. Shields are made to take punishment, and mine was really made for it. The titanium shield hummed like a tuning fork, and every flash of gunfire was met with a report of warping metal. Unseen waves of energy blanketed the air before me, causing every bullet that was flying through the air to whip and whirl to my shield. The flash and sound exchange went on for what felt like an hour. I heard the guns click on empty, and I made my move.

Well, I tried to. I lowered my shield to see one thug reloading and one coming at me. The thug coming at me was a big guy. He was at least as tall as me and built like he could arm wrestle a bear. Shoving people out of his way to get to me, he came at me with a serrated hunting knife. He stabbed forward, and I brought my shield around to block. Sparks flew from my shield, and the thug recoiled. I back stepped, and he advanced while swinging his knife savagely. He had no form, but each blow came down with the force of falling tree.

There were too many people around for me to swing my sword. I hated fighting in close quarters, but I didn't have any other option at the moment. I drew my own knife as I backed away. No sooner did I have the blade out from its sheath than the thug grabbed the top of my shield with his left hand. He yanked my arm forward and down. I had no choice but to follow. I lost my balance and stumbled forward at the same time that he thrust his knife at my head.

"Anziehen!" I called on the magic of my shield once again, and the thug's knife arm curved as he slammed his knife into my shield. He had committed to the strike, and when it was redirected, he overbalanced and stumbled forward past me. His weight forced my shield to the ground where I managed to plant it like a crutch so I could get my feet back under me. I pushed off and came up swinging my shield high. The flat of my shield came around with my full weight behind it and smashed across the thugs head. Just for good measure, I followed through with the blow and drove his head into the ground.

Even after that blow, the guy wanted to get back up. I couldn't have that, so I kicked him in the head. He fell over and stopped struggling. Something whipped past me, and I remembered the other thug. I got back behind my shield, and once again gunfire was met with the sound of warping metal. I charged ahead as the gunman fired.

"Michael, on your left!" Kerri screamed.

I was so focused on protecting the crowd I forgot to think through my defenses. I looked to my left when I heard Kerri's warning. The gunman had moved, and I had just run past him. I was beside him with my shield ahead of me. He was barely three feet from me when he leveled his gun and fired. The shot hit me in my upper back near my right shoulder. I fell down and bounced off my knees to skid to the side.

I felt like a baseball bat had hit me in my back. My training as a knight saved me. My grandpa had drilled it into me to cover my back, especially when I had a shield. I swung my arm behind my head just before bullets began to rain down at my spine. I had to use my right arm to balance myself, and doing that hurt more than being shot had. My arm screamed with pain, but every muscle on my right side from my neck down felt like it was made of Jell-O. I couldn't take much more.

"Anziehen!" I screamed for the third time in as many minutes.

The gunfire stopped, and I felt something heavy clank against my shield. I swung my shield back around and spun on the gunman. I looked over my shield and saw a collection of bullets, a knife, and a gun all stuck on there.

The gunman looked perplexed as he stared at his unarmed hands. "What the hell?"

I couldn't keep the smile off my face when I asked, "Want it back? Abstoben!" I roared.

Bullets surged off the surface of my shield along with the knife and the gun. They all smacked against the shocked gunman. They weren't flying with anything nearing lethal force, but it was enough to scare the crap out of him. I even got lucky with the knife when its blade slashed across his shin. He grabbed his leg, and I got back to my feet.

We squared off. When he shot me I dropped my knife, and now I had no idea where it was. That was my favorite knife, and I really hated being shot. I ran at him and threw a straight right punch into his gut. The gunman wasn't as big as his partner, but he didn't budge when I hit him. In fact, it hurt my hand when I did because my right arm was as useful as a wet noodle. He hit me with an uppercut that lifted me off the ground. Then he grabbed my right shoulder and laid into me with half a dozen punches to my face and chest.

I may have lost consciousness during that fight. My body hit the ground, but I only know that because my head hurt when it smacked against it. A heavy boot stomped repeatedly into my chest and stomach causing me to cough up blood. The gunman must have noticed my guns while he was stomping me into the ground. He reached down to my Desert Eagle with a cruel smile on his face.

My right hand still felt limp, but I didn't need much strength right now. My fingers curved around a familiar handgrip, and I clutched it for all I was worth. Ignoring the pain in my abdomen, I sat up fast. The gunman recoiled, but he was worried about his vitals like his heart and neck. I shoved the blade of my dagger into his kneecap. He howled in pain, and I gripped the dagger harder. My arm didn't have enough strength for me to press the advantage, but I could always use gravity as a backup. I fell backward again but turned to the side letting gravity help me rip the knife across and out of the side of the gunman's leg.

He screamed and swore in pain. His howls were louder than the music. I just lay there listening for a moment. The gunman's screams went from profane, to monosyllabic, to noises of animal rage. He looked at me with hate in his eyes. I couldn't move, so I just stuck my tongue out at him. That drove him off the deep end. He rolled over onto his stomach and began crawling at me. I lifted my eyebrow as I realized that I really was in trouble. My body just did not want to move right now.

The gunman had just reached me and was reaching for my throat when Aaron calmly palmed the back of his head. The Vampire snapped his arm forward and smashed the man's head against the ground with enough force not only to crack the ground but to spray me with blood. Aaron lifted the head to inspect his work. The nose and jaw were broken, the face would swell, but other than that, the man was fine. Blood was all over his cheek, and I realized that it wasn't just blood on me. The gunman had a huge zit on his face that I hadn't notice during the fight. So I wasn't just covered in blood but puss, too. Great.

Aaron stepped over to me and offered me his hand. I took it, and he pulled me to my feet. "You okay?" he asked me.

"I'm good. He just shot me, that's all," I said.

Aaron checked my back and reported there was no injury. My layers of armor had stopped the bullet, but the impact had left my arm in pain. We walked into the crowd to find Eden and Kerri. They were standing together over one of the thugs that had come after us. He was lying on the ground holding his groin. Kerri was holding my hammer. Aaron and I reflexively covered our own groins.

"The ritual is on the top level. The demon and sorcerer are there," Eden told us as we approached.

Aaron held his hand out to the downed thug. "He told you that?"

Kerri smacked the hammer against her palm. "I told him that if he talked I wouldn't hit him again."

I knelt down to speak to the thug. "Do you and your buddies know what's going on?"

He nodded.

"Tell me."

"We get these kids to dancing and partying," he said in a wheezing voice. "Then the boss kills them all to summon some more demons. The demon told us to kill your friends on sight but to take you alive."

That bothered me. They wanted to kill my friends but wanted me alive. Did Ophalistis want to screw with me that badly? That, however, was not what made my blood boil.

"So you knew you were going to kill these people?" I asked.

"Yeah," the thug said.

I felt the sneer on my lips before I yanked the thug to his feet by the front of his shirt. Rage fueled my strength as my quivering arm held him there. My muscles tensed with the desire to beat this thug to within an inch of his life.

"They are innocents! They are living, breathing beings," I roared. "What right do you have to kill them?"

The thug looked at me with a blank expression. "The boss pays us, so we get the job done," he said.

I could taste the bile in my mouth. Guys like this just got to me. I hated it when anyone hurt someone else just because they could. To do it for money was just as wrong. These people were innocent of the surrounding evil. They may not have been innocent of mortal crimes, but they had no idea that they were being used in a ritual to open a portal to Hell. This thug and every one of his cohorts had robbed them of their free will. They had tried to kill my friends. Each one of them had just made my shit list.

"Aaron, please dislocate both of his arms and do the same to the rest of them," I said.

I shoved the thug over to Aaron, and the vampire took him by the shoulders. Aaron's arms snapped down, and I heard a sickening sound. It was a wet popping sound followed by screaming. We took their ammo and cash. These assholes could go to the unemployment line in the morning or beg for money. At least they would be alive to have an option.

"New rule," I said. "Disable them if you can, but if you have to kill one of them in a fight go ahead. They *are* the bad guys."

I kept giving people the benefit of the doubt, but these guys were playing for keeps. It was time I did the same. We took the ramp up to the next level, and each of us had a gun in our hand.

CHAPTER 29

ARON TOOK THE rear. He was the fastest and could get to one of us if we were overwhelmed or hurt. I led the way. The ramps were clear for the most part. There were several cars with incredible sound systems. Each one was hooked up to a Wi-Fi system and streaming from a live feed. Whoever the DJ was, his set up was pretty innovative. Seven or more cars on each ramp blasting music had the entire building jumping. The flat areas of the parking deck were where we encountered more and more victims. The higher we climbed the less family-friendly the crowd became. By the time we hit the third floor no one was trying to dance anymore.

"I don't see anything for a ritual. I can still hear that strange beat, but that's it," I said.

"They must have everything set up on the upper levels. The people and building are just the fuel and a box for it," Eden said.

"Does anyone else feel like they are getting high?" Kerri asked.

Both Aaron and Eden agreed. I looked back at them and shrugged.

"You don't feel like you're high?" Aaron asked.

"Maybe…I don't know what 'high' feels like," I said.

"Boy scout," Aaron said.

"Church Boy," Eden said.

"Michael," Kerri said.

Everyone just shook their heads at me. Then we got back to business. Security must have planned to take us out on the first floor, because the second and third floors didn't present any problems. I hit the fourth level in a sprint. The guard at the top of the ramp hadn't been paying attention, and I backhanded him with my shield. He went down, and that got the attention of every guard on that floor. They all turned to me while drawing their guns.

Eden came up behind me to my right. She thrust her staff forward in her right hand. She screamed a word of power, and an unseen force smacked into three guards. Kerri came up on my left and fired four times with her confiscated gun. Four shots, and four mean went down clutching their right legs.

"Arms and wallets," I said. Aaron blurred past us and began injuring people and looting them.

Eden was shaking her head. "I don't like this."

The hairs on the back of my neck began to stand up. I looked at the wizard and was about to say something when Kerri spoke up. "I know. You would think they would have more guards or something."

I leapt over to my two friends and started waving my hands like a mad man.

"Don't say it! Don't!" I yelled.

They both looked at me as if I was insane. "Do you really think we would say something that stupid?" Eden asked.

"I'm just making sure. The last thing we need is for someone to feed the universe a straight line."

"I would bet my SUV against your truck that you would say it before we did," Kerri said.

Aaron walked back over and handed me a bunch of cash to go into my loot sack. He looked around at our faces and then settled his eyes on me. "Michael, did you really say it?"

"No!" I said.

Kerri hooked her thumb at me. "He almost did."

"I did not!"

Eden sighed. "Give him enough time and he will."

"What? No I won't!"

All three of them looked at me and rolled their eyes. I pulled my hat down over my eyes and swore. I pulled it back up and started toward the next ramp. "You guys all suck, you know. I admit that I mess up sometimes. It happens. Anyone can make a mistake, but this is my *job*, it's what I do! How big of an idiot would someone have to be to say that this was too easy?"

The music stopped. Not for an instant. Not as though the power had gone out. There was a squelching sound like a record being forcibly brought to a stop, and then everything was silent except for the base beat that had been in the background. The only other sound in the building was the thunderous roar of the stares I was getting from my friends.

"That doesn't count! That was a question, not a statement," I said to my friends. Then I looked up at the ceiling and yelled, "You are supposed to be the one boss that doesn't take things out of context!"

Kerri's face turned blood red, and she stomped over to me. Before she could say a single word, my eyes caught sight of her shadow. It elongated and began to rotate around her body. The light in the room began to increase, and I felt heat on my neck. Kerri began to yell at me, but I wasn't paying attention to her words. Instinct took over and I lunged at her. I scooped her up in my arms and leapt ahead. I turned so that my back hit the ground and my shield was in front of Kerri.

Searing air filled the area. It rushed at us, and I felt Kerri shudder in my arms. It was a second ahead of my own shudder. She was tough. When the fire washed over us, she yelped but did not scream. I felt the flames wash over my legs, and though it wasn't enough to injure me it still hurt like hell.

"New pain!" I screamed as I retracted my legs. They were burned, but I could not tell how badly. If the red-hot metal of my greaves were any indication then I was in trouble. My pants were burnt, and one of my boots was burning. I could feel the hot metal of the steel toe on my actual toes.

I looked around and saw Aaron had leapt back almost fifty feet. He was crouched down as if he was ready to pounce on something. His eyes were dark, and I could feel him snarling. Eden was behind a barrier of blue light. Her staff was planted on the ground in her right hand while her left hand was extended before her as if it alone could stop anything from approaching her. Both of my friends had sensed the attack coming and reacted to protect themselves just as I had.

Kerri may have been the best shooter among us, but she was not equipped for this. She didn't have any training in fighting the supernatural, and she was completely ignorant about what our enemy could do. It was my fault she was here and my fault that she was ill-equipped. With that in mind, I would punish myself for the rest of my life. But whatever had just thrown a fireball at my girlfriend would only have to deal with that for a few more seconds.

I looked up toward the top of the ramp and saw Alistair Dyhart, dressed in black robes, standing in front of a cargo van. His eyes were blood red, and he had a sinister grin on his face. He glared at me like he wanted to kill me, and all I could think of was that his fake-ass wizard robes were better than my fake-ass wizard robes. Seriously, his robes were as dark as my boots had been a few seconds ago, except that his V-cut collar was dark gray, and he had a purple rope around his waist. I had made mine from an old bathrobe and a sewing kit. I had to admit that he looked pretty bad ass.

"How did you find this place," he asked me.

I whispered, "Kerri, I need you to get up and get behind me. I want you to slowly back up until Aaron is ahead of you. Got it?"

I looked down at her, and she looked into my eyes. "Are you going to kick his ass?" she asked.

"Yep," I said.

Kerri started to get up, but she whispered into my ear, "Go get 'im, tiger." She got behind me and waited for me to get to my feet. My legs wanted to give out, but I held my balance. All of my friends were behind me, and there was an evil sorcerer watching me. I couldn't show weakness. Once I was up, Kerri began to back away from me.

"Did you not hear me, fool? How did you find this place?" Dyhart demanded.

"Oh, I heard you," I said.

"You probably shouldn't answer him when he calls you a fool," Aaron yelled.

"Thank you, Aaron!" I yelled sarcastically.

"You're welcome, buddy."

The light shifted again. I snapped my head back around to look at the sorcerer, and he was holding a ball of fire in his palm. "Perhaps another blast will help you to focus," he snarled.

"Eden, shut this guy down," I said.

Eden dropped her shield and took up her staff in both hands. Before she could begin to gather energy to her will, the sorcerer hurled the fireball at her. The fireball came at her faster than I could move to defend her safely. I swore and set myself to leap into its path so that I could take the hit for my friend.

Eden had called Alistair Dyhart a second-rate mage, and she showed me what she meant in their first exchange. I felt a wave of magic surge forth from the little wizard and didn't understand what was happening. There was no flash of light, no roar of power, and no clash of wills. The fireball just snuffed out in mid-flight as if it was a match being stomped on by a boot. My eyes darted between the two mages, and I saw Eden's mouth twist into a wolfish grin.

"You must be the wizard," Dyhart said. "I thought you would be taller."

"So did I," I said. "I mean, they say big things come in small packages, but I really didn't expect her magic penis to be that much bigger than yours, Al. Can I call you Al? I mean, wow. It must be embarrassing to shoot your load and have it smacked down like that."

The sorcerer snapped his attention back at me and snarled a word. Fire flew from his hand toward me but snuffed out a foot from his outstretched arm. His eyes went wide.

"Wow, twice in a row? Did she even do anything that time? It's completely understandable to have performance problems after a chick shows you up that badly," I said.

"Alistair Dyhart," Eden roared. She strode forward with all the confidence of a lioness hunting a lamed gazelle. "My name is Eden Freeman. I am a member of the International Council of Magi, also called the White Council by some. I hereby accuse you of the practice of unlawful magic. You will lay down all of your weapons and surrender to me."

I had no idea what Eden was talking about. The only White Council I had ever heard of was from the Tolkien books. To hear that there was an actual organization of real wizards by that name was a surprise. Personally, I figured they would be a guild or maybe a union. It then occurred to me that if Eden captured the sorcerer I could avoid killing him. It was a win in my book.

"I guess this was easier than I thought," I said.

Dyhart looked at Eden with a scowl of contempt. She advanced a step and, although he was at the top of the ramp while she was at the bottom, he backed away from her. For all his boasting and plotting, this confrontation with an actual wizard had lasted less than a minute. Eden had shut him down cold and fast. The sorcerer threw fire at her once again, and the same thing happened. The spell snuffed out as it left his hand.

"Is that the only trick you have, Alistair? I have seen carnival magicians with more talent than you," Eden said.

"I like carnival magicians," I said.

"Shut up, Michael," Eden snapped.

The sorcerer screamed in outrage and began to stomp his foot wildly on the ground. He snarled and spat. He swore incoherently and flailed his arms violently.

Eden began to laugh. She stopped advancing and had to use her staff to find her balance. "Are you actually throwing a temper tantrum?" she asked. "Illegal magic, temper tantrums, and gaudy-looking sinister clothing. This is textbook sorcerer behavior. Did you watch a children's cartoon one day and decide to be evil?"

Alistair Dyhart stopped throwing his tantrum and focused his eyes on me. "This is *your* fault. You couldn't just die like you were supposed to. You just had to interfere with my business. You had to meddle in my personal affairs like a school yard bully," he snarled.

"Dude, you came to my house and threatened me," I said.

"You are nothing but a common thug, a roach that needs to be crushed. It is people like you that have ruined this world," he screamed. Even from the bottom of the ramp, I could see spittle and foam flying free of his lips.

"You kill people *and* summon demons. Look man, I have no idea how bad your life must have been, but *you kill people and summon demons*. That has to be on every faith's top ten list of things not to do," I said.

"Kill him! Kill him!" the sorcerer yelled. The doors of the cargo van behind him exploded, and out leapt a stone sculpture. It was eight feet tall and detailed to look like a roman gladiator. In one hand it held a sword that bore no cross guard to speak of, a gladius I think. In its right hand it had a weapon that was a little more modern, a Kalashnikov.

"You had to say it, didn't you?" Aaron yelled.

"Everyone move," I yelled.

The statue leveled the large rifle in one hand as if it was a pistol. Aaron sprinted over to grab Kerri. He picked her up and sprinted back toward cover. Eden's shield flared to life, but I saw her running after Aaron. The statue started walking forward and pulled the trigger. Bullets rained down at us as I lifted my shield and yelled at the top of my lungs. "Anziehen!"

I felt the magnetic pull of my shield flow over the area ahead of me. I poured all my faith and will into the shield to increase its power. Normally my shield could attract, deflect, or repel small amounts of metal, but I had never used it this much.

I felt bullets smack against my shield, and each one felt like a baseball bat slamming into my arm. There were odd whistling sounds to my right, and I saw bullets striking the ground at odd angles, as if they were being fired from a completely different direction. One whipped in and cut across my right bicep. I grimaced from the pain and instinctively backed away from the assault. My legs were still burning, and the hammering from the Kalashnikov was not helping me. My legs wanted to give out.

"Darn it, why didn't I just shoot that jerk when he started talking?" I asked myself.

I was still backing up when the assault stopped. When I lifted my head over my shield, I watched the gladiator flip the rifle in its left hand like a spear. It hurled the weapon down the ramp at me, and the rifle flew as perfectly as any javelin. My body was quivering from weathering the gunfire, so I just barely managed to get my shield braced before the gun's barrel struck me. The thrown gun hit with enough force to knock me to the ground, but I managed to roll with the blow so I came back up in a crouch.

I looked up just in time to see that the gladiator was airborne with its sword in both hands and the blade angled down. I dove forward just as the gladiator crashed down with its sword impaling the ground where I had been just seconds before. When I hit the ground, it wasn't graceful. Turning sideways, I rolled like an awkward barrel as I tried to put some distance between the animated statue and me. The gladiator stood and wrenched its sword free of the ground. It whipped the stone blade through a fast routine to the check the weapon.

"Eden, can you dispel this thing please?" I yelled.

"No. It's demon magic. There aren't many wizards in the world that can dispel demonic magic on the fly, and even if I could, I would have to stop crippling the sorcerer," she called back. It was only then that I noticed a steady pulse of power coming from her staff.

"So you aren't going to be much help with this guy, are you?" I asked.

"No," she said.

"Aaron?" I asked.

"He got shot," Kerri called to me.

The stone gladiator started toward me. I pushed up and got to my feet. My friends were out of the fight for now. Aaron was seriously hurt if he wasn't answering me. So that left me and a stone gladiator. Game on.

"Alright Rocky, let's dance." I closed my hand over the grip of my sword and drew the blade out like I had done a thousand times. This time, however, the light that came forth from my sword was blinding. For an instant, the world turned into a pure white plane. The music started up again and my swords light toned down to a manageable level of luminous flux. "Well, welcome to the party!" I said to my sword.

On came the stone gladiator. It charged at me faster than I could have imagined a statue moving. Any thoughts I had about countering his size and strength with speed went out the window with that first rush. As I backed up, it opened up with a right to left slash that forced me to duck the attack. I flung my shield over my head like a roof just in case. The stone blade clipped one edge of my shield. The gladiator reversed his slash but came in at my midsection. I jumped straight up and kicked my legs out to either side. Then I brought my sword down in a hammers blow to strike the moving stone blade. It dipped down and cut into the ground beneath us. I landed and back peddled as the gladiator withdrew his weapon from the ground once more.

Fighting draws more out of the human body than anything else. I am not talking about a fight you have with your friends or when two people have a disagreement. I'm talking about when you meet a person's eyes and realize that if you do not kill this person then they will kill you. I am talking about fighting for your life. When we fight, our bodies attempt to ignore everything that is wrong with us. I couldn't feel the bullet wound on my arm or the burns on my legs. I knew I should be tired, but I thought at that moment that I could run a mile. The human body is amazing!

But the human mind is freaking more amazing! In that first exchange, I learned that the gladiator had an advantage on me in the reach department, and though it was just an animated statue, it had a basic understanding of the science of combat. It was worried that I would be faster than it would, so everything it had done up until now had been to slow me down. The barrage of bullets, the thrown Kalashnikov, the high slash that caused me to shorten the strides of my retreat, and the low slash that fully stopped my retreat were all meant to keep me within range of its attacks. Some might think this meant it didn't want me to get too far away. What it really didn't want was for me to get too close.

I took a gamble and darted ahead. The gladiator responded with a thrust at my chest. My shield was already up, so when I sidestepped to the left the blow struck the right side of my shield. The deflected strike added to my momentum as I spun to my right to bring my sword around in a wide slash. It shambled backward, and my sword struck its calf. The sculpted greaves that it bore held true across the front of its leg, but I saw a trickle of stone blood oozing from the nick beside the armor.

The statue planted its feet and hacked at me until I backed off. Its blows were stronger than mine, and each one struck my shield sending me stumbling back. Once I was far enough away, the statue reset itself for battle. It was smart and knew that it held the advantage in a drawn out fight. I had defeated its heavier blows and survived its opening barrage. This thing wanted to kill me, but it wasn't about to make a mistake by fighting on my terms. I took the offensive and rushed it with my shield. When the gladiator brought its sword down in a cleaving strike, I lifted my shield to block. The blow halted my charge but not my blade. The Sword of Innocence shot forward at the statue's gut. It leapt backward but I dashed forward.

We traded blows. The gladius darted in at my stomach and chest. I parried one blow with my sword and the next with my shield. Launching an overhand cleave of my own, the stone sword met my attack with a sound of metal striking stone. Turning my sword so that the flat of the long sword rested against the flat of the gladius, I swept my sword back toward the gladiator's sword hand. When my blade struck the statue's finger, it swung its sword out wide. That's when I roared and stepped in to open the statue's guts with a backhand slash.

The gladiator's stone foot came up in a rising kick. I stopped my advance and leaned back just enough to avoid the blow. The gladiator tucked its leg back toward its body and thrust it forward like a massive piston. Thankfully, I managed to get my shield in front of my sternum before the stone foot hammered in. The force of the blow sounded like a car wreck. My body went flying backward and did a full flip in the air. When I hit the ground, I bounced off my back to land on my stomach before skidding a few feet.

"Can you please never do that again?" I asked the statue. I got to my feet and only stayed there because of the overload of adrenaline in my body.

The gladiator ran up and jutted forward with a thrust. I parried with my sword and sprang ahead. It backed and then swung wildly to back me off. Another blow struck my shield, and I turned and ran to the ramp. It chased after me. As I darted up the incline, I began to swerve from side to side, and the gladiator followed my lead. Once I as out of its attack range I swerved one last time. When it tried to follow, I spun around and dove across the ground at the statue's legs. I came in behind the blow and swung my shield and sword out to their respective sides. Both blows struck opposite ankles, and the sound of metal shearing stone filled my ears.

The stone gladiator overbalanced. I heard its stone ankle crack and break. It fell to my right, down the ramp. Its trailing right foot came up and clipped off my head. I went down along with the statue. We both rolled down the ramp and sprawled out in heaps. It got to its knees first and brought the stone sword down at my head. I was on my right side, so I took my sword in both hands and rolled left with everything I had. Stone and metal clashed, and I forced the gladius out far enough to miss my body.

I sprang to my feet, and the gladiator recoiled from me. Its blade came up defensively, but I batted it aside with my shield. I brought my sword up and around to take the head off the statue. Stone blood spurted out for all of a half second until the whole thing drained of magic. In the end, the statue settled on its knees, the sword out wide and its head in the air with a fountain of stone connecting the decapitated head to the body.

An instant later Aaron's scimitar erupted from the chest of the statue. It stopped two inches short of impaling me. Aaron's head popped up over the statue's shoulder, and he smiled at me. "Saved you buddy!"

"I hate you," I said.

Aaron withdrew his scimitar and stepped around to look me over. There was a bloodstain on his dark shirt, and I realized he had been shot in the chest. His shirt was soaked down to his pants. I could see blood staining his left pant leg and could hear the squish of blood in his boot when he walked. He wasn't bandaged anywhere, and he was moving just fine. I looked at him in the shifting light and saw blood on his face.

"Are you carrying blood?" I asked.

Aaron didn't look up from inspecting my body when he said, "No."

I looked over and saw one of the thugs on the ground. He wasn't moving. Aaron had eaten him. My friend hated eating people, but he was hurt. To heal he needed blood, and the thug was a readily available juice box for vampires. Cautiously my gaze shifted over to Kerri's now pale face. She had probably watched and may have even helped Aaron reach the thug. I don't know if she had ever seen someone die before, but watching a vampire eat someone was a gruesome way to be introduced to death.

Eden sprinted over to me and looked up the ramp. "The sorcerer?" she asked.

I looked back up the ramp. He wasn't there. "Probably rabbited. He can't leave, and you shut off his magic, so now all we have to worry about is if the demon keeps his word or not," I said. I turned to the ramp and started up to the next level.

"I locked down his magic, but he still has those demonic powers, Church Boy," Eden said. She fell in beside me, and then Aaron and Kerri fell in beside us.

"So instead of being a three trick pony, he is a two trick pony. Maybe a one trick pony, since he needs a sculpture to use one of those tricks. I'm betting the gladiator was his heavy," I told them.

"Why?" Kerri asked.

"Because he tried to take us on himself first. The statue was the backup plan," I said.

When we walked onto the fifth level, we found everyone on the floor. There were at least fifty completely nude people engaged in the biggest orgy I had ever seen. Men were having sex with women. Women were having sex with other women. Men were having sex with other men. One guy was masturbating as if he was a pervert hidden in the girl's locker room.

"Oh my," Eden said as she covered her eyes.

"Oh my," Aaron said as he licked his lips.

"Oh my," Kerri said as she grabbed my arm.

"Lions and tigers and bears," I said, way too late, but I said it.

There were no guards that I could see. I opened my mind once more to feel how badly the ritual was getting. I can't see magic, but I saw fire. Fire rose from the floor in waves and trenches. I yelled and darted to the side. The walls were ablaze. The ceiling was burning. My eyes darted around, and all I could see was fire. I swung my sword at the flames in primal fear when I realized that it was all around me. Something powerful got hold of me and flung me into the air.

I heard Eden yelling, "Close your mind, Michael! Close it now!"

I stopped trying to understand the world around me and the fire went away. Aaron had put me into a full nelson. His fingers were locked behind my head, and he had lifted me into the air so that I couldn't get any traction or try to throw him. When I calmed down, he let me go.

"Sorry," I said weakly. "I don't know what that was."

Eden looked at me with cold hard eyes. I couldn't read her expression, but I felt she knew something I didn't. I wanted to ask her about it, but I didn't have a chance. Something howled on the floor above.

Kerri looked up and asked, "Do they have dogs?"

"No," I said. "They have worgs."

CHAPTER 30

KERRI HAD PICKED up more guns, and she had one in each hand. She had three or four more tucked through her belt. Eden had her .22 out, and Aaron drew his mini Uzi. I sheathed my sword, shouldered my shield, drew both of my Desert Eagles, and charged ahead. Well, I tried to charge ahead. There were just too many people on the floor having really elaborate sex. Basically, we had to scoot, shuffle, and slide around people in order to move forward. This was no place to have a fight.

The howling grew louder, and I could feel the ground shaking under the pounding feet of running beasts. We reached the bottom of the next ramp just as they reached the top. They were four-legged beasts more akin to mutant bulldogs than wolves. There were at least two dozen of the beasts, and they leapt at us with fearless abandon. We didn't hesitate— we all lifted our guns and opened fire. The worgs howled in defiance as fire and thunder filled the air. Eden had the smallest gun among us, but she had her wand as well. She loosed bullets along with bolts of flame that set the worg's fur and skin ablaze. Aaron's weapon had the most killing potential, and combined with his vampire speed the automatic Uzi laid down a constant stream of death. Kerri was firing two guns at once, and each shot seemed to kill a worg. They were constructs of magic, so when we dealt them a lethal blow their bodies dispersed into a combination of ectoplasm and mortal elements.

When I say 'we,' I meant my friends. I had my two Desert Eagles and was firing like a mad man. I don't know if I have mentioned it, but I am not a gun guy. I am pretty sure that I missed with every shot. In my fight with Anfalar, the demon was the size of a small barn and was right in front of me, so even I could hit him. Now was a very different story. The worgs were big, but they were a good distance away and fast as hell. I picked out one and unloaded both of my magazines on it only to have it come within a few yards of me. When it leapt at me, both of my guns clicked on empty.

Kerri put four neat holes into the worg. One in the monster's head, one in the thick neck, and two in its massive chest. While fumbling with my guns in an attempt to reload, I turned to thank Kerri and saw her acquired guns click empty. She ejected the magazines, flipped each gun in her hand, and smacked their ends together. Each gun broke apart into its individual pieces, and she tossed them aside. She drew two more guns and started firing. The little gunfighter started firing again as I continued to fumble with reloading. I finally managed to slap a magazine into each gun and leveled them once again.

The worgs were dead. Bullet shells and discarded magazines littered the ground. I saw scorches from Eden's spells scattered across the ramp. Playing it cool, I checked my gun's slides and holstered them. "Good work guys," I said.

"You missed every shot," Aaron said.

I looked over at him and smiled. "No I didn't."

"Yes you did. You shoot like a girl," he said. Kerri and Eden both cleared their throats. "Well not like those girls. They can shoot. You can't. You should probably stick to playing with dolls."

"What?" I asked.

"Dolls. They are probably a little more your speed," the Vampire said.

"I hate you," I said.

He blew me a kiss. Kerri laughed so hard that she nearly fell over. She stopped when power washed over us. Unseen energy hit us like rain. Along with it came feelings of abandonment, fear, and misery. I had felt this before. I looked to the top of the ramp and watched as a too-thin man with features too angular to be human stepped into view.

"I thought you might bring allies," the demon said.

"I brought friends," I said.

Ophalistis looked at me as if I had switched to a language that he did not understand. He looked over our group. First, he looked at Aaron and narrowed his eyes. When he looked at Eden, he sneered. It scared me when he looked at Kerri. He smiled at her.

"Look behind you," he said. I didn't want to look away. I knew taking my eyes off the demon was a bad idea, but something about the way he was standing, the way he composed himself, told me that I really did need to look behind me. Turning slightly, I felt my eyes grow wide.

The naked people we had just tiptoed through were standing behind us. They all had blank looks on their faces, and they stood still. Not perfectly still, but as still as a living person can manage. I looked hard at the eyes of one man and saw pain. In those eyes were anger and confusion that can only be brought on by intense fear. He was enthralled.

"You will release whatever hold you have on me, witch!" said a shrill and whining voice that could only be Alistair Dyhart. I looked up at him, and the little weasel was hiding behind the demon. He wasn't clutching him like a coward, but he was standing far enough behind Ophalistis that he seemed more like a lurking shadow than a sorcerer.

Eden ignored the sorcerer. She looked at me and asked, "Can you free them?"

In the hospital, I had to focus on each person individually. I just was not use to using the power of my sword. I could probably blanket them all with the simple truth that they would be protected. Fifty people at once would take a lot out of me, probably more than I had to give, but I couldn't leave them like that. My hand moved to my sword and I opened my mouth to speak.

"Kill the wizard," Ophalistis said.

Aaron had never taken his eyes off the demon and the sorcerer. His head snapped to the left, and he leapt at Eden. There was a crack of thunder as something whizzed by me, and then a there was a thump. I watched as Aaron and Eden fell to the ground. Eden screamed, and the gentle pulse of her power stopped. I turned around and found Kerri with a blank expression on her face. Her Baby Desert Eagle was in her hand, and she was training on Eden to finish her off.

I leapt and managed to grab her arm, but she fought me. She punched and kicked at me with a viciousness that I don't believe she could have normally managed. Her free hand came up to rake my eyes, and I was forced to lean back. Kerri tried to wrench her gun hand free, but I held on.

"Kerri, stop!" I yelled. She tried to knee me in the groin, but I blocked with my hips. Her free hand darted down, and she pulled out the hammer I had given her. She lifted it right from her hip in a vicious blow. I managed to get grab her wrist just before she cracked my jaw open.

"Kerri stop, it's me! It's Michael, your boyfriend!" I pleaded. She started banging her head into my chest and roaring with determination to get past me to shoot Eden.

"Enough!" yelled Dyhart. He was standing beside Ophalistis now. He sneered down at us as Kerri struggled against me. "Kill them as you see fit, but bring me the knight and the sword. Bring his pretty bitch, too. I want her to watch him die. I am going to finish the ritual."

The sorcerer walked away and left us alone with the demon. Ophalistis looked down on us and said nothing. Long moments passed before anything happened other than Kerri struggling. She kept trying to bull through me, but that was like a toddler trying to move a truck. I had her in the size, strength, and weight categories. I wasn't going anywhere.

"Stop struggling against the knight," the demon said. Kerri stopped.

I looked over at Aaron and Eden. Aaron had her cradled in his lap. "Is she…" I started to ask.

"Her arm is broken, she's concussed, and when she comes to she's going to be pissed," Aaron said.

My friend was alive. Good. Go team. I looked up at the demon and snarled. "Let her go! We had a deal."

"Yes," he said. "I am altering the deal."

"Oh hell no! You are not going to Darth Vadar me!"

Again, the demon looked at me as if I was speaking a language he did not understand. He looked at the horde of thralls and said, "Kill the vampire and dismember the wizard." As one, the thralls began to move forward. Their blank expressions changed to ones of murderous rage.

Aaron drew his Uzi and grabbed Eden's gun in his free hand. He set her down gently then spun on the thralls.

"Aaron, wait!" I cried. My friend didn't begin opening fire, but he kept the guns up and ready. "What's the new deal, you bastard?"

"Halt," the demon said. The enthralled horde stopped advancing. "You will come with me, and you will fulfill your end of the deal. But you will leave your underlings behind, along with your armor and weapons with the exception of your gun and sword."

"That's it? You still just want me to kill the sorcerer?" I asked.

"Yes," he said in a matter of fact manner.

"Release the girl," I said.

"No. She is to carry your sword. I will not touch it and do not trust you with it," he said.

"How do I know you won't harm her?" I asked.

"You do not. But those two will be left unmolested," he said with a nod of his head toward Aaron and Eden. "They may even try to leave this place if you like."

I really didn't have a choice. I could shoot him from this distance, but then again I could miss. We were outnumbered by the thralls, and Kerri was one of them. I couldn't fight her. One way or the other I was going to be making a huge mistake. Either I work with the demon or I take my chances with being his enemy. I looked at Kerri and wondered if I could free her.

"Agree or I will tell the girl to kill herself," said Ophalistis.

"I agree!" I blurted out. If I could have seen myself, I bet I would have looked as white as a ghost. I let Kerri go and began to take off my weapons. When I got around to taking off my armor I said, "Aaron, take Eden and figure a way out of the building."

"I am not leaving you," he said.

"You can't help me, Aaron. I want you to find a way to get out," I said. I walked over to Kerri, fished her keys out of her pocket, and tossed them to Aaron. "Get Emory and Priest Greyshadow. Get out of town."

"Michael..." Aaron started to say something, but I cut him off.

"Don't you go getting all gushy on me. Get Eden out. I don't need you. Go!" I said as I dropped the last of my armor to the ground. When I was done, I was wearing only my hat, Darkwing Duck tee shirt, pants, and boots. I ejected the fresh magazine I had put in my black Desert Eagle. I loaded in my last magazine and slipped the gun into my pant waist behind my back and pulled my shirt down over it.

"Michael...I just want you to know something. It's really important," Aaron said as he gathered Eden up in his arms.

"What is it?" I asked.

"Emory and I never really thought you were gay," he said. "We just liked having you at our parties, and you creeped the girls out, so we told everyone you were in the closet."

I bit my bottom lip and shook my head. "Aaron, you are my best friend. That's saying a hell of a lot right now."

201

"I love you too, man," said Aaron. Then he turned to leave.

I turned to Kerri and handed her my sheathed sword. I looked up at Ophalistis and shrugged as I said, "Alright, let's go kill a sorcerer."

CHAPTER 31

WALKING WITH A gun in your pants feels weird. I don't see how people do it. I took the first fifty or so steps thinking that at any second I was going to move one of my legs too much and shoot myself in the butt. The safety was on, but even that did nothing to help. I was going to be the first knight in history to shoot himself in the butt. In addition, it wasn't fooling anyone. My gun is huge. If I turned even slightly sideways Dyhart was going to see it.

We walked across the next level of the garage, and it was empty. There were no victims, no goons, and no cars. That did not take away from the desecration of the floor. Arcane symbols were written up and down the floor, on the walls, and on the ceiling. I couldn't read them, and I didn't have to. They were symbols of pain and death. I knew that because, in my experience, those are the only kinds of symbols that are always written in blood. There were hundreds of symbols, and every single one was written in blood.

"Where did you get all the blood?" I asked.

"From mortals," the demon said. His tone was no different than at any point before now, but that simple statement was said with an absolute lack of emotion.

"What mortals?" I asked with a growl to my voice.

"Mortals from this city," he said in the same tone as before.

I grabbed Ophalistis by the shoulder and spun him around to face me. He did not so much as blink an eye when I did.

"Why?" I asked.

"Why what?" There was no emotion to his voice, no flavor, no accent, nothing! It was as if he was a digital recording for a suicide hotline.

"Why did you kill those people?" I asked.

Calmly and as if speaking to a slow child, he said, "Because mortals have blood and are easily slaughtered."

"How many people did you kill to do this?" I growled.

"Enough to finish the necessary amount of symbols for the ritual," Ophalistis said.

I let him go. There was no point in questioning him. It was an odd feeling to realize I was angry with a being that could not understand why I was angry. Demons are by their nature evil. They are created from and for death, depravity, hatred, and unspeakable actions. To be angry at a demon for murdering anyone would be the same as being angry at a baby for crying. It was a waste of my energy.

The demon turned around, and we resumed our slow march to the top floor. As we walked, I went over everything in my head. A sorcerer had started throwing raves to gather people together as sacrifices. What bothered me about all the raves was that only three demons had been summoned, and not many people had been killed when you thought about the fact each rave had upwards of two hundred people. Furthermore, both the sorcerer and the surviving demon had come to see me. When you finally get a moment to think, you get to figure out things that you normally wouldn't. I might be a private investigator, but this wasn't some who-dun-it noir. This was a train wreck, and I was on the tracks. These guys didn't try to avoid me, they didn't try to hide from me, and they didn't kill me when they had the chance. Multiple chances really. They wanted me here, and they wanted me alive.

They had me right where they wanted me.

When we reached the final ramp, I looked up expecting to see the stars in the sky. There were no stars. The sky I knew was gone. Where the sky was supposed to be was a span of red that looked like it could have been the sky if we were in a world filled with fire and lava. Or a plane of pain and punishment, like Hell. I looked at that blazing sky and saw dark nebulous swirls spotting the expanse. Those dark swirls were in the exact spots where stars should be. I guess that in Hell they make it a point to snuff out any light that may resemble hope.

That sky terrified me. I am a Knight of the First Order, a reasonably good Christian, and I once tried to be a boy scout. I was kicked out of the scouts, and as for the other two groups, I am sure they would love to get rid of me. Standing in a place that was being claimed by Satan and his crew, I had to wonder a few things. Did my faith matter at all here? Would my sword still glow with the power of God and Heaven? Did the Devil have a special place here for me? To fight against those thoughts, I thought about Kerri and how I might save her. Then I thought about the two of us finding Wild West Mars and having ourselves a good old time in a barn…in Wild West Mars.

I looked over at Kerri and wanted nothing more than to save her. Here she was in the middle of a trap set for me and enthralled by a demon. She didn't deserve to die here. She didn't deserve to be tied up in a world of magic, mayhem, and monsters. She deserved to live a fabulous life. She deserved to see art, hear music, and read books. She deserved a guy that had a stable job, a nice car, and normal friends.

Right now all she has is you, I thought. I think. My head was pounding.

The sound of an asshole pulled me out of my contemplation. "Finally, the knight is here," cackled the sorcerer.

I looked up to see Alistair Dyhart standing at a small altar in the middle of a magic circle drawn in blood. It had a fifty-foot diameter, and there were dishes of burning herbs spaced around the circle. Some dishes were not filled with herbs. They were filled with the remains of the people that had been killed to make that circle. The smell of burning blood and flesh mixed with exotic spices that were never meant for such things.

To the side of the circle was a bunch of equipment crates and tables stacked with digital equipment. I am a homebody, so I have no idea what all of it was called, but I do know that it was all DJ equipment. Turn tables, laptops, synthesizers, and stacks of records. None of that really mattered. The drawn-looking young man with dark sunken eyes was what caught my attention. He was bloody, but that blood was old. I could smell him over everything else in the building. He was wearing torn rags that smelled horrible. They were black and brown with filth and sweat. There was a metal collar around his neck, and it had a chain attached to it that lead down to a cement block on a pushcart. His nails were long, and he had a scraggly beard that was filled with clumps of blood and dirt.

"Look around you, slave of God," Dyhart continued. "This is the new world. This is a better world." He spun around to take in the sky and the surrounding evil. He had his arms out wide and held a curved knife in his hand. Finally, he spun around to face me and said, "Or it will be once you die and I bring Hell onto earth."

Chapter 32

MY ODDS WEREN'T good. The sorcerer was standing inside an empowered magic circle, which meant I probably couldn't shoot him. A demon wanted to use me as an assassin. Said demon had my girlfriend enthralled. My girlfriend had my magic sword. We were in a building that was slowly being taken over by Hell. In addition, I had this poor dude behind the turntables to worry about.

If things weren't bad enough, this was the point where the burning herbs started setting off my allergies. I reached into my pocket and pulled out a bottle of over-the-counter allergy meds. Once it was opened, I tossed a few into my mouth. They were tablets, not capsules. That meant they were chewable even though they tasted horrible. When your allergies are as bad as mine are, you get used to doing whatever you have to just to get through the day.

"What are you doing?" Dyhart asked.

"I have allergies," I said. "Don't let me stop your tirade; just keep talking and explain your evil plan…or plot…yeah plot. I'll jump in when I'm ready to thwart you."

That threw the bastard for a loop. He stuttered a bit as he processed what I was doing. Meanwhile, I walked over to the turntables and spoke softly to the young man. It was a blessing my nose was stuffed up, because the smell coming off him was almost homicidal.

"Hey man. What's your name?" I asked.

He didn't answer me. Fear caused him to shrink away. You could tell from his slack skin and drawn face he hadn't eaten in weeks, not properly at least. His eyes were hollow, as though hope itself had been ripped out through them with pliers. Dyhart yelled some threat at me, but I ignored him. I reached into my pocket and pulled out a protein bar. The young man watched me wearily as I held the protein bar out to him. Then suddenly his hand darted forward, and he snatched the offered food from me. It went straight to his mouth where he ripped into the wrapper with his teeth...what was left of them.

"You will answer me, knight!" Dyhart yelled.

I stiffened and took a deep breath before saying, "You came to my house to talk, but instead you ruined my door and my neighbor's lawn ornaments. You decided to sic a three-headed snake on me at the police station. You threw fire at me downstairs. You had your three strikes. I will get to kicking your ass in a minute."

Again, the sorcerer stuttered. I smiled at the young man as he licked the wrapper clean. I held out another protein bar in my right hand. He looked at it hungrily.

"What is your name?" I asked again.

"Na...na...na...Nathan Swa...Swanson," he said.

I knew something about names. Names were power. They were identity. They were given to you at birth by those that loved us before we existed. Sometimes they were given by those that wanted to love us. Sometimes they were forced upon us. Sometimes they were things that we chose for ourselves.

"What is your real name, Nathan?" I asked.

He looked at me as if I had just opened a vault of gold. He smiled with his broken teeth and bloody gums as he said, "DJ Straight Base."

I tossed him the protein bar. "Well, DJ Straight Base, I am going to get you out of here and get you some help. Just hold on a minute, okay?"

He looked at me and trembled. His words came out in sputters and squeals, and he was on the edge of breaking. "They kill people. They beat, rape, and kill them! They have guns and fire, and they keep making me watch them kill people. There are demons!"

I widened my smile so he could see that I wasn't afraid. Then I said, "I know. None of that matters. I am going to put a stop to all of it." Straight Base looked at me as though I were a lunatic.

I turned to find Alistair Dyhart trembling with rage inside his magical circle. His right hand was wreathed in green fire. I never stopped smiling as I spoke. "Now we can talk. Surrender and I won't have to hurt you."

"Surrender?" he asked.

"Yeah. It's easy. Surrender and we can stop this insanity," I said.

The fire around his hand erupted to engulf the length of his forearm.

Alistair Dyhart ground his teeth when he spoke. "So arrogant. So self-righteous. You are so used to getting everything you want, aren't you?"

I scratched my head. "No…I pretty much get told no a lot. I also get called names and told to go away."

"You just ram your religion down people's throats. You bully people and do whatever you want," he growled. He wasn't listening to me.

"I know that as a knight I should be more devout, but religion isn't a big thing with me. I pretty much just let people believe what they want and leave them alone. As for the bullying, I am anti-bullying."

"LIES!" he screamed. "YOU LIE AND YOU JOKE AND YOU ACT LIKE YOU ARE SO MUCH BETTER THAN ME!"

I got the sudden feeling that this wasn't about me. His anger was directed at me, but not in the least about who I was. This was about *what* I was to him.

"Alistair, stop this!" I screamed back at him. "Whatever problem you think you have with me or anyone else will not be solved by unleashing Hell on earth!"

"That's where you are wrong, knight! Once I open a portal to Hell, the odds will be evened. You and your kind will finally get what you deserve," he preached. "No longer will the strong outnumber the weak. No longer will the privileged prey upon those that have to earn their keep. No more war, no more famine, no more lies! The true chosen have promised me an end to God's falsehood and tyranny."

Okay, there were definitely some lies going around, and I was starting to get the feeling it wasn't just Dyhart that was being lied to. On a side note, it wasn't just me that was being manipulated. I looked over at the demon and saw a too-wide grin on his too-perfect face.

"But before that," the sorcerer said, "before that I am going to hurt you. You who thought you were so powerful and so righteous."

I started edging to my left so that Straight Base wasn't directly behind me. "What are you going to do? If you throw that fireball, you will break your precious circle. I'm no expert, but I know that once you do that I can kick your ass," I said. I was baiting him, because I needed him to break the circle since I didn't know how to do it myself. As long as he stayed behind it, he was going to win. "So why don't you just pipe down and put away the tiny bit of magic you have managed to scrape together. Leave the spell slinging to the big kids like my wizard friend. You don't have the brains to pull off a real spell anyway."

"Brains? What would you know about brains, you muscle-bound fool? Did you even finish high school?"

I grinned. "Yeah…actually, you and I have a lot more in common than you think. You're a district attorney, right? Well, I have a law degree!"

"Huh?" he asked.

"Yeah…I studied law. You keep calling me stupid and saying I'm an idiot, but I have to tell you, dude, that you are in the wrong profession. Law is all about memorization, research, and litigation. All you do is parrot case studies and debate issues. It's kind of simple," I chuckled.

Alistair Dyhart started shaking, and his green spell fire roared up his entire arm. "What did you say?" he growled.

I slipped my hands casually behind my back and lifted my shirt. I put my right hand on my gun and got ready to push the sorcerer over the edge. "I said that law was mind-numbingly boring. That's why I got a second degree in architecture. Seriously, it takes skill to build a tool shed. To have an assistant research precedent or even better to google it? Man, that is easy mode!"

Alistair Dyhart screamed, and I got ready to do the most awkward draw of my life. I didn't take the safety off or put my hand on the trigger. I was still convinced that I was going to shoot myself in the butt if I did. Fire roared, but Alistair didn't throw his spell at me. Instead, he grinned at me and chuckled.

"You would love for me to break this circle, wouldn't you?" he asked. He dropped his spell and the green flames vanished. "If I break the circle, you think you can run in and stop me. No fool. No."

Darn it! So close. I relaxed my grip before I shot myself in the butt.

"Is that your whore?" Dyhart asked as he turned his gaze to Kerri.

"Don't you ever call her that!" I barked. Every muscle in my body tensed as if I was going to charge at him.

"I remember the first night you stuck your nose in my business. You hit Ophalistis in the eye with that hammer she has, didn't you?" he asked. "Ophalistis, make her hit herself in the eye with the hammer."

"No!" I yelled.

I looked at the demon, and he grinned at me. I turned my attention to Kerri as she drew out my hammer. Calmly she held it out low and in front of herself. She brought it up to her face with all of her strength. I didn't think I could stop the blow by grabbing her wrist, so I buried her head in a massive hug. The hammer hit me in the kidney and I screamed. I don't know how I moved fast enough to get to her, but I had and I was thankful. Then she tried to hit herself again and hit me right where she had a moment before.

"Kerri, stop it!" I yelled. She struck me again.

Ophalistis spoke softly. "Kill him and I will make her stop."

Dyhart screamed, "That's right you stupid cunt, beat him bloody!"

Kerri hit me again, and I stumbled down to one knee. I darted back up when I felt her rotate her shoulder. I took a blow to the back of my head. The blow knocked my hat off, and I fell to the ground. I grabbed my skull in pain as Kerri lined up for another swing.

My hat flipped and spun in the air as it fell. Kerri's arm began to move toward her face. All I could do was watch. Alistair cackled with joy, and I screamed in defiance. My hat landed on her head. It was a bit lopsided and too big for her, but it flopped right into place atop her head.

White light erupted into the world. My sword could cut through darkness, but this light was ten times brighter than my sword had ever been. That hat, a run-of-the-mill baseball cap, was a symbol of my faith. I wore a crucifix, and yes it represented my belief in Christ, but it was nothing compared to what that hat meant to me. Baseball was my favorite sport, and it was one of the few times that I felt the power of faith as a child. When I played or watched baseball, I saw people put aside differences and struggle toward a goal. I felt triumph and defeat. I felt what it meant to be alive! My hat reminded me that God loved us because he gave us simple things like baseball.

Ophalistis screamed and ran away. He wasn't looking where he was going, and he hit the waist-high barrier that separated us from the ramp. He flipped over it and went head first down the ramp. Alistair screamed in pain as well.

The light only lasted an instant, and when it faded, Kerri was holding the hammer in her hand with no intention of striking herself. She looked down at me and dropped to her knees. My sword and the hammer fell to the ground between us, and she wrapped her arms around me.

211

"Michael! Michael, I'm sorry!" Tears streamed from her eyes, and her pleas for forgiveness drowned out the demon and sorcerer's screams of pain in my ears.

I smiled at her. "I'm fine. Don't worry," I said. I didn't show her the blood on my glove when I pulled my hand from my head. I pulled the hat down on her head and straightened it. Then I grabbed my sword and forced myself to stand up. "Go over there with the DJ and stay out of the way, okay?"

I helped Kerri to her feet, and she wrapped her arms around me. "No, no, no. We have to leave."

I hugged her. "Kerri, go over there and get down. When this fight starts, I need you out of the way. Please?"

"How are you going to fight a demon and a sorcerer?" she asked as she sobbed into my shirt.

I couldn't think of anything to say to her. She was scared. I was scared. With all the cliché heroic things I usually thought of and all the battle cries that I played around with, nothing came to mind. I couldn't even lighten the mood.

"I don't know, but I can't win if I am focused on you. Go. Trust in me. Trust in Jesus. Trust in God. Trust in The Holy Ghost," I told her as I kissed her forehead.

She pulled me down into a full kiss on the mouth. She said nothing when she pulled away and ran over to hide behind the turn tables with Straight Base. I flipped my sword belt over my chest so that my sword handle was over my right shoulder. Then I reached behind my back and spun the handle of my gun so I could draw it with my left hand.

Ophalistis came up the ramp. He had dropped the human disguise. He stood a full ten feet in height. The demon was built like a warrior, with lean muscle from head to hooved foot. His skin was black-orange, and he had no hair anywhere on his body. His face was humanoid, but he had sharkish features. His teeth were all sharps, and his mouth looked more like a snout or beak. Twin-ridged horns three feet in length were atop his head. He had claws on each of his five fingers, and he was completely naked. His four-foot cock was shriveled like he had just taken a cold shower.

Alistair Dyhart had gotten back to his feet as well. The sorcerer began to rant and rave as he screamed, "Kill him, Ophalistis, kill him!"

I watched the demon look at the sorcerer and then at me. He sneered as he asked, "Why have you not raised a hand to the sorcerer?"

I smiled. "Because I figured out that killing him was the point. He's a pawn. You wanted me to kill him because...well, I haven't figured that out yet. But you never cared if I stopped the ritual. You could have done that much."

The demon sneered. "Perhaps you are not as idiotic as you seem."

"That, or maybe bad guys are stupid and ugly."

"KILL HIM OPHALISTIS!" Dyhart screamed.

"If you aren't going to kill the fool, then I have no use for you," the demon said.

"I know. I'm not doing your dirty work or playing your games anymore," I said as I spread my feet apart.

Ophalistis reached the top or the ramp and said, "You are outnumbered, human. You are so close to Hell that your God has forgotten you. This time I will not be drunk on blood or beer."

"Kill him!" the sorcerer screamed again.

"I have God on my side," I said.

"And the force!" yelled Kerri.

"Yeah!" I said.

"God and Sith Lords!" yelled Kerri.

I looked back at her with one eyebrow lifted. "Really? Sith?"

"The dark side has cookies and lightning. It's not evil, it's just passionate," she said.

To each her own. "Yeah. I have God and the Sith on my side."

"Kill him! Kill him! Kill him!" the sorcerer screamed.

Ophalistis bellowed a battle roar that shook the building. Straight Base cried out in fear.

Kerri yelled, "Michael!"

Me...I still had nothing to say. I had an irate sorcerer at my back, a demon charging my front, and I was standing in between the mortal world and Hell. I had nothing! All I could do was drop into a battle stance, grab my sword's sheath with my left hand, and grab the Sword of Innocence's handle with my right.

The moment my hand touched my sword, my voice rang out like a trumpet. The words weren't mine...but they were. I knew them as well as I knew my own name, my own choices, and my own direction in life. They flowed out of me as if I had been born for the sole purpose of saying them. They were not fancy or elegant. They simply were an expression of who I was and what I did.

When I saw danger, I did not turn away. When someone asked for help, I stepped forward. When life got hard, I didn't complain—I rose to the challenge. It did not make me special or make me a hero. It simply made me, me. So when a demon and a sorcerer decided to kill me, when they decided to open a portal to Hell in my city, when everyone cried out as the battle began, and when all the noise started, I spoke those words.

"BRING IT!"

CHAPTER 33

OPHALISTIS DID JUST that. He charged me like a freight train. I bent my legs, shifted my weight onto my toes, and charged straight at him. He had me beat in weight by at least 200 pounds of solid muscle, and he was moving faster than I could if I dropped into a dead sprint down a steep hill. Charging him was a foolish and suicidal move, which is why it was perfect for taking on a demon that was used to completely overpowering mortals.

When Ophalistis opened his arms wide to rake both claws at me, I sprang forward inside his reach and ducked low. My left hand grabbed his collarbone while my right grabbed his groin as he started to barrel over me. I yanked down with my left and pushed up with my right to lift the demon over me in a high arch. Using his own momentum, I threw him over my shoulder and straight at Dyhart. He hit the invisible barrier that was protecting the sorcerer, and the violent energies contained within surged at him like a plasma ball. Orange lighting struck him without a crack of thunder, and the demon screamed before falling to the ground.

Smoke rose from the demon's flesh, and for an instant I thought he was done. Glancing behind me, I saw his feet had cracked the ground as he ran. I turned back to Ophalistis, and of course he was getting up. He roared in anger as he climbed back to his feet, and an idea came to me. If this was going to be a boss fight, I was going to make it one to remember.

"Hey DJ!" I yelled. "How about dropping a phat beat for me to kick some demon butt to?"

"Music?" yelled Dyhart. "You want music? Something to die to? A funeral march? He is a demon, you Christian fool! We are in Hell! When you die, I will watch your shade rise from your body to suffer an eternity at my Master's hand!"

I gripped my sword and sheath. I wrung my fingers on the handle. *Don't let them see you sweat*, I thought to myself.

The demon got to its feet and bellowed. I wrung my fingers again as fear began to set in. There was no way I could match the demon in speed or strength. I had my sword, but if it came at me like that again I wasn't going to get in another lucky throw. I was going to have to go toe-to-toe with it, and I didn't have armor, back up, or anywhere to run. Ophalistis wasn't a weakling, and he wasn't stupid like Anfalar was. Then there was the sorcerer. He was right. For all intents and purposes, we were in Hell. The bad guys had the home field advantage. I started to loosen the grip I had on my sword as Ophalistis' roar died away.

That's when a chorus sang out "Do do do doooo" not once but thrice. Then Bonnie Tyler demanded to know where all the good men had gone and where were all the gods. I answered by drawing my sword and letting the Sword of Innocence show that the power of God was indeed here. The sword's light pressed against the red light of Hell's sky, and all around me white lighting danced with orange lightning. The bolts did not strike anything but each other, and when they did, the night of the mortal world showed like a shattered window in the air. I cut a look at Kerri and saw her holding up a record album proclaiming me to be a hero. To be her hero.

Ophalistis didn't rush me this time. He summoned orange flames into one of his clawed hands. The flames took a spherical shape the size of a bowling ball, and I could smell brimstone and sulfur over the burning flesh and drugs of the summoning circle. Every mortal creature knows that smell. It is buried somewhere in the most primal and fearful reaches of our minds. The demon stepped forward and threw hellfire at me.

"Batter up!" I yelled as I took a right-handed batting stance. I stepped into my swing and hit the hellfire with the flat of my blade. The orb of hellfire met the light of my sword and exploded into burning embers and stinging sparks. They spread around me and hit the ground harmlessly.

"And that one is out of the park people! This young rookie is batting a thousand!" I said in my best announcer voice. The demon threw another ball of hellfire, and this time I put a little English in my swing. My sword struck the orb, and the shower of hellfire exploded to rush past me.

"Oh, that one had some heat to it folks, but White still put it in the hands of a fan in center field! Maybe the home team should consider going to their bullpen—oh wait, their bullpen is an idiot sorcerer with a weak curve!" I said.

That made Dyhart scream, "Kill him, you stupid demon! He is just a man, a depraved fool!"

Ophalistis looked over his shoulder at the sorcerer. I saw another ball of hellfire form in his hand and dropped into a batting stance. "My orders were to make sure the knight killed you, but I never liked that order," the demon snarled. He spun on the sorcerer and shoved the hellfire at him.

Dyhart screamed in terror as the air before him exploded in fire and fury. The heat was intense, and even from thirty feet away my skin felt like it was burning. I crossed my arms defensively and backpedaled from the heat. Fire washed out to the left and right of the demon. It surged into the sky and scorched the ground. When the flames finally died away and the smoke cleared, Dyhart was splayed out on the ground with his hands up in an attempt to shield himself. He didn't need to—his magical circle had protected him from the demon's treachery. He sat there on the ground perfectly healthy and unburnt. The look of shock on his face was genuine.

"This circle isn't supposed to keep out demons or magic," Ophalistis said. "I told you how to erect the circle to keep the knight out."

"It…was too involved," the sorcerer said. "It was too complicated. I just made my normal circle but bigger. I figured it would work fine."

Ophalistis' fist struck the invisible barrier of the magic circle. Again, orange lightning struck his hand, and he kept pounding on the barrier. "You insufferable fool!" he bellowed. "You bastardized the entire ritual! You have ruined the portal!"

"Ruined? But the sky," Dyhart argued.

"A byproduct of your ignorance! The Master gave you power, and you wasted it! You pathetic mortals are all the same. All of you are stupid, foul smelling, and worthless. I will kill you for the Master's revenge!" The demon pounded away at the barrier with blows that would have put dents into a tank.

"Ki…ki….ki…kill me?" Dyhart asked softly. The reality of his choice to make deals with the minions of Hell was setting in.

Ophalistis raged at the barrier, and the sorcerer whimpered in terror. I, being a most honorable and noble Knight of the Crucifixion, allowed this to happen as I charged the demon's back with my sword drawn. I closed the distance to the demon with speed and stealth and plunged my sword at Ophalistis' spine.

"The knight!" screamed the sorcerer.

Ophalistis caught my attack out of the corner of his eye at the last possible second. He leapt to the side just as my blade would have entered his back. I swore and leapt out to my right opposite the demon. We faced each other for an instant before I dared to look over at the sorcerer. I screamed at him, "He wants to kill you, Dyhart!"

"He wants to kill *you*!" the sorcerer said. "You are the enemy here!"

My eyes snapped back to Ophalistis just as his left hand came at me. His raking claws met my blocking sword, and a dull sound of bone striking steel filled the air. Sparks flew up from the point of impact to mix with the white and orange lightning warring all around me. His right claw came in low and swept up high. It was a blow designed to disarm me, but I parried the attack and rolled with it. I came back with my own left to right slash that would have taken the demon in the gut, but he was fast and darted back from the blow.

"Kill him, Ophalistis, while I fix the ritual," the sorcerer said. The little worm scurried away to the small altar he had set up in the middle of the circle and began chanting.

"Dyhart, you dumbass, don't you get you are being used?" I roared as I charged the demon.

I worked my sword furiously, striking with sweeping blows that the demon countered with slashes of his claws. I juked left in the middle of a strike and stepped into a side kick to the demon's right calf with my right leg. He lifted his leg to avoid the blow, and when he did I hopped, planted my right leg, and swung my left in a wide sweep to catch his raised ankle. The collision almost stopped my momentum, but I turned my whole body into the strike. The demon overcorrected as I spun his body on his off balanced leg. He lurched awkwardly and fell. He scrambled on his hands and knees for an instant in an attempt to regain his balance, but he couldn't and hit the ground hard.

I charged ahead with my blade low. The demon looked at me and kicked out his leg at me to keep me back. I let the blow come and jumped up into the air. I meant to come down on that leg and break his bones but that didn't happen. The demon spun up onto his hands with the grace of a professional dancer. His legs whirled around and kicked me across my back with a leg as thick as a car bumper. I arched my back and screamed a breathless scream of pain. My vision flared with pain, and all I could see was red. I hit the ground, bounced, and rolled back up to my feet. I didn't plan to do that, it just happened. God was definitely with me in this fight.

My vision cleared just as the demon hit me with a clothesline in the chest. Half an inch higher and he would have taken my head off, so I hold to God favoring me. I don't know how many times I spun, but it didn't stop when my head skimmed the ground. I came back to my feet, and they scrapped the ground before I fell on my back.

I could see stars, and not the cool ones you see when you hurt your head. I was in a nexus between Hell and the mortal world, so the stars I saw were dark and evil. They were jerks. They told me to stay down and to stop fighting. That made sense. I was in pain, and I really didn't know which way was up, so how could I get up to fight. Maybe those stars were cool guys after all.

Ophalistis stood over me and lifted his claw before me. Five clawed fingers came at me, and five clawed fingers went through me. Three went through my chest, one went through my gut, and one got me just above the groin. I tried to scream, but my mouth filled with blood. The demon lifted me above his head and shook me vigorously.

"Drop the sword mortal," he said as his claws ripped longer trenches into my flesh, muscle, and organs.

I looked down at the demon and sneered at him. I gripped my sword and called upon Truth. My voice carried the power of the heavens when I said, "Go back to Hell."

Ophalistis roared and slammed me into the ground. I felt my ribs break. The power of Truth was still in my voice when I screamed, so my pain echoed through the heavens. But I held onto my sword! I swung my blade in desperation and cut into the demons chin. He jerked me back into the air and slammed me down repeatedly. I lost consciousness, but I regained it when he lifted me up to his lips and bit into my right arm with his double row of two-inch teeth.

I screamed as blood ran freely from my mouth. My arm went numb, and I heard my sword clink against the ground. The duel between white and orange lightning ended as the Sword of Innocence fell silent. The demon pulled away and took my arm in its hand. It lifted my mangled limb before me, and I realized that my tattoos weren't going to heal that anytime soon. The bones were broken and my muscles were severed at odd angles. Looking at it reminded me of a microwaved hot dog. My skin was ruptured in places where muscle, tendon, and bone darted out where they were never meant to be. I couldn't scream anymore; my lungs were filling with blood.

The demon laughed. I could hear Kerri screaming. She called my name and yelled at the demon to release me. "Let him go!" she screamed. "Stop it! Let him go!"

"Your lover? I can smell her on you," said Ophalistis. "It is your faith that protects her. Hers alone was nothing to me. When you die so will your faith, and I will make her a gift to the master."

That was never going to happen. I drew my gun and pointed it at the demon's ugly face. Its eyes went wide as I pulled the trigger. Then my eyes went wide when I realized that the safety was still on. On reflex, the demon shoved me away from him. My body flew free of his claws, and they hurt just as bad coming out as going in. Blood trailed from my body as I flew through the air. There was a dull thud when I hit the ground.

My eyes were closed. I opened them and lifted my neck to look around. Ophalistis was standing a good distance away. He looked pissed. I bent my neck back and saw Alistair Dyhart kneeling two feet away from me. He was still chanting and trying to fix whatever he had messed up with the ritual.

I clicked off the safety, lifted my gun above my head, and said, "Stop it." The sorcerer kept chanting. I thumbed back the hammer on my gun and said, "Stop it!" The sorcerer continued to chant. Sweat rolled down his brow, and he trembled with fear. I gritted my teeth and spoke to him one last time, "Stop it now!"

The sorcerer shook his head. He glared at me, and I saw hate in his eyes—hate that came from a lifetime of torment. Hate that came from being bullied for being smaller and weaker than the other children. Hate that was tempered by being forced to practice the religion of his tormentors. He had been persecuted for no reason other than being different, being smaller, being weaker, being quiet, being interested in learning. He had prayed for help, and his prayers were not answered with a magic sword. He did not have a friend willing to devote her life to him. He didn't even have the support of his family. They had bullied him as well. The hate had driven him to pursue vengeance, and his lust for it had been a form of prayer. Demons had answered him. Demons had given him power, and demons had given him an enemy. The man pointing the gun at him now.

I pulled the trigger…and eased the hammer back down. I couldn't kill someone that was so messed up in the head. I wanted to stop him, and I knew that killing him would do it, but I am not that guy. I am not the monster Alistair Dyhart thought I was. In the end, he was a mortal man, lied to by demons, driven mad by torment, and in need of help. He…was an innocent. If not for my family and Kerri, I could be the one trying to bring Hell to earth.

"Kill him, knight," Ophalistis said. "Kill him. He is a fool. He threatens your precious mortals. Kill him and save them. Kill him and end this farce."

I watched as Alistair Dyhart finally caught on to what was happening. He didn't stop chanting, but he did look up at Ophalistis as if the demon had slapped him. Then he looked at me, then back to the demon, and then back at me. A better person would have told him not to be afraid or not to worry. A better knight would have tried to calm him down. But I was bleeding out and in too much pain for that, so I just told him the truth.

"Yes, you dumb fuck! He's a fucking demon! A DEMON! They lie! They kill for no reason, and you thought he was your buddy! YOU FUCKED UP!" Saying that many words at once nearly made me pass out. I took a breath and calmed myself. Then I said, "Don't worry. Just stop chanting. I'll handle this."

It surprised me when the sorcerer actually stopped chanting. If everything started going right, then we might really be in trouble.

"I broke the barrier when I crossed it, didn't I?" I asked Dyhart.

"Yes, but—"

I cut him off. "Well that's fine. Like I said, I got this."

"But you don't understand!" he yelled.

"You were lied to. They manipulated you. I get it. I am not going to hurt you. Now be quiet and let the ritual die out. I have a demon to kill."

"You reject your soul, knight! You reject the truth of who you are! You have failed the Master!" roared the demon.

I stood up. Everything hurt. My right arm was useless. My sword was behind the demon. I still had my gun, and I had a job to do. I walked over to the edge of the circle and looked at the seething demon walking straight at me. He growled at me, and I spit blood on the ground at my feet.

"Hey, Ophalistis, who is your master?" I asked.

He stopped marching, looked at me with a puzzled expression, and said, "You know whom I serve, mortal."

I shrugged. "Hell is a big place. Demons exist in many different forms and go by many different names. I just want to know who you report to."

"I serve the one true Master. Lucifer, Greatest of the Fallen." The demon smiled when he said it. He was pleased with himself, with his master, and with the thought of killing all of us.

"Well tell your master this city is off limits. He has no claim here. If he so much as wants to take a stroll down one of Baltimore's streets, he had better check in with me first," I said as I leveled my gun.

The demon laughed at me again. "You think your mortal weapon can harm me?"

"Yep." I took a deep breath. I exhaled half of it, pulled the trigger, and put an explosive round in his kneecap. Flesh and bone went flying in every direction, and his lower leg fell off. I had aimed for his chest.

The demon howled. The kickback from my gun sent a wave of pain through my body that almost dropped me to the ground. I gritted my teeth and rose back into a shooting stance. Now I am a horrible shot, but even I can hit a target on the range once in a while. Right now Ophalistis was struggling to stand less than fifty feet from me. When the demon pitched over I calmly took another deep breath and shot his other knee. This time on purpose. He howled again as his remaining leg blew apart. Again, the effort nearly dropped me, but I was ready this time and grunted through the pain.

I stalked over to the demon and fired into each of his arms. He was already healing, but I wasn't going to give him the chance. I knelt down to the demon and said, "Tell your master that Michael White will never serve him."

The demon laughed. "If you strike me down, I will just return for you later, mortal."

"When you do, I will cut off your head." I pulled the trigger and put a bullet in the demon's forehead. Blood, gore, and blue fire filled the air as the fiend burned. Its body would return to Hell whole, and he would be furious.

Everything went quiet. The battle was over. Good had triumphed over evil. Lives had been saved. Kerri ran over and hugged me. I wanted to scream when she wrapped her arms around me. My bones were setting themselves, but touching them was only going to cause them to fracture. Firing my gun had been painful enough. Now I had the woman I love crushing me in a hug as if I was some sort of hero. I winced through the pain. She had been through enough without me screaming at her touch. I soldiered through her embrace.

When she let me go, I turned to Alistair and said, "Okay, now that this is all over you can release everyone and give me the key to the DJ's chains, Alistair."

"No," said the sorcerer.

I looked at him hard for a moment. My mind raced to where my sword lay on the ground behind me. I thought of pushing Kerri away and sprinting over to my sword. If I had to fight this sorcerer now, I would have no choice but to fight with the intent to kill him. Anything less and I would be forfeiting the lives of everyone in the city.

"Alistair, I don't want to do it, but I will kill you if you don't stop the ritual right now," I said. I put my hand on Kerri's shoulder to get her out of the way when things went down. I shouldn't have bothered; she already had her gun out down by her side.

"I can't stop it," Alistair said. "The ritual is done. It's beginning."

CHAPTER 34

I PICKED UP my sword and walked over to the altar where the sorcerer was standing. Kerri had her gun ready and was standing at my side. I looked Alistair in the eyes, and he shrank away from my gaze. I didn't have any patience left for the man. He may have been an innocent, but he was a pain in my ass.

"How will it happen?" I asked.

Alistair held up his curved knife. "I was supposed to kill someone upon the altar. Their soul would be bonded with Hell, and when I burned the body that energy would be released into the air. The portal would open merging Hell with Earth."

"So…since the demon wanted Michael on his side, he wasn't going to let you sacrifice him—and you didn't want to anyway. You wanted to kill him outright. Which means you were going to sacrifice me," Kerri said. The sorcerer started to say something in his defense, but Kerri put her gun in his face. Seriously, she put the barrel right in his eye. "Just so you know, everyone here has figured out that the demon wanted Michael to kill you on that altar. That was the Devil's order. Get it? The guy you worship tossed you out like a pimp does a used-up whore."

That was probably the harshest thing I had ever heard Kerri say. I saw the fear of death fade from Alistair's eye, and it was replaced by something else. Something sad. He had been betrayed. The poor bastard had been betrayed by everything he believed in. I felt sorry for him, but I am an idiot. In my idiocy, I put my hand on Kerri's gun arm and pushed it down. She pushed her gun back up, but I forced her arm down. I shook my head and she started to argue. I held up my hand.

"No. We have bigger problems." I turned back to Alistair. "What happens if you don't kill someone with the knife?" I asked.

"The spell will rebound and…" he said. He turned pale and choked on his own words.

"It will kill you," I said.

"Serves your ass right," Kerri said.

"Kerri!" I said.

"No! It serves him right! He kills people! He was going to kill both of us! You are the knight, not me! I say we dance a fucking jig on his grave."

I couldn't blame her, but that wasn't going to happen. "Judge not less ye be judged," I said.

"Then someone judge me!" she snapped. "No one has the right to kill anyone, and this asshole does not deserve our sympathy or help, Michael!"

I looked her in the eyes and said, "Everyone deserves help. I have to believe that. If I don't, then I will end up being more lost than the people I should be helping."

Kerri shook her head, but she did not argue further. Alistair was just standing by waiting for us to make a decision with his life.

"What happens if the knife is used but doesn't kill anyone?" I asked.

He shook his head. "I don't know. Probably the spell would merge with the soul, but that would be like having a piece of Hell inside them. No one could survive that. As long as the body didn't burn, I guess the portal wouldn't open."

"Okay, this is what we are going to do. First give me the knife," I said. He did, and I nodded to him. "Next I want you both to go unchain DJ Straight Base. Then I want you all to go get Eden. She can fix this."

No one argued. They both got a move on and took the stairs instead of the ramps. That would be a lot faster. We hadn't taken them up for fear of bullets being fired down on us. They would be back in a few minutes. That was good.

I managed to take the knife in my right hand. Then I gritted my teeth and pressed the tip of the knife into the palm of my left hand. Eventually this knife was going to cut someone. When something is imbued with magic for a purpose, it tends to fulfill that purpose one way or another. So I wasn't about to let some poor innocent nick their finger and end up with their soul merged with Hell. It would probably kill them outright. I didn't think I would fare any better, but I could at least die doing my job.

Something touched me. It wasn't physical. It wasn't supernatural. It just…was! I felt it in my throat. No, that isn't right. I felt it where my throat should have been, but it didn't fit. It was too vast, too broad, and too sharp to be in my throat. That touch was in my spine as well. I felt it in my heart and then my groin. Something was touching me all over.

I swallowed and told myself I could handle this. Then I started to pull the knife away from my hand. However, that strange touch gently pushed the knife further into my flesh. The knife slid deeper into my palm as I tried to pull my hands apart. That strange touch turned my arms so that I could watch the knife emerge from the other side of my hand.

As blood ran from both my palm and the back of my hand, I bit my lip to keep from screaming. I pulled with all of my strength, but the knife would not come out of my hand. As I struggled, a voice more beautiful and confident than any I had ever heard before whispered into my ear. I couldn't describe it. It was cold and distant, but at the same time it was warm and close. It only said one word, and it was enough to let me know that I could not handle this.

"*Perish.*"

I screamed. I screamed like a mad man. I screamed like a coward. I screamed like a baby. I screamed! I knew that voice. Everyone knew that voice. I don't know how, but I knew exactly who had spoken to me. I knew who was touching me!

"Lucifer!" I screamed.

"*You are mine now,*" the voice said.

I fell to my knees, and every muscle tensed up. My body began to shake, to panic. Worse, I could feel my heart slowing down.

"*False Knight. Judas reborn. Fake Christian. You were never his. Always were you mine,*" the voice said.

I looked into myself for my faith. I closed my eyes and reached out to touch...nothing! There was nothing there. My faith, my belief in something more than myself, was gone.

"*Faith? You? When has God touched you? Was it when the boys in your school tied you up and threw you into the dumpster? Was it when the nurse switched your booster shot with chloride? Or when your teacher beat you with the wooden pointer?*" the voice asked.

"None of that had anything to do with God," I said. Tears were rolling from my eyes as the voice recanted just a few of the things that had happened to me as a child.

"*God does not care for you. He has never shown you love or favor. He* abandoned you to a world that hates you. A world that wants you dead, but only after it harms and tortures you," the voice said.

"God loves me!" I whined.

"*No Michael. I love you. I have always been with you. You used to pray that people would leave you alone. That you could be normal. That you could be loved,*" the voice said.

"Everyone prays for that!" I said.

"*Please forgive those that are angry with me. Please let me stop harming them. Please protect them. Please make me normal. Please give me friends. Those were your prayers,*" the voice said.

I fell over. Those were my prayers. My private words to God. The Devil had heard them.

"*Come to me, my child. Come to me, my Knight,*" the voice said.

I felt his touch begin to lift me. My body did not move, but I felt myself shift. The motion of sitting up felt strange. When I turned my head, I found myself looking down at my own body. It was as if my soul was doing a sit up while leaving my body behind. His touch gripped me harder and began to peal my spiritual legs away from my physical ones.

A firm hand touched my shoulder. It was different from the devil's touch. I looked up to see a young man around my age squatting down in front of me. There were sandals on his feet. He wore dark jeans and a gray tee shirt. His dark eyes looked at me, and a well-kept beard framed his face. The thick and curly hair atop his head went well with his dark skin. I couldn't place his race at all. There were too many features that didn't fit into any standard dynamic of modern race.

"This isn't like you," he said.

"*Mine,*" the voice said.

"Not yet. Not today," the young man replied. "Michael, you need to get up. Well, first you should lie back down in your body. Then get up." He smiled when he talked to me.

"*You are alone. Only I want you,*" the voice said.

"Alone?" the young man asked. He looked around at the infinite darkness surrounding us. I hadn't noticed it before. "That isn't right. Let me borrow that."

Reaching down, he took my sword in his left hand. Then he stood up and looked all around us. The young man lifted the Sword of Innocence before his eyes. He examined the blade for a moment and then held it out before himself. When he nodded to the sword, it began to burn with white fire. Then he slashed the sword horizontally above my head. The darkness directly around me shattered like glass. I never felt my body shift, but I could see that I was lying on my back. Aaron was kissing me…no he was breathing into my mouth. When he rose up and started compressing my chest, I realized that he was performing CPR. I saw Kerri holding Eden around the waist. The wizard was swinging her staff with her one good arm at Alistair Dyhart.

"If he dies I will kill you, motherfucker! I swear I will kill you, and I will do it so slowly that you beg me a thousand times to kill you before I'm done!" Eden roared.

"That's not what he would want, Eden!" Kerri yelled.

"Three out of billions," the voice said.

The young man laughed a deep and hearty laugh. It didn't inspire me or fill me with mirth, but it was genuine. "Hey Michael, this has been one hell of a year for you, hasn't it?"

He slashed the air again and the darkness all around me shattered. I saw myself over the past year. I saved a baby that fell off a roof and a little girl that a demon had possessed. I met Aaron, Emory, and Eden. Priest Greyshadow had trained me as a detective and had started asking me why I did what I did. I drank moonshine with werewolves. I fought goblins with my grandpa, his friend Griff, and my dog Rex.

I had saved people. I had fought evil. I had learned the difference between being a monster and being different. I had been hurt. I had been stupid. Nevertheless, I had come out with everything I had ever prayed for. Except being normal. I would never be normal, because if I were, I wouldn't have adventures or friends.

I saw Kerri. She had been furious with me. She had cried, she had begged, and she had screamed at me. But as always, she had loved me. She had waited four years for me, and I had a lot of time to make up for.

"One year of small pleasures weighed against a lifetime of persecution," the voice said.

The young man rested my sword on his shoulder and said, "One year. What do you say Michael? Is one year enough to build on, or are you going to let him win?"

I looked around at everything I had accomplished in a year. I looked at my best friend trying to breathe life into me. I looked at Eden trying to kill my perceived enemy. I looked at the world around me and saw Hell receding. I shrugged my shoulders and said with all the strength I had left in me, "I think I am going to get back in my body, go home, and sleep for a week. I can do that, right?"

The young man smiled at me.

"*Nooooo!*" the voice screamed. It was filled with hatred and malice, but it faded away like a gentle breeze. The feeling of being touched all over went away.

"You sure can, Sir Knight. Rest well. You have earned it," the young man said.

I began to lie down, but something was bothering me. "Who are you?" I asked. "I feel like I know you, or at least that I should."

He smiled all the wider at me and said, "You don't know me, but I know you. Don't worry about it. You aren't going to remember me. It's just not time for us to meet. I only came because you performed a selfless act and your usual guy couldn't come here."

"Okay, but don't I perform selfless acts all the time?" I asked.

He laughed again, but this time he bent over and slapped his knee. He had to catch his breath before answered me. "Oh no, you don't. You are a man with dreams of being a superhero and an overzealous sense of right and wrong. You are usually just being stupid when you try to save people. Every once in a while, though, you do end up being selfless."

"Oh…well…that is not reassuring at all," I said.

"Get some rest, Michael. You will be needed again soon enough," the young man said.

I slipped back into my body and everything went black.

Chapter 35

W HEN I WOKE up, I was in my bed. There was an IV in my left arm, a Mountain Dew with a cheese steak from Kate's on my nightstand, and a laptop playing cartoons on a loop on a stack of crates. My right arm was in a cast from my shoulder down to my knuckles. My left hand was bandaged but functional. Standing up, I turned off the laptop, almost falling over from the effort, but I used the IV stand as a support. I managed to walk into my living room and found I wasn't alone. Aaron and Emory were cuddled up on my couch watching Doctor Who. Priest Greyshadow was sitting in a chair enjoying what I guessed from the bottles next to him was his fourth beer. Eden was setting my table, and Kerri was cooking.

"So it's a magic telephone booth with a pocket dimension within it?" Eden asked.

"It's a time traveling ship that's bigger on the inside," Aaron said.

"So it's a magical hole in space and time that should, by all reason, terrify everyone, but instead everyone wants to get inside it?" she asked.

"Yes, just like a vagina," Emory said.

"Hey," I said. Everyone jumped up when I spoke and ran over to me. Aaron was first, and he lifted me as if I weighed as much as a newborn. Eden and Kerri scolded me while Aaron and Emory fussed over me.

It was Priest Gregory who set them all at ease with true words of wisdom. "Get the kid a beer and let him be." I don't know if it was gospel or not, but it could have been. Probably from the New Testament.

Kerri got me a beer. Emory got me my food. Eden got me a blanket. Aaron set a bunch of pills on my tray, took my beer, and gave me a glass of water. Aaron is an evil, evil vampire!

Apparently, I had been asleep for a week. My friends filled me in on what happened after I stabbed myself. I had passed out and wasn't breathing. Aaron had managed to resuscitate me, and he suspected that my brain wasn't developed enough to suffer any real damage. The ritual had ended without being fully completed. No one had died because of me taking the full blow of the spell upon myself—a spell that was designed to open a gate to Hell at the expense of all those lives had been fully focused into my soul. I didn't really understand it, but as far as victories go, I will take what I can get.

Kerri explained that all the charges against me were dropped since the district attorney that was so hyped up to railroad me was found to be the mastermind behind the rave murders. On top of that, Detective Clay had woken up. He had been questioned by the investigating officers and had explained that, not only did I not shoot him, but that I saved his life. Which was kind of true, I guess. Kerri had hired a lawyer for me, and I was now involved in a lawsuit against the city. One that after only a week was in talks of settlement.

The downside of everything came down to over forty cases of rape or sexual assault being filed. People's lives had been turned upside down or ruined because one man decided to make a deal with demons. Women were pregnant, diseases had been spread, and marriages had been ruined. This part wasn't a victory. It was a testament to my failure as a protector of the innocent.

The sack of loot from our adventure was on my living room table. It came out to roughly $4,000. I asked Emory to take it and buy new lawn ornaments for Mrs. Faraday. The rest I wanted to donate to the youth center where I volunteered. Nathan Swanson, aka Straight Base, was home and safe. Priest Greyshadow had petitioned the Church to cover his medical and dental expenses since he was a prisoner of war.

I could live with the turn out only because people were still alive, but I had two really important questions. "How did you all know I was going to wake up tonight?"

Everyone's eyes turned to Priest Greyshadow, and he took another pull of his beer before saying, "Bill Fred stopped by this morning and said you would probably be up tonight."

"I got the cheese steak because you get cranky after something beats you to a pulp," Aaron said. "But you have to take your medicine first."

I took the pills and drank some water. I even took a bite of my cheese steak. I looked at the beer Aaron was still holding, and he shook his head.

He put the beer on the end of the table farthest from me. Aaron is an evil, evil vampire!

I drank some water before speaking. "So the world is safe?"

Greyshadow coughed up some beer. "The world is never safe, kid."

"Well, I know that. I mean this time. I saved the world."

Eden snickered. "Well...not the world."

Kerri agreed as she forced the water bottle back to my lips. "Yeah, it was more like the city."

Aaron had settled into Emory's lap with my beer where he happily shrugged and argued, "Not really. No one ever said how big the portal was going to be. For all we know it could have been the size of a kiddie pool."

I shook my head. "No. It was a portal. It would have been a gaping hole the size of a stadium."

The vampire shrugged. "I say tomato. You say tomahto."

"But tomahto is wrong!"

Aaron snapped his fingers as he pointed at me. "Exactly!"

"Well, let's give him the benefit of the doubt," Eden said. "Let's say it would have covered the area of the building. It would have probably been open for an hour at most before some other power intervened. So I would say you saved, maybe, a city block."

"A city block?" I asked.

Emory was absently playing in Aaron's hair when he threw his two cents in. "That's not a good measurement. A city block is a term that covers a different amount of ground in every city. Best to say a neighborhood. That's more standardized, right?"

The evil vampire was laughing again. "I could see Michael saving a neighborhood. The world, not a chance. But the neighborhood, sure."

Everyone began to nod, and they even raised their drinks in a toast to me. "Congratulations, baby, you saved a neighborhood." Kerri kissed me on the top of my head and hugged me. Just like that, my greatest victory was downgraded from saving the world to saving the neighborhood.

Over the next hour, everyone wished me well. They all said that they would check in on us periodically, and Aaron said he would be available if my recovery had any problems. No one stayed long—they really just wanted to see me to make sure I was okay. Priest Greyshadow was the last to leave.

"You did good, kid," he told me. "You make your report as soon as you can. The Church is expecting it."

"Sure," I said. I was in no hurry to contact anyone from The Church other than my grandpa.

"So, Michael, why do you do it?" he asked me.

I thought about it for a moment. There were many reasons to fight the good fight. There were plenty of reasons to stand before terrible things and defy them. There were lots of answers. However, none of them were my answer. "I don't know," I said honestly.

Priest Gregory Greyshadow shrugged into his trench coat and put on his fedora. He looked back at me and said, "Well you're young kid. You've got time to figure your shit out."

When he left, I was finally alone with Kerri. There was no sorcerer walking the streets, there were no demons waiting in the shadows, and there was no one to save. There was just her, me, and four long years of us being apart. She locked the door and looked back at me. I looked back at her. Our eyes met. She started toward me as I began ripping out my IV with my teeth. I got it out and ripped my arm cast off with a growl of effort. My arm was raw and bruised, but it was whole and strong enough to catch Kerri when she leapt into my arms to kiss me.

We made love there on the couch. We tumbled onto the floor and had sex there for a while. The dining room table was next, and then the kitchen. At some point we found my bed, and we stopped making love. We just fucked like animals! It was hot, rough, sweaty, and it was amazing. We went to sleep when the sun came up. We woke up at noon, ate, and made love until the sun went down. For two days we laughed, lived, and loved harder than either of us ever had.

On the third day, there was a knock on our door. My right arm had just gotten its full range of motion back. I walked to the door in jeans and nothing else, wanting just to get back to bed with Kerri. I was so fixated on her that I opened the door without thinking. Her dad was standing there with her brother Chester. They were both just under six feet tall, and both as broad-shouldered as I was. Her dad was holding a revolver in his hand, down low against his leg.

"Where's my daughter, you bastard?" he said. His eyes were blood shot and his words were slurred. He was drunk.

"Mr. Briscoe," I said. My eyes were fixed on his gun. "She's here. How about you put down your gun?"

"How about I put a bullet in your fucking head?" he said as he raised the weapon. His hand was unsteady, and the effort of aiming the weapon had him swaying back and forth. I tried to move out of the way of the barrel but he tracked me. He did it horribly bad, but he tried. He was waving the gun back and forth like a mad man.

"Daddy?" asked Kerri from behind me.

Mr. Briscoe swerved his head to see his daughter. He pulled the trigger. Fire flew from the barrel of the revolver. Mr. Briscoe hadn't meant to fire, and it surprised him. He fell backward into his son's arms. I fell away from the shot and scrambled back on my hands to get my balance. Mr. Briscoe started struggling with his son, and I jumped into the tangle to wrestle the gun away from him. I got my hands on the revolver and yanked it up then down. I wrenched it from his grip, but he turned and slugged me in the mouth. He fell over from the effort and I caught him. He slugged me again.

I gritted my teeth and accepted the third punch. He was drunk, and even if he wasn't, he was no threat without the gun. I shoved him back into his son's arms. Then I emptied the bullets out of the revolver.

Mr. Briscoe broke free of his son's grasp and came at me again. "Give me my daughter, you son of a bitch!" he yelled.

This time when he swung at me I blocked his punch. Then I decked him across his jaw. He went down in a heap. I had hit him with my right hand, which was still healing. I felt like I had just punched a brick wall, but I shook off the pain.

"Don't you ever call my mother that word, you asshole," I growled.

"Michael," Kerri said weakly.

I turned to look at her. She was standing with my covers wrapped around her. I can't say much for anyone else, but she was beautiful covered in nothing but my bedsheets. There was no one in this world more beautiful. My eyes were drawn to the bullet hole in the wall a few inches from her. I spun on Kerri's dad and lifted my foot to crush his head.

"Michael, don't!" Kerri yelled.

I froze. I wanted to hurt him. I wanted to hurt him more than I wanted anything. I pulled my foot back, but my body started shaking with anger.

Chester pulled his dad up to his feet, and Mr. Briscoe focused his eyes past me onto his daughter. "Kerri?" he asked. He turned back to me, "You raped her, you bastard!" He tried to break free to attack me again.

"Daddy, he didn't rape me! He's my boyfriend!"

Mr. Briscoe stopped struggling. He looked at his daughter with a look of utter disgust. "No. Not him. Not him. I would rather you be dead than be with him."

"Daddy, don't say that." I could see the tears filling her eyes.

"You are my daughter! But you are dead to me if you are with him."

"Daddy, you don't mean that."

"DEAD! DO YOU HEAR ME? DEAD, YOU ARE DEAD TO ME!" he roared drunkenly. He pulled away from his son and stumbled away from my home.

Silence fell. I had experienced Insight with Kerri's dad before. I knew he hated me. I knew he hated the thought of his daughter being with me. I had ignored all of that because I loved her. When I turned to face her, my heart fell. She was crying and trying to hide her tears.

"Kerri, we came to take you home," Chester said.

"You let him drink. He can't drink. You know that," Kerri said.

"You try stopping him. Especially when he tracked your GPS and found out you were here with him," Chester shot back. I turned to look at him, and he added, "Why can't you just leave our family alone, you retarded fucker? You're lucky I don't beat the shit out of you."

I clenched my left hand into a fist. It hurt to do so, but it was still a solid fist. "Want to try it?"

"I used to kick your ass every time I got the chance. I don't care what you think you are, fucker, you're still the same piece of shit that me and everyone else used to knock into the dirt," he said as he flexed his fingers in anticipation.

"Michael!" Kerri-Lynn said. I glanced back at her. "Chester, I need a minute. Michael, please close the door." I closed and locked the door before Chester could open his mouth. I started walking over to Kerri, but she held up her hand to stop me.

"It's stupid. All my life I have been in love with you. You were this nerdy skinny little boy with glasses that were too thick and a heart that was too big. You grew up to be something amazing. You grew into a good man, a great man. You have a body that pro athletes would kill for, and you are so kind. Damn it, Michael, you are every little girl's knight in shining armor and every woman's fantasy," she said.

"Okay," I said with the suave sophistication of a rock.

"But this isn't a fantasy. This is real life. I am not a little girl looking for a knight in shining armor, and not every woman gets her fantasy," she told me. Tears were running down her face now. "I know the hero is supposed to get the girl, but that's a fantasy too. I'm sorry, Michael."

"Sorry? You came here to see me, to be with me! Didn't you?" I asked.

"Yeah…but I can't forsake my family. My little brothers. My father. If it was just them being mad I could do this, but I can't give them up," she said.

"So what? You just leave? That's it?" I asked.

She looked up at me with a weak smile and said, "Sorry, Michael, your princess is in another castle."

Being the idiot I am, I laughed. It was a weak laugh, but it matched hers. We just stared at each other for a while. Kerri looked around my living room and shook her head. I looked around at it too. The place was a mess from the wild sex we had all over the apartment. I believe we were both thinking about that.

"I am going to get my stuff," she said. I nodded.

Half an hour later, she was dressed and packed. I walked her to my door, and she let Chester take her bags. She turned to me and looked me in the eyes. There was no Insight. I wish there had been.

"There is plenty of food in the fridge. I made a few meals and froze them—spaghetti, pot roast, beef stew, and lasagna. I cut up some steaks for you, and you will find the rest. I bought lots of sports drinks, Kool-Aid, and apple juice. I know you like apple juice," she said.

"Thanks," I said. "That should hold me for an hour or two." We both laughed.

"The pantry has all those nutrition bar things, but I stocked it with cookies, fruit snacks, and canned fruits. Lots of canned fruits. I made you some Jell-O for tonight. It's got peaches in it," she told me.

"Thanks," I said.

"God, it sounds like I'm feeding a little kid." She laughed. "I just wanted you to have things you liked."

"Thanks," I said.

She shook her head, "Can't you say anything else?"

I looked her in the eyes and frowned. I never said it to her before, and it had hurt her, so I said it now. "Kerri-Lynn, I'm sorry. I can't be your boyfriend. I'm no good for you, and you deserve better than me."

She slapped me. She slapped me hard and it hurt.

"Don't you ever think that. You don't get to think that. You are mine, even if we can't be together. I love you, and any girl you find after me is on borrowed time. The same if I find a guy. One day we will fix this," she said. "Right?"

I looked at her, at her dad and brother standing by their truck, at the hole in my wall, and then down at my feet. I nodded.

"Say it," she told me.

"Right," I croaked.

She hugged me and I hugged her back.

"I'm sorry," she said. "I love you, Michael."

"I love you, Kerri," I said.

She started walking toward her truck. It felt like every hope I ever had was slipping away. I barely noticed when she stopped walking. She didn't look back at me but spoke clearly so that I could hear every word.

"I know that there were twelve apostles, and each was given a sword. Your sword is The Sword of Innocence. Whose sword was it?" she asked.

I felt the tears in my eyes as I lowered my head and said, "Judas."

Kerri stiffened as I put the final nail in the coffin of our relationship. She started walking away again, and I watched her get into her SUV. Her dad got in the passenger side. Her brother got into his truck. They drove out of my parking lot, and Chester nearly clipped a guy in a dark red business suit that was walking along the sidewalk.

"Hey, sir, are you okay?" I asked him.

"Yeah, I am fine. It's sad when a person can't even walk down the sidewalk," he said.

"I know, man. Sorry about that. Enjoy your walk," I said.

He nodded. Then he started whistling as he walked away. It was an odd tune. It sounded kind of like *The Devil Went Down to Georgia*.

I went back inside and looked around my apartment. My girl was gone. My gear was stowed. My place was a wreck. But my city was safe.

That's what mattered. I plopped down on my couch and picked up a pen and paper. I could take my mind off everything by writing my report.

I was utterly alone.

"You grotesque human bastard!" a voice said that sounded British, cartoonish, and country all at the same time.

I sprang to my feet to find the source, but there was no one else in my apartment. I didn't have a TV or a computer. My phone was off. I was alone.

"Up here, you little shit!" the voice said.

I turned to my right toward where the voice had come from. I looked around and saw nothing but my bookshelf and my teddy bear. The teddy bear that Kerri-Lynn had fixed up and brought to me. The teddy bear that was holding a chef's knife and baring teeth that it shouldn't have had.

"Horace?" I asked.

"Time to die, asshole!" yelled my teddy bear. He leapt off the shelf at me as he brandished the knife in the classic style of a slasher-movie killer.

"Seriously?" was all I could say.

My name is Michael White. I won't tell you my whole name because that can get you killed. I am the grandson of a Paladin. I am the owner and sole employee of White Knight Construction. I am a part-time private investigator. I am a Knight of the Crucifixion. When you have a problem that seems too big for you, when you think the police can't help you, when the shadows are surrounding you, or when you hear something go bump in the night, just ask for help. I will be there.

The Adventures of New World Dave
Chris Cervini

In the spring of 1519, Hernán Cortés arrived at the shores of Mexico to conquer the Aztec Empire and claim its gold for Spain. That's what the history books tell us. But sometimes, right in the middle of the history we know, somebody goes and does something to change one important detail, and the world is never the same…

A Third Kind
J.C. Campbell

He was to have been an immortal undead, to have power and strength like he'd never known in mortal life. The Vampyrs lied. When he awoke he was something else, a creature so foul they abandoned him to die alone in a crypt. When the local ruling Vampyr clan realizes what is living in their midst, they come in force to destroy Kaleb and wipe every last trace of his existence from the face of the earth.

Time Starts Now
Michael Walsh

Professor Cal Sutherland's research on time travel elicits snide remarks from fellow philosophers and rejection notices from journals. Even Cal would admit that time travelers probably aren't real—until he encounters one inside his neighbor's burning house. Cal soon learns that, while the past cannot be changed, there is much a time traveler can do in the past. Unfortunately for Cal, this includes the possibility of dying there...

Bonebelly
Christine Lajewski

A sinner transformed into a hideous creature, with an unfortunate craving for human flesh, condemned to a private hell in a wooded corner of Rhode Island; An outdoor haunted attraction—the creature's only respite from his suffering; Two young aspiring graphic novelists trying to record it all. Will the sinner find redemption by stopping the evil he chose to ignore so long ago...

www.ingramcontent.com/pod-product-compliance
Lightning Source LLC
Chambersburg PA
CBHW071301250626
47159CB00004B/1257